PRAISE FOR *NO HONOUR*

'A stunningly written, immensely important book that offers a powerful insight into a world where women and girls are murdered in the name of "honour" ... An outstanding re~~~ ~~
earn its place at the pinnacle o~~ ~~
recommended' A.A. Chaudh~~~ ~~

'*No Honour* is a beautifully wri~~ ~~
you, anger and sadden you, but ~~ ~~
the power of love to triumph ov~~ ~~ ... in the race of
seemingly insurmountable obstacles' Anthony Frobisher

'A gripping read with a broad appeal and incisive writing that doesn't mince words. *No Honour*'s compelling main characters make it memorable, and the heavy subject matter is handled the way it should be – with empathy' *Mashable Pakistan*

'Awais Khan has written an immensely powerful, important and significant book. But what also comes through is his compassion. A sense of wanting to bring a difficult subject to light, so that society can tackle it and make the changes and progress that are so urgently needed' *Daily Times*

'Awais Khan has crafted a deeply engaging story that keeps you hooked from the first sentence to the end. It is a masterful story of courage in the face of seemingly impossible odds' Sopan Deb

'Awais Khan's *No Honour* is a deft novel about physical and emotional survival in Pakistan – between women and men, as well powerless men and powerful men – and a fascinating plunge into unfairness, sexism, patriarchy and misogyny' Soniah Kamal

'*No Honour* is remarkable on many levels ... perfectly paced story structure and eloquent dialogue ... shocking, deeply moving and hugely important. Highly recommended' Carol Lovekin

'An absolute belter of a novel ... Hypnotic, atmospheric and by the end, so hopeful. Loved it' Sarah Sultoon

'Beautifully written and immersive, *No Honour* starts with a powerful opening that propels you into the shocking themes and leaves you rooting for Abida' Sarah Pearse

'Addictive, brave and powerful. A page-turning book, it opened my eyes to the horrific practice of honour killings that are still carried out today. Bravo!' Louise Fein

'A beautifully rendered, moving and insightful novel, *No Honour* takes us deep into lives that many of us in the West probably know little about. Highly recommended, this book is not always an easy read but it is a compelling and rewarding one' Neema Shah

'I was hooked from the first page. Fabulous writing!' Qaisra Shahraz

'Khan presents us with a shocking portrait of lives lived under the shadow of threat and prejudice. A brave book' Vaseem Khan

'A novel that explores misogyny and honour killing, but which is also a compelling and compassionate story. Congratulations, Awais Khan!' Anna Mazzola

'This is a powerful and shocking story ... A compelling, brave and uplifting read for our time' Eve Smith

'This is a book that will stay with me for a long time, especially the opening chapter ... I was horrified by what I was reading but literally couldn't put this book down' Madeleine Black

'This novel dives deep into the leitmotifs of story – memory, love, loss, betrayal – and you are left reeling from an experience which is soul-deep, mind-blowing and heart-wrenching' Faiqa Mansab

'With surgical precision, Awais Khan exposes a culture poisoned by misogyny ... A brilliant, unforgettable book that starts with perhaps the most shocking opening scene I've ever read in a literary novel' Alan Gorevan

'Khan is an icon, pioneer and inspiration. This book is devastating, vitally important and beautifully written. Astonishing' Rob Parker

'Delves into the ingrained practices of Pakistani culture and its approach to women, both their deaths and their fight for survival in a world where they are possessions, objectified and used as bargaining chips ... Passionately written and truly unforgettable, you will be absorbed until the last page!' The Reading Closet

'The writing is just so supremely evocative ... without losing himself in detail he knows how to paint a picture in such a manner that you almost feel like you're watching a film. *No Honour* is stunningly beautiful and extremely readable'
From Belgium with Booklove

'It's difficult exactly because of the very nature of the book – a complex and emotive subject that has been handled in a careful but challenging way ... A difficult story to read, but an important one to be told. Prepare to be taken on quite the memorable journey'
Jen Med's Book Reviews

WHAT THE READERS ARE SAYING

'Beautifully written and immersive ... A must read'

'An important ... eye-opening read. A real insight'

'A captivating story!'

'A beautifully rendered, moving and insightful novel'

'Compelling and rewarding'

'A beautiful story'

'Such a special book. I will be very surprised if it doesn't win several awards'

'Another unputdownable thriller by Awais Khan'

'A heart-wrenching tale'

'A breathtakingly powerful story, and powerful characters ... truly remarkable'

'A terrifying opening ... will leave you emotional and sad ... Incredible'

'It will surely blow you away'

'Khan has taken his writing skills to the next level ... a masterpiece'

ABOUT THE AUTHOR

Awais Khan is a graduate of the University of Western Ontario and Durham University, and studied creative writing with Faber Academy. His debut novel, *In the Company of Strangers*, was published to much critical acclaim, and he now regularly appears on TV and radio. Awais also teaches a popular online creative writing course to aspiring writers around the world. He lives in Lahore and is currently working on his third novel. Follow Awais on Twitter @AwaisKhanAuthor.

No Honour

AWAIS KHAN

**ORENDA
BOOKS**

Orenda Books
16 Carson Road
West Dulwich
London SE21 8HU
www.orendabooks.co.uk

First published in the United Kingdom by Orenda Books, 2021
Copyright © Awais Khan, 2021

A catalogue record for this book is available from the British Library.

ISBN 978-1-913193-78-2
eISBN 978-1-913193-79-9

Typeset in Garamond by typesetter.org.uk

Printed and bound by CPI Group (UK) Ltd, Croydon CR0 4YY

For sales and distribution, please contact *info@orendabooks.co.uk*
or visit *www.orendabooks.co.uk*.

For Begum Shamim Akhtar Sahiba (Amaji),
who lives on in our hearts...

'It is never too late to be what you might have been.'
—George Eliot

'He who does not know one thing knows another.'
—African Proverb

Khan Wala Village, Pakistan
6.30 am

It was when they snatched the baby from her that she realised how serious the situation had become. She watched her twin brother, Aslam, wrap her daughter – his niece – in a filthy rag that he might have picked up in the stables. She could smell the damp fabric from where she lay on the floor. He tossed the knitted shawl she had made for the baby onto the ground.

Tears burst from her eyes.

'Give her back,' she said, her voice hardly more than a whisper, her legs thrashing weakly on the floor. The midwife was cleaning up, her eyes darting towards Aslam as she hastily pulled a shalwar over Shabnam's legs, buttoning it at her waist.

'Please, tell him to give my baby back to me. She needs me,' Shabnam begged.

The midwife averted her eyes. 'It is none of my business. You should have thought of that before you brought this filth into your home. You should be grateful your family asked me for help. Girls like you get thrown into the river if they're lucky. Burned alive if they're not. Pray that your brother is merciful. A lot of brothers aren't.'

'Oh, she's one of the lucky ones,' Aslam said. 'Fortunately for her, Pir Sahab doesn't like fire. It draws too much attention.'

The midwife drew herself to her full height. 'If that is what you had in mind, why did you ask me to help with the birth? What was the point?'

'To make sure she doesn't avoid her real punishment,' Aslam

said, his eyes gleaming. 'Dying in childbirth is too good for the likes of her.'

The midwife's face drained of colour. She hurriedly packed up her things and left the house without a backward glance.

With a herculean effort, Shabnam managed to prop herself on her elbows. The birth had utterly drained her. Every muscle in her body screamed. Her throat was parched, but she was too afraid to ask for water. There was no telling what Aslam might do. For now, he was captivated by the baby, playing with her tiny fists. *Maybe he loves her enough*, she prayed.

Maybe.

Their mother had her back to Shabnam, her heaving shoulders the only indication of her emotion.

'How could you, Shabnam?' she whispered. 'I begged you to run away.' One glance at her son, and she changed gear. 'How could you?' she said, louder this time. 'Your father must be turning in his grave.'

Shabnam closed her eyes, her mind travelling back to the day when she had been goaded into giving herself to that man, the one she had been engaged to marry. He was fifteen years older than she was, over thirty, but when he suggested they take a walk down the river, no one batted an eyelid, least of all Aslam, whose eyes were fixed on the cartons of mangos The Man had brought for him. The Man – she refused even to think of him by his name – had promised her the world. He had promised to take her to the big city.

Her mother had done nothing to warn her about men and their ways. When Shabnam had come of age, she had simply thrust a dirty rag at her and ordered her to use it to soak up the blood that came every month. But now she had accepted lavish gifts from The Man, and had sent her fifteen-year-old daughter down the path of destruction. Shabnam didn't hold her greed against her. She only wished her mother hadn't raised her to be so naïve.

Shabnam had tried not to let her surprise show when The Man

had led her into the fields, when his soft words tickled her skin, when he whispered fond things into her ear, making her blush with a mixture of fear and pleasure. Despite her ignorance, she had seen a few Punjabi films, and knew it was not commonplace for a man to ask a girl to shed her clothes. At first she resisted, but then she saw a shadow settle on The Man's face, and her heart quailed. She thought of the cartons of mangos at home, the countless rolls of silk and chiffon he had brought them, the satisfaction on her mother's face, and smiled her assent. Even then, she didn't know what she was agreeing to. It wasn't until she thought she was being split in two that she screamed, but there was no one to hear her.

And now here she was at age sixteen, with a fiancé she'd not seen since that day and a newborn baby ripped from her arms.

'All he wanted was your virginity,' Aslam said. 'Don't fool yourself by thinking it was love. It wasn't even lust. These city boys are all the same, Pir Sahab says. They come prancing in with sweet gifts and try to buy our daughters' innocence. And you spread your legs for him at the first opportunity.'

Her mother slapped her palms against her forehead. '*Haye*, why did this happen to us?'

'Because you gave birth to a *kanjari*, that's why? A *kanjari* who sold her honour for a few gifts.'

Shabnam didn't have the energy to argue with them. Her ears were trained towards the door. She could hear raised voices outside. Men's voices. Her mother shuddered as if something had blocked her windpipe.

'They're here,' she whispered to her son, her voice choked with fear. 'Quick, open the door, or they'll burn the house down. Try to talk them out of it.'

Aslam smirked. 'Gladly.'

'Aslam, no!' Shabnam raised herself to her feet. The room spun in front of her, and she almost lost her balance. 'Give me the baby, please. I promise I'll leave and never come back.'

Aslam scratched his chin. 'What puzzles me is how you managed to hide your fat belly for so long. But, then, you've always been lazy. It was no real surprise to see you gaining more weight.' His eyes darkened, and he directed his gaze at their mother. 'Did you know?'

Their mother put a hand on her heart. 'Of course not. What do you take me for?'

She had known for months, of course, and had said nothing, hoping against hope that The Man would return. When seven moons had passed since Shabnam's last blood, her mother had thrust a pouch at her, containing her life's savings and some jewellery, and pleaded with her to run away. By then it was too late. There were rumours of gangs of rapists prowling the neighbouring villages. Every day they heard of women being kidnapped and raped. Even if her mother had accompanied her, they wouldn't have been safe. These men had been known to rape women in their seventies, and there was no way she would have put her mother through something like that. Shabnam decided to face her fate. She wasn't going to run away.

Now she wished she had. What a fool she had been to think her brother would support her. As the knocking became urgent pounding, she turned to her brother again.

'I'm her mother,' she said. 'Have you no heart?' When he looked away, she tried the one thing she knew would get a response out of him. She took a hold of his free hand and held it on her breast where her milk welled. 'See? Can't you see she needs me?'

Aslam sprang away from her as if he'd been electrocuted. 'What kind of *kanjari* would try to seduce her own brother?'

Shabnam wanted to slap him across the face, anything to make him understand, but he held that precious bundle in his arms.

Every thud on the door intensified the beat of her heart till she felt she would collapse. She leaned against the wall for support. The room was thick with the smell of blood. The coppery taste of it clung to her mouth. Time was running out.

As soon as Aslam opened the door, everything happened quickly. Her baby was shoved into the hands of a stranger, and Aslam, with a couple of other men, dragged Shabnam out of the house. Day was breaking and there was a nip in the air. She felt it on her exposed arms as she was pulled towards the village square. She was so weak that her vision was clouded and she caught only glimpses of the crowd of people who had gathered in the village square. It was only when they brought her face to face with the pir that she saw the smile on his face, his hands folded over his belly.

'Take her to the riverbank,' he said mildly.

The cold morning air seemed to settle around her heart. Just beyond the row of thatched houses was a clearing by the river where the villagers often congregated for festivals. At this time of the year, the water would not be frigid, but it wouldn't be warm either.

'Courage,' she whispered to herself. 'For my baby.'

A few of the older women spat at her as she was led down the road, the mud clumping around her ankles. Children threw dirt in her eyes, pulled at her hair.

'*Haramal*,' they called her baby. 'Born outside marriage. Shame.'

'Filthy *kanjari*, Shabnam.'

'Burn her alive.'

'Shoot her.'

'Drown her.'

Her brother smiled all through the procession, the beads of sweat on his forehead the only proof of his anger.

'Shooting her would be too easy,' he replied to a man baying for her blood, the smile still fixed on his face. 'She needs to understand what she's done, and I need to restore my family's honour.'

'Hear, hear,' the crowd cheered. 'There's a man who knows what he has to do.'

The jeers continued all the way to the clearing. It may have been a carnival ground, with the trees cut back and the packed earth beneath their feet, but this place carried a hint of foreboding even at the best of times. Shabnam knew full well how many women had been tortured here. The current must be strong as she could already hear the water.

Shabnam pleaded with Aslam with her eyes. She didn't have the energy to open her mouth. She pleaded for her baby. She knew she would die, but at least her baby could live. A part of her...

Her brother seemed to read her mind. He held up a hand to silence the crowd. 'First' – he removed the rag that wrapped the baby – 'bring a bucket of milk.'

No, she thought. *You wouldn't dare.*

She didn't think she had the energy to speak, but when they lowered her child into the bucket, she wailed. The little one's cries died as soon as she vanished into the bucket, but Shabnam couldn't stop screaming. The milk sloshed over the edge, splashing onto the bare earth. Small bubbles rose to the surface, but soon the ripples settled.

'Good riddance,' the pir said. 'We must never let such filth tarnish our village. The baby was born out of wedlock, an abomination on this earth. Good work, my son.'

Aslam grinned, and for a moment he looked like the sixteen-year-old boy he was, not the demon he had just become.

Shabnam hardly felt the breath leave her body as she was thrown into the river.

She embraced the coolness of the water, and let it pull her down, away from the madness and pain.

Peace, at last.

Jamil

As they had every day for years, Jamil's eyes opened to the sound of a baby crying. His youngest, Shugufta, this time. His wife, Farida, tried to muffle the sound by swaddling the baby inside her kameez, close to her heart, but the shrill cries persisted. And to think babies were considered weak.

Jamil rolled his eyes and shifted on his *charpai*, trying to go back to sleep. It wasn't yet April, and his kameez was already soaked in sweat. They should start sleeping outside soon. Through the open window he could see an orange dawn breaking over the wheat fields, rows of sparrows lined up on the wire that supplied electricity to their house. Jamil both loved and hated living so far from the village proper. While the distance allowed them some degree of freedom, it also meant that they faced the longest and most regular power outages. They seemed innocuous enough now, but in the heat of June, the absence of a fan could mean the children wailing the entire night. Jamil sighed. The day hadn't even started yet, and already he was thinking doleful thoughts. It would be time to get ready for work soon.

Blood, feathers and innards. That was his life as a butcher. No matter how hard he scrubbed underneath his nails, the smell of blood never quite left him. In the soft light he examined the palm of his hand: calloused, the skin as rough as sandpaper. His children cried if he stroked their cheeks, so he had stopped doing that. Besides, what father had ever shown affection for his children? He didn't want to appear weak.

Beyond the rag hanging across the doorframe, in the second

room, the other children were beginning to stir. Too young, all of them. Jamil sighed. After Abida, they had tried for years to have another child, but without success. Just as they had given up, Farida had told him she was with child. The much-awaited son, Yousaf, came, followed by Abbas a year later. And then, the four daughters: Farhana, Nasiba, Saeeda and Shugufta. Jamil couldn't remember what Farida had looked like when she was not expecting. He was afraid to get too close to her now, for fear that they'd have another. Her body was plump and inviting, but her eyes were vacant, and Jamil knew she didn't have it in her to carry another baby. They had been celibate since the birth of Shugufta.

'Is Abida up?' he asked Farida, trying to ignore the sound of the suckling baby. He felt as if he was invading a private moment. 'She is supposed to help me with the chickens.'

Farida sighed. 'When has that girl ever helped you? Tell her to collect the birds for slaughter, and she'll play with them. I worry for her, *Ji*.'

'She's only sixteen, Farida. And for God's sake, you can say my name when we're alone.'

'I was married at fourteen, Jamil.'

'That was different. Times are changing.'

Farida huffed, shifting the now-sleeping Shugufta to her shoulder and rubbing her back. 'Don't tell me a girl is too young to get married once she's had her blood. And Abida has been having her blood for years now. We ought to find her a husband.'

Rage stirred inside him at her tone, but he swallowed it. 'As soon as we have some money saved, we'll start looking for a suitable boy.'

'Sell my jewellery and we'll make her a dowry. Don't forget, Jamil, you have six other children to worry about. Marrying her off would mean one less mouth to feed.'

Stung, he threw out his arm and gave her a sharp shake, disturbing the baby on her shoulder so that she fell into Farida's lap.

Thankfully, Shugufta didn't wake up. 'How could you say that about your own daughter?'

Farida began to cry.

Jamil pulled at his hair. 'Farida, please forgive me. It's not like I slapped you. Come now, everything will be as you say. I will spread the word that we are looking for a suitable boy for Abida. Now stop crying. You'll wake the other children.'

'She is sixteen, Jamil. We need to find someone now. You need to stop dawdling.'

His hand itched to smack her, but instead he pressed it against the thick jute of the charpai they were sitting on.

'Why do you think I let Pir Sahab order me around? His son has just returned from Faisalabad. He has more than fourteen years of study under his belt.' He had heard that Pir Sadiq had proper beds with feather mattresses in his home, and he hoped that one day his daughter would have one too. Jamil didn't have money for something so lavish. And anyway, the charpai was good enough for him and Farida. And in the punishing summer, the air circulated under the jute.

Farida's eyes were as round as dinner plates, and the *dupatta* slid from her head, revealing the thick brown tresses he adored. 'Fourteen years. *Ya khuda*, he must be a genius.'

Jamil smiled. 'Nothing less for my beloved daughter.'

'But how will you manage it? The pir is so rich and influential, his servants probably earn more than us.'

'He's my friend, Farida,' he replied coldly. He waved away her protests. 'Just leave it to me.'

'Do you think he would hire our Yousaf as an apprentice?'

Farida was a good wife, a doting mother, but sometimes she could be dense. Jamil sighed. 'I'm trying to fix our daughter's marriage with the pir's son, and all you can think of is Yousaf's apprenticeship.'

'Has Pir Sahab given you any hint that he wants the same thing?'

'No, I just dreamed the entire thing. Have some sense, Farida.'

She wasn't fully convinced, but the way her frown settled and her eyes went dreamy, he knew she had lapsed into her world of dreams, most of which had remained unfulfilled. Jamil intended to fulfil this one. He covered her hand with his. 'And I'm sorry. I shouldn't have shaken you like that. You know violence is not my style, but sometimes you go too far.'

But Farida's tears had dried long ago and, laying down the now-sleeping baby, she opened her arms to him.

'It's forgotten, Jamil.' Her dark eyes glittered, making her look a decade younger. The old playful Farida. 'Why don't we celebrate this decision? The children will sleep for a while yet.'

'Are you sure? We can't afford another baby.'

'Of course, I'm sure. I've picked up a few things about my body over the years. You may think your wife is a *ullu* but I have some sense.'

Despite himself, a smile spread across his face as he took her in his arms.

❧

His high spirits evaporated when he opened his shop. The village was abuzz with the news of a *karo kari* – an honour killing. Jamil's heart sank as the neighbouring shop's owner, Naeem, recounted the events of the previous day. He closed his eyes when he learned that it was the brother who had pushed his sister into the river. And for what? Something that wasn't the girl's fault. All in the name of honour. He marvelled that the man's contribution to the woman's plight went largely unnoticed.

'Tied her hands and threw her into the water like she was a sack of trash,' Naeem said, his bottom lip quivering. Jamil interpreted it as distress, but then Naeem let out a loud laugh. 'The little *gushti*. Thought she could get away with it. Giving birth to the spawn of Satan. Unmarried. Setting a bad example to other girls. It was a relief when Pir Sahab intervened.'

Jamil was sharpening his knife. His head jerked up and he set it down. 'Pir Sahab was behind this?'

Naeem grinned. 'Why, of course. If it wasn't for him, this village would have fallen prey to evil ideas from the city long ago. We're lucky to have him as head of the *jirga*. Who else would have the guts for something like this?'

'What did they do with the baby?' Jamil asked quietly, not wanting to hear the answer.

'Drowned her in a bucket of milk. What else? Exactly what she deserved.'

Jamil closed his eyes.

Just a baby. It wasn't uncommon, and *karo karis* happened more frequently than anyone in this village would care to admit.

His mother's face swam before his eyes and he thought of her back then, forever looking over her shoulder for the cousins who would murder her. He shook his head and opened his eyes again. He couldn't think of her while Naeem was watching. Any display of emotion for the dead girl could damage his reputation forever. Word would travel back to the people in the *jirga* and to Sadiq, the pir himself.

'Are you sure Pir Sadiq was behind the murder of the girl?'

'Don't call it that.' Naeem's tone was sharp. 'It wasn't a murder. Besides, can you blame a brother for trying to protect his family's honour? Every man has the right to marry a chaste wife of their choosing and raise his children with a family name that is pure. If his sister was dumb enough to get pregnant before marriage, she deserved to die. Some women are no better than animals when lust overcomes them, I tell you.'

'Most men too,' Jamil countered.

'Men are allowed to be whatever they want. That's how it has always been and will always be.'

'And doesn't that right extend to women?' The words were out of his mouth before he could stop himself.

To his surprise, Naeem laughed, his eyes crinkling up with a hundred lines. 'Jamil Bhai, that was a good joke. Imagine if the women in this village were free to choose. Aren't things bad enough in the cities that you want our villages polluted with this too? It would be chaos, Jamil Bhai, chaos!' He drummed his fingers on the wooden slab where Jamil kept his knives. 'We are lucky that the *jirga* here takes honour seriously.'

'Honour.' Jamil didn't like the way the word rolled over his tongue. 'Such a tricky thing.'

'Without it, we are lost.'

'Of course, Naeem Bhai.' Jamil set down the knife he was sharpening. His hands were shaking and his heart thumped as if he'd run miles. Why, he thought to himself, did he care so much about the girl who had been drowned?

The answer came to him hours later as he was closing the shop. The ill-fated girl could just as easily have been Abida.

Abida

'Enough, Kalim. Let go of me now.' Abida pushed against his chest, but only half-heartedly. In truth, she wanted him to hold her and never let go.

Kalim tightened his grip. 'Really? A few moments ago you couldn't get enough of me, and now you're pushing me away.'

Abida giggled into his chest, breathing in his earthy scent, like sunshine and cinnamon. 'Are you calling me devious, Kalim Sahab?'

He tapped his chin, breaking into a smile. 'I suppose I am,' he said, rolling on top of her.

Abida wished she could have held on to that moment for ever. It reminded her of the first time they had seen each other, in these same mustard fields. It was last June, a month when the sun scorched the earth. There had been no rains and the roads had baked in the constant heat, making it impossible to walk barefoot. With their homes heating up like furnaces, most of the village women had taken to spending time at the tube well, where cool, running water soothed their frayed nerves and short tempers. It was a place to relax, a place so far from the prying eyes of the village that the women could afford to remove the *dupattas* from their heads and fling them in the water. There could be as many as twenty women playing in the small pool, taking turns to hold their heads beneath the running water. It was sheer bliss.

Abida had been soaked, her cotton kameez clinging to her, revealing every contour of her body. She knew she couldn't face her father like that, so she walked through a nearby mustard field and lay in the shade of an old oak, waiting for her clothes to dry.

'Just so you know, this oak tree is where the *jirga* meets sometimes.'

She almost leapt out of her skin. 'Who's there?'

A man emerged from the fields and stood before her with his hands on his hips. He was young, only a few years older than her, but what took her completely off guard was the way he pretended they were having a routine conversation. His eyes did not travel down her body like any other man's would. Instead, he lowered his gaze. 'My father is in the *jirga* and they're all coming down here today for the meeting. It's cooler here, away from the village, and this oak is a favourite.' He held out his hand. 'I'm Kalim, by the way. I just returned from Lahore.'

Abida had stared at him. He had good manners, but how on earth could he expect her to shake his hand. 'I don't know you.'

Kalim withdrew his hand as if remembering. 'Ah yes, I sometimes forget. I'm Hafizullah's son. I was studying in Faisalabad. You probably don't even remember me, but I've seen you around. At least I think it was you. You've grown.'

Abida was now extremely conscious of the fact that she wasn't wearing her *dupatta*.

As if on cue, he'd nodded at her *dupatta* drying on the ground. 'You better get that and follow me. You don't want to end up bumping into the men from the *jirga* in this condition. Not when they are probably going to be deciding the fate of women who've been' – he clicked his fingers – 'erm … naughty. To put it mildly.'

She was in such a daze, her heart pounding in her chest, the heat making her lightheaded, that she took his hand and let him lead her into the fields and away from the savage old men. The way Kalim had behaved that day was how her father would describe a gentleman.

There had been no turning back from there.

Now, Kalim lay on his side on the coarse blanket they had spread deep inside one of the mustard fields. Despite the arrival of spring, the bare earth was still cold to the touch. He watched her as she shook the insects off her clothes and started to put them on.

'What are you looking at? Haven't you seen enough?'

'I could never see enough of you.' He winked at her.

Abida blushed. Their banter was partly why she loved spending time with him. He made her feel like a princess, not that she knew what a princess was like. In the village, even the richest man could be seen milking his own cows or mending a damaged wall. Still, when she was with Kalim she could be herself. She could speak her mind without any fear. At home, her mother was always scolding her for being outspoken, blaming her poor father for spoiling her.

'I tell you this girl will be the death of us,' she'd wail at Jamil whenever Abida forgot to cover her head or said something out of turn. 'Look how she walks with her chest thrown out. What will people say? You've spoiled her, *Ji.*'

But, then, she was spoiled, wasn't she? What pious, God-fearing, unmarried girl would ever contemplate having an affair? Each time she met Kalim, she told herself that they would soon be married, yet the niggle remained that she would be abandoned. A girl holds her own honour between her legs she had always been told. And yet she had given it away so freely. Girls had been murdered for less. A shiver crept down her spine.

'Do you love me?' she asked, without thinking. Taken aback, she shifted her eyes away from him, focusing on straightening her scarf over her head.

Kalim didn't speak for a moment, which made her heart skip a beat. She was about to burst into tears, when he said, 'Look at me.'

Her vision blurred with tears, and she blinked several times before turning to face him. He looked serious, his beautiful mouth set in a grim line, the forehead that had been smooth now lined with concern or anger, she couldn't tell.

'If I didn't love you, do you think we would be doing this?' He sat up and spread his arms. 'Do you think I would be hunting for a job in Lahore if I didn't love you?'

'Kalim, I didn't—'

In one deft movement he was up, his fingers encircling her

wrists. He laid one of her hands flat on his chest. His heart was thumping like a frightened animal's.

'This is what you do to me when you question my love.'

Now she allowed the tears to fall down her cheeks. 'Oh, Kalim, forgive me. I wasn't thinking. It's just that I have been distracted lately.'

Before she could elaborate, Kalim's pocket buzzed. Kalim was one of the few, proud owners of a mobile phone in the village, even though coverage was sketchy at best. Abida knew it made him feel like a city boy – which he yearned to become. She wanted him to though. She wanted to be far away from the villagers who breathed down her neck. Nosy people who would have accompanied her to the bathroom if it wasn't for the stench, satisfying themselves by staring instead.

Kalim was talking rapidly to someone, his face a mask of worry. But after he ended the call, he averted his gaze, claiming it was nothing.

When she asked him for the tenth time – sternly – he looked at her feet. 'I suppose you'll hear about it in the village anyway, so I might as well tell you.'

'Did someone die?' Abida breathed.

'Your house is a bit of a distance away, so the news might not have reached you yet. They killed a girl called Shabnam yesterday. Her brother threw her into the river.'

Abida clapped her hands to her mouth. 'But why? Poor Shabnam. I used to see her in the square sometimes.' Their village was not a large one. The muddy alleys all led into an open space where a couple of towering shisham trees shaded a few stalls, most of them selling fresh fish and vegetables. The village's few shops all faced the square, so it was only natural for people to bump into each other there, even people as reclusive as Shabnam. Now that she thought about it, Shabnam had been keeping to herself for the better part of the year. Abida sighed. 'She was such a gentle soul. It doesn't make sense.'

This time Kalim met her eyes. 'She had a child out of wedlock. Abida. We need to be careful as well. Are you sure you're not...?'

Before he could finish, Abida turned away from him. She felt as if she was about to be sick. Kalim embraced her, his relief palpable from the way he squeezed her gently, but she still didn't say anything. Maybe she had temporarily lost the ability to speak. It was as if a knife had sliced through her heart.

Even as they parted before the fields ended, she remained silent, giving Kalim a short wave. She couldn't bring herself to tell him that she had already missed two periods.

Jamil

They said that the body was bloated beyond recognition. It appeared that Shabnam had been cursed in death too.

The pir had agreed to a burial because the body had snagged in a fishing net and was pulled out of the river a couple of days ago. The smell was unbearable. The villagers didn't want the girl's sinful flesh to contaminate their precious water supply.

'*Kanjari*,' they still shouted, whenever Shabnam's killing came up in their talk. 'She deserved it.'

The baby had been so small that with just a couple of hacks into the ground the burial was done.

Poor child, Jamil thought, as he watched them lower the girl's body into the grave. Although it was wrapped in starched white cloth, the roundness of the corpse was clear, and no matter how much they perfumed it, the odour was thick in his nostrils. This was what death smelled like, rancid with a peculiar sweetness. Like bitter honey, he thought. They had tried to clean the body as best as they could, but a brownish fluid seeped from it, soaking the fabric.

Shabnam's mother's eyes were dry, but there were dark circles underneath them, and Jamil knew from the grip her son had on her shoulder that she had been forbidden to cry.

'I pray I never have a daughter,' his mother used to say. 'There is no greater punishment than to be born a woman in this place.'

She had got her wish. Her mother didn't have any children after Jamil. For a long time, the absence of a sibling had puzzled Jamil, especially when he saw women with legions of kids in tow, but gradually he began to realise that his mother was ahead of her time. He remembered her keeping track of the days she had to use the bloody rag between her legs. She obviously knew something most women in the village didn't, something Farida seemed to have figured out only now, after years of marriage.

Jamil closed his eyes when he thought of all those kids at home.

'What a waste.' The pir sighed, walking up to stand next to Jamil. 'It hurts me to see the youth die like this.' He pointed a henna-stained finger towards the mother. 'No parent should have to bury their child. That's not the way things are meant to be. Yet Shabnam doomed her mother to this fate when she frolicked in the fields with a man.'

'Wasn't he her fiancé?' Jamil asked in a small voice. 'He might have forced himself on her.'

The pir laughed, the pure white turban on his head quivering. 'My dear Jamil, words like these make me wonder whose side you are on. Having had so many children yourself, I'm shocked that you still haven't understood how base and insatiable a woman's desire can be. A man is helpless in the face of it.'

'I'd like to think that I have my own desires as well,' Jamil started, but the way the pir's eyes flashed made him reconsider. What was Shabnam to him, anyway? Why was he arguing with the man over a girl who was already dead and forgotten? He backtracked. 'Of course you are right, Pir Sahab. Women can be clever creatures when they want to be. Imagine if they were as physically strong as men are. I'm certain they would rule the world.'

'Women will never rule the world,' the pir said quietly.

Jamil cringed. Pir's hatred of women made him wonder about his past. Did he really want Abida associating with people of his kind? He was about to step away from the pir when Farida's face swam into his mind, with her dire warnings about Abida. Sixteen years old. His daughter was on her way to becoming an old maid. He lowered his head in respect. 'Of course, Pir Sahab.'

People were beginning to scatter now that the body had been buried. Jamil saw a few boys looking crestfallen, no doubt having waited unsuccessfully to get a glimpse of the corpse.

Jamil stepped on a large beetle. It gave a satisfying crunch. One less insect to feast on the body, he thought.

'I hear Khalil is back from the city,' he began, desperate to change the conversation, and to his relief, the pir brightened instantly. The edges of his white moustache perked up as his face broke into a genuine smile. Up close, Jamil noticed for the first time that his eyes were an electric green. No wonder he mesmerised whoever he met.

'He has just come back from Faisalabad after studying there for four years. He has a bachelor's now.' He looked sideways at Jamil. 'You do know what that is?'

Jamil knew, but he also knew that his ignorance would give the pir more pleasure. 'All I have heard from the villagers is that he has had fourteen years of education. Forgive me, Pir Sahab, but having spent just a few months in school myself, I don't know much about education.' Another lie, but on someone as self-obsessed as the pir, it worked like a charm.

The pir's chest puffed out, and his smile grew wider. 'A bachelor's means he has a proper degree from a chartered university. He can go anywhere and he will get a job.'

'Anywhere in Pakistan?' Jamil asked, astonished.

'Anywhere in the world,' Pir Sadiq boomed. 'He could go anywhere in the world and people will be bending backward to accommodate him. I've spent a fortune on his education and, with the grace of God, it is being repaid in kind.'

'Farida was telling me that Begum Sahiba is in search of a suitable bride for Khalil.'

'I don't recall Rukhsana being friends with your wife, Jamil,' the pir quipped, but he was grinning.

Jamil smiled back. 'It is a small village, Pir Sahab. Word spreads, especially when it has something to do with your family.'

He was laying it on thick, but to his astonishment, the pir was lapping it up.

'Why don't we sit and talk somewhere more pleasant,' the pir sniffed, 'than this shithole? Our work here is done.'

They made their way to a nearby stall where tea was being served. It was another warm day, the sun high in the sky, the heat starting to bite the skin. Soon, it would be impossible to sit and enjoy the sunshine. Pir Sadiq bought them both steaming glasses of milky tea. Jamil had to blow on his to push away the thick layer of cream on top. Having a large family and not so large a business, he seldom had the chance to drink something so rich. He took a sip and almost groaned. It tasted like heaven.

'Not that I ever notice any females, but I have heard from Rukhsana that your daughter has turned out beautiful and dutiful.'

'She's the apple of my eye, Pir Sahab. My firstborn.'

'Indeed,' the pir said, slurping noisily. 'Not too educated, is she?'

'With so many children and a small butcher's shop, I'm lucky to be able to make ends meet, let alone think about sending my daughters to school. The boys go, of course.'

'Good, good. Why bother giving women an education if they're going to stay at home and look after children?' He leaned closer. 'I'll tell you a secret. My daughter, Bushra, had the preposterous idea of going to school when she saw her older brother leaving for college in Faisalabad. I nipped that idea in the bud. And now she's happily married with two children.' He leaned back and slurped more of his tea. 'Abida sounds like an obedient daughter, well trained in household tasks. I'm sure my wife would like to meet her.'

Jamil didn't know if this was his cue, but he took it as such. 'Why don't you and your family come to my home for lunch? The house is small, but I have a decent seating arrangement outside, with shade from a large tree, and my wife can prepare the main room for the ladies.' He knew he was babbling. He did that when he got nervous.

But Pir Sadiq seemed to be enjoying his awkwardness. 'Why, of course, my dear man. Rukhsana and I would be pleased to come for lunch.' He checked his watch ostentatiously, to show off its glinting gems. 'Let's say Monday next week? I'll bring Khalil and my daughter as well.'

Jamil swallowed when he thought of the expense such a lunch would incur, but he kept his smile in place. 'It would be a pleasure, Pir Sahab.'

Abida

She had once heard a midwife say that after two months of pregnancy, the baby was the size of a bean. She had been accompanying her mother, who'd gone to see the woman complaining of labour pains. But the midwife had scoffed.

'You have a case of gas, *beti*. The baby isn't due for another month. Believe me, I know.'

And she had gone on to enlighten them about the various stages of pregnancy. Abida looked at her naked belly in the mirror. She could see no change. Her stomach was as flat as it had ever been ... or was that a slight curve low down? She couldn't be sure. If she stood up straight with her chest thrown out, the curve was undetectable. But she couldn't walk around like that – she was a girl. What would people say?

Her mother banged on the door to the bathroom, and she hastily covered herself.

'What is it with you? I have never known a girl take as long as you to get ready.'

If only you knew what I am doing right now, Abida thought, willing the baby to dislodge itself. The news of Shabnam had hit her hard. There was no place in this village for unmarried girls with child, and if Kalim didn't marry her soon, her humiliation would be sealed. Probably her death too.

Don't think that. Her father would never let any harm come to her. He had spent his life defending her from her mother. Surely, he wouldn't let them drag her through the square? But then, she was with child out of wedlock. No respectable man would ever support her.

Stop it, she thought again. Things weren't that dire.

Besides, when she slid into a fitted shirt, it fit her perfectly. She stood in front of the spotted mirror for a moment, taking pride in her slim figure. Covering herself with a *dupatta*, she smiled at herself. She was still slim, so why worry?

Only for a few more weeks, a voice whispered in her mind. She ignored it. She would think about it later. Right now, there was a lunch to get ready for.

By the time she emerged, her mother had vanished back to the outside kitchen. Usually she could smell only smoke and lentils inside, but today the scent in the air was so rich that Abida's mouth watered.

Meat. That was what it was. She hurried outside to confirm it and, sure enough, several steaming pots were standing on the ground, each containing a different delicacy: lamb and cauliflower, chicken in a spicy gravy and beef stewed in spinach. Her mother must have been up since dawn to prepare all this. Abida's cheeks burned: she hadn't lifted a finger to help, too busy dreaming about a life with Kalim.

Her eyes filled with tears when she saw her exhausted mother sitting in front of the fire, roasting lamb chops over a spit with one hand while with the other she pounded a mound of dough. Her younger sisters, Farhana, Nasiba and Saeeda, were nowhere to be seen. Maybe her mother had drugged them and they were now sleeping in the fields. Abida chuckled at the thought, and when her mother looked up, she hurried over to take over the dough, sitting on a small stool to avoid the earthen floor.

'I don't understand, Ammi,' she said. 'Who is this important person for whom you've gone to such lengths? I don't remember the last time I tasted lamb – probably at Eid – but here we have three dishes of meat. Surely we can't afford this. You could have sent the little ones to school with this money.'

'The boys already go to school, Abida,' her mother snapped. 'And girls don't need to study. Between your father's shop and my embroidery business, we are managing.'

'I would have liked to read,' Abida mused. 'When I see Yousaf and Abbas reading their school books, I wish I could do the same.' She didn't tell her mother that she had already started learning secretly from Yousaf. He was all of ten years and growing up fast, but at heart he was still a little boy. He was supposed to be a child, but the village had a way of forcing children to grow up before their time. Only last night, they had read a page from his Urdu storybook, Abida whispering the words in Yousaf's ear.

'You read like a robot, Aapi,' Yousaf had told her, sniggering behind his fist. 'You're human, you know.'

Despite herself, she had laughed at the cheek. She remembered praying that he wouldn't grow up to become a criminal, like so many boys in the village. Or a murderer, given the sins his sister had committed.

She hadn't even noticed that she had stopped kneading the bread. Clearing her throat, she added, 'Farhana, Nasiba and Saeeda are already old enough to go to school.'

Her mother frowned at her. 'Honestly, Abida, wherever do you get these ideas from? Pir Sahab would have a heart attack if he heard you.'

'What's Pir Sahab got to do with it?'

Her mother's cheeks reddened. 'Pir Sahab has a hand in everything that happens in this village.'

Abida stood up. 'That's not what you meant. Pir Sahab makes everyone's business his own business, but your tone suggested something more personal.' Her heart sank. 'Pir Sahab is coming for lunch, isn't he?'

Her mother wiped the sweat from her forehead with the back of her hand. '*Ya Khuda*, I'm sweating in this weather. What will happen to me when summer really arrives? And yes, Pir Sahab is coming with his entire family.'

'When were you going to tell me?'

'There is no need to tell you. They are simply coming to meet us. You are only going to greet the pir's wife. At this point, that's enough.'

Realisation dawned on Abida just as the sound of tyres crunching against gravel reached her ears. 'You want me to marry his son, don't you? Oh, Ammi, have you even seen him? I will not marry him, not in a million years.'

In one swift motion, her mother rose and slapped Abida's cheek. Hard. 'You will not make things more difficult than they already are. Do you have any idea how much we have spent on this feast? And just for your happiness, so that you can have a better chance at life.' She dug her nails into Abida's upper arm. 'Now go to your room and stay there until I call you outside.'

Nausea rose in her throat, and Abida almost vomited. She took deep breaths. 'You don't understand. I can't just marry anyone you please.'

'That is exactly what you're going to do,' her mother said, her voice brokering no argument. She pulled her into the room Abida shared with her siblings.

Abida made a beeline for the window looking onto the courtyard, just in time to catch a couple of black jeeps coming to a halt in a cloud of dust. The occupants of the jeeps remained inside until the breeze had carried the dust away into the wheat fields. When they stepped out, Abida recognised the pir immediately. There was no mistaking that starched white turban and that puffed out-chest, as if he was doing the world a favour just by existing.

'*Kanjars,*' Abida whispered. 'The whole lot of you.'

A pair of burqa-clad women climbed out next – presumably the wife and daughter – and as they stood shaking the dust from their clothing, Khalil emerged. Abida nearly gagged again. She could see his flabby stomach dancing behind his white kameez, and when he knelt to retrieve the sunglasses that had fallen off his head, the kameez became lodged in his ass. She laughed, hoping this would be enough to stop her father committing her to this man – this family.

As her father rushed over, hugged each of the men and bowed in front of the ladies, Abida thought she could hear his soft, respectful voice. She was too far to make out what was being said, but no matter how much her father sucked up to the pir, she was never going to marry Khalil.

'Get away from the window,' her mother hissed from the doorway. Abida turned to see that she had already managed to put herself together for the guests. That must be a record time, even for her mother, who was always the first one out of the door. She could see the excitement bubbling in her eyes. She had made a clumsy attempt at putting on makeup, overdoing the foundation and lipstick so that she looked like one of the monsters the village elders warned them about. A snort escaped her, and was replaced with a sob. She wanted to bang her head against the wall to make them understand, but they never would.

Instead she watched her mother bustle outside to greet her female guests. Abida sat down on one of the many *charpais* lining the room, running her hand over the old cotton sheet. It was flimsy enough to tear and she could feel the coarse jute underneath that held the bedstead together. She raised her knees and wrapped her arms around her legs. She had never felt so alone in her life. Conversation began in the other room, which her parents had converted into a living space for the day. In addition to her mother's earnest voice, there was a thin one, which most likely belonged to the pir's wife. There was a lot of scraping and scratching of the bamboo wicker chairs on the brick floor before the ladies settled in. Since there was just a rag separating Abida from them, she could hear every word.

'Spring is here in full swing already,' the woman with the thin voice exclaimed. 'God knows what will happen with us come June.'

'Would you like a hand fan, Rukhsana Apa?' Farida asked. 'I can have Abida fetch it in a second.'

Abida heard the desperation in her mother's voice, and her stomach lurched. She turned her face away from the curtain. Sitting on the *charpai* had calmed the nausea, but she couldn't believe what was happening. How could she even begin to consider this proposal given her current state? And what about her love for Kalim?

Rukhsana seemed to have refused the offer of the fan, for the women had lapsed into silence.

'It must be difficult,' Rukhsana spoke up, 'to fit the entire family into two rooms.'

'Oh, not at all,' Farida replied, unaware of the attack that had just come her way. 'We have all this open space outside. And there is the courtyard too. The children are outdoors most of the time. It's just my husband and me in the house.'

'I see. Well, then, it's no wonder you have so many children. If I had been alone with Pir Sahab so much, I don't know how many I would have had.'

Abida heard her mother laugh, but the sound was hollow. It seemed she had finally got the message – Rukhsana was here to insult her.

'Human nature is funny,' Rukhsana continued. 'We are so consumed by our desire for the flesh that sometimes we fail to take our circumstances into account. Just the other day, I was visiting my cousin, and I discovered that she had ten children. Ten. And her husband is a pedlar.' She allowed a pause for effect. 'Naturally, they're struggling to make ends meet and rely on handouts from people like us.'

'We manage just fine,' Farida said in a small voice.

Abida clenched and unclenched her fists. The nerve of that woman. And this was the kind of home her parents wanted her to go to.

'Oh, of course you do. Your home is wonderful,' Rukhsana replied. 'I'm dying to see your daughter. Pir Sahab was so full of praise for her. You've heard of my son, Khalil, I presume? He's just returned from Faisalabad with a bachelor's degree.'

'I'm afraid I don't know much about education, Apa, but my husband told me that he is very well educated. I can imagine any girl who marries him would be very lucky.'

'Speaking of girls, where is your Abida?'

The unwelcome sound of her mother's flip-flops grew louder as she hurried in Abida's direction. Abida noticed the flush on her face as she entered the room. She was breathless.

Abida turned away. 'I'm not coming out,' she murmured.

Without warning, her mother took a good amount of her hair in her fist and pulled – hard, but not hard enough to make her scream. 'What are you doing?'

Farida bent close to her, so close that Abida could smell the fear and excitement. 'Don't you dare do anything to ruin this. You will meet with Rukhsana and do everything that is expected of you or, so help me, God, I will tear you limb from limb.'

All of this was whispered in Abida's ear. It was so comical that for a moment Abida wanted to laugh, but she pressed her lips together to stop herself. 'I don't want to marry into that family. Did you notice how rude the woman was or were you too dazzled by the expensive jewellery I'm certain she is wearing?'

Farida's grip on her hair tightened. 'I'm warning you, Abida.'

'Well?' came Rukhsana's voice from outside. 'What's the girl doing? Primping herself? She can't be that bad. Tell her I've seen worse.' Then a laugh, light and conceited.

'See,' Abida said, freeing her hair. 'This is who you want me to end up with?'

'Shut up and come out.'

'What kind of mother would want her daughter to marry into such a family? Money isn't everything, you know.'

In the end, Farida had to half carry, half drag Abida out of the room, but as soon as she lifted the piece of cloth, she let go and Abida righted herself. Had the situation not been so serious, she would have laughed at her mother's behaviour.

She covered her head with her *dupatta* and stepped forward, keeping her eyes aimed at the guests, even though the firmness of her mother's grip on her wrist told her to lower them.

'Ah, the celebrity finally shows up,' Rukhsana exclaimed. 'Come closer, girl, so that I can take a good look at you.'

Other than her voice, there was nothing thin about Rukhsana. Her large frame easily filled the wicker chair. She had removed her *chaddar* and Abida could see how her belly and breasts strained against the fabric of her kameez. She looked ready to explode.

Abida swallowed another snort, careful to keep her face neutral. Rukhsana's small, button-like eyes were intelligent, and right now they were focused on her. Beneath all the layers of makeup, Abida could tell that she had once been a striking woman. If her son was anything like her, he wouldn't be too bad. Unfortunately, from what she had seen, he wasn't.

Don't go there, her mind told her. She was committed to Kalim. She loved him. How could she even entertain the thought of another man? In any case, anyone who discovered she was with child would probably kill her.

'You have handsome features and a well-shaped body,' Rukhsana observed. 'Wide hips well suited for giving birth.' She turned to Farida. 'If her body is anything to go by, Farida, I would assume she's as fertile as you.' Another of those rude laughs. She held up a finger. 'Not a bad thing, mind you. At least you're not like my slip of a daughter.' She pointed at the hunched, silent girl wrapped in an embroidered *chaddar* – Abida hadn't even noticed her. 'She's already had several kids, but, looking at her, you'd say she'd never experienced any of it. No, I want my girls to be hale and hearty, to represent the wealth of the family they belong to.'

The glittering eyes swivelled back to Abida. 'Educated, are you?' Abida shook her head.

Rukhsana nodded. 'Just as well. Wouldn't do having a girl with fancy ideas in the house. My silly daughter once had lofty ideas of getting educated. Nipped them in the bud, didn't we, Bushra?'

Bushra nodded.

'Speak up, girl!'

'Yes, Maa Ji.' The girl's voice was barely more than a whisper.

'Abida, pour the tea,' Farida said, gesturing to the steel teapot and mismatched cups. Abida chose the chipped one for Rukhsana.

Rukhsana sighed. 'If God was only going to give me two children, I would have wished them both to be boys. But he saw fit to give me Bushra. Slim and stupid. My bad luck.' Another extravagant sigh. 'You can't imagine the beatings I endured for giving birth to her. A daughter. Poor Pir Sahab hung his head in shame for weeks.'

'And what's wrong with having a daughter?' Abida asked, staring at Rukhsana. 'My parents have plenty of daughters.'

Farida clapped her hands over her mouth. 'Abida!'

For a moment, Rukhsana's mask slipped, and Abida thought she caught a hint of admiration in her gaze. 'You've got quite a tongue on you. It will cost you dearly if you're not careful. In our society, girls are not meant to speak their mind. Surely your mother must have told you.' She shrugged. 'None of my business. At least my daughter is married now. That's a relief.'

Abida saw a solitary tear run down Bushra's cheek.

Rukhsana lowered her voice. 'Did you know that Shabnam tried to lure my poor daughter into friendship? The nerve.'

'Shabnam?' Abida asked. The cup shook in her hand and some of the tea sloshed into the saucer. Her mother narrowed her eyes at her.

'That tart who ended up being drowned by her own brother,' Rukhsana continued, holding out her empty cup to Abida and nodding at the tea pot. 'Serves her right. Bold as brass, she was. Having a child out of wedlock and then expecting the world to accept her and the evil thing she gave birth to.'

Abida saw her mother shake her head and focus her attention on Rukhsana again. 'Such a sad thing to see a girl sink so low.'

'Sink?' Rukhsana edged forward in her seat. 'The girl was the devil's spawn. Lured her fiancé into the fields, had her way with him, and rumour has it she killed him or something. And drank the blood. She deserved to die.'

'But how could her own brother—?' Farida began.

'Are you trying to question honour, Farida? Do you think the poor, unsuspecting brother who had to kill Shabnam to save his family's honour did a bad thing? Do you?'

Farida looked horrified. 'Of course not.'

'Then don't spout unnecessary rubbish.'

Abida bristled, and the cup that was supposed to go into Rukhsana's outstretched hand landed instead in her lap, upturned, the hot tea tracking a brown stain on her starched kameez.

Rukhsana yelped, jumping out of the chair as she shook her dress. 'You fool. You burned me.'

Abida smirked as she saw her mother steer the almost hysterical Rukhsana to the makeshift washroom outside. From the corner of her eye, she saw a smile spread across Bushra's small face.

Farida apologised all through lunch, right until the moment Rukhsana huffed her way into her jeep, looking ahead as Farida stood next to her, bent and broken. Seeing her mother like this now, Abida wished she hadn't spilled the tea. As a final insult, the jeep screeched its way down the dirt track, raising a cloud of dust that settled on her father's head and her mother's beautiful embroidered *chaddar*. Rich *kanjars*, Abida thought. They never could stop themselves showing off about owning one of the few vehicles in the village. She wanted to spit on the ground, but she knew that would earn her a slap across the face.

Her mother's shoulders shook as she wept silently, her father's face creased with worry, but when their eyes met, he gave her a small smile. That more than anything broke her heart, but she still didn't regret what she had done. *You taught me to have a backbone*, she thought, watching her father wrap an arm around her mother.

She had caught barely a glimpse of Khalil, except for a moment outside when their eyes had met. Short and flabby, Khalil had none of his mother's striking features; neither did he have his father's height. He had a round face with an oily forehead and chubby features. But judging by his toothy smile, he seemed to like what he saw of her. It turned her stomach.

She couldn't marry someone like him, no matter how far along she might be.

Jamil

Despite Abida's blunder, Jamil hoped the response from the pir would be favourable. After all, it was his Abida they were talking about. Rude or not, she was attractive enough to turn heads. Besides, she had learned her lesson. Farida had beaten the poor girl to within an inch of her life.

'Rukhsana criticises everything,' he assured a panic-stricken Farida. 'If Pir Sahab liked her enough, then nobody will dare question his decision.'

It had been three days since the pir's family had visited, and Farida was still refusing to eat, which was a pity because they seldom had meat. The children enjoyed the rich gravies for two whole days before the meat went rancid, and it was with a heavy heart that Jamil had scraped away the food from the pots before asking Farida to cook the usual – lentils.

He spooned some lentils into her mouth, but she simply burst into tears. 'I can't believe she would do this to us. After all we spent on that lunch.'

Jamil closed his eyes, striving to maintain the self-control he had exercised for days. He wanted to shake Farida, just to knock some sense into her, but he restrained himself. What kind of example would he be setting for the children? But if he didn't beat her, how would his sons learn to become real men?

Jamil flushed at his thoughts. What would his mother say if she saw him beating his wife?

He remembered the time when he was in class five, and his friend, Jabbar, had shown him a blooming blue bruise on his upper thigh. 'Got it from Abba Jaan,' he told him. He'd only smiled when Jamil gasped. 'You should see the bruises on Amma's body. They are all the colours of the rainbow.'

'Why would your father beat your mother like that?' Jamil was horrified.

Jabbar shrugged. 'My father says that all men beat their wives. They need to be beaten or they can end up forgetting their place.'

Jamil still remembered his chest expanding with pride. 'My father has never lifted a finger to my mother.'

Jabbar blinked once before bursting into laughter. 'Your father is not a man, then.'

They'd fought with fists until a consensus was reached to consult their fellow classmates. To Jamil's shock, every single one of them swore to seeing beatings in the house. Some had seen their mothers cowering on the floor while others had seen them shaking with fear – one so violently she cut herself with the vegetable knife.

'Only weak animals beat their wives, Jamil,' his mother told him when he complained his father was not a man. His mother always wore kohl around her eyes because his Abba liked her eyes that way. She narrowed them at him before patting the dust out of his school clothes. 'Sometimes it is good to stand apart from the crowd. Just because everyone is doing something bad doesn't make it right, Jamil. Always remember that. Your father is a real man, God bless him. He has never dared raise a hand against me.'

Before Jamil could interrupt, she had held up a finger. That is how he remembered his Amma, her kohl-lined eyes burning with a silent strength, a *chaddar* on her head. 'No matter what nonsense the villagers talk, always try to be like your father or pray you get a wife like me, who will keep you in line. Someday, I'll tell you our story.'

Not only had Jamil married an obedient woman, he had also been influenced by the villagers, persuaded to beat his wife just to assert himself. His mother would have spat in his face had she lived to see it.

Jamil clenched his fists. He would not raise his hand, ever again.

As if on cue, Farida opened her mouth and swallowed the food. Her eyes, so full of pain for the last three days, shone with hope. 'Are you telling the truth? Did Pir Sahab really like our Abida?'

Jamil embraced her. 'Of course, my love.'

The way she shuddered against his chest, Jamil didn't have the heart to tell her about the other thing that was worrying him. For a few weeks now, he had been suspicious of Abida's movements, the way she disappeared for hours on end. He had questioned her once, but her answer was vague, her expression dazed as if she was in another world. Jamil recognised that look: it used to appear on his mother's face whenever she mentioned his father. It was the look he wished to see on Farida's face, but with the countless children and the struggle to make ends meet, Farida could barely spare him a second glance, let alone a look soaked in passion.

His daughter was in love with someone, he suspected, yet he kept silent. What kind of man did that make him? What would his mother say? He knew exactly what she'd say. She would be proud of Abida.

Jamil closed his eyes, squeezing Farida tight against him. The softness of her frame gave him comfort.

When Jamil didn't let go of her, Farida understood. He felt the tension deflate from her body as she whispered, 'Let me check on the children.'

Jamil released her then, waiting for her to bolt the door as she shooed them outside. Abida, Yousaf and Musa were already out on errands and the rest relished the chance at being sent outdoors. Only little Shugufta remained in the room, asleep with her thumb in her mouth.

Sweat dripped down his body in streams, and his mind screamed *coward* at him, but he didn't say anything. He waited until Farida returned, her face set in determination of fulfilling her duty as a wife. He knew she had long since lost any urge for it, but he was desperate for distraction.

Anything to make him forget what he suspected of his daughter, who might very well be doing the exact same thing at that moment.

Abida

Abida lay next to Kalim, waiting for his breathing to return to normal. Lately, she had noticed that he was merely concerned with fulfilling his own urges with no regard for hers. He had no idea, she thought, that she hadn't been enjoying it. Her mind had been adrift the entire time, her eyes staring vacantly at the yellow petals of a mustard flower. She had wished for weeks that she could lose the baby. She had jumped around, pushed her stomach against a slab of marble, even tried to swallow mouthfuls of castor oil, but it was as if the baby were lodged somewhere deep in her body, refusing to let go. All she got was stomach ache. The more she tried to get rid of it, the more resilient it seemed to become. A bit like her, maybe.

Her thoughts turned back to Kalim. Perhaps all men were like that, she thought. After a time, they all forgot that a woman was a living, breathing person with her own desires and thoughts, not just a vessel for them to satisfy their needs.

Maybe she was being unfair to him, but she couldn't help it. Ever since she had been pregnant, her emotions had been all over the place. She wanted to strangle Kalim one moment and bury her face in his neck the next.

He turned to her, a sleepy smile playing on his face. His nose was slightly crooked at the tip, but somehow it seemed to enhance his good looks, complementing the eyes, which were an uncommon grey, specked with green, so that when he looked at her, she could feel herself melting. He ran his fingers through her hair. 'What are you thinking?'

Reaching for her scarf, she threw it over her sweat-drenched body. She didn't want to mince her words. Not any more. She guided his hand towards her lower abdomen, where a small bump was beginning to form. 'I'm with child. More than three months along.'

The confusion that clouded his face was so profound that for a moment she expected him to ask who the father was. Instead, he muttered, 'How?'

'How? Really? I just told you that I am with child and all you can say is "how"?'

'Abida, I – I don't understand. We have been using protection. Why didn't you tell me this before?'

Abida turned away from him, focusing her attention on the mustard flower again. The way he said 'protection' grated at her, as if she didn't know what it meant. *Yousaf has been teaching me how to read,* she wanted to say. Instead, she said, 'I wanted to be sure. And, besides, even a roadside beggar will tell you that the plastic things you use are not complete protection. Especially not the cheap ones.'

'I can't believe you didn't tell me. Three months. Wow.'

'I told you I wanted to be sure.' Abida couldn't bear to look at him.

Behind her, Kalim let out a long sigh. 'This changes things, I guess.'

Now Abida turned to glare at him. 'You guess? Of course it changes things. We need to get married. And fast.'

'Whoa, whoa, hold on.' He shifted in the makeshift bed they had made, scrambling to get into his clothes. 'Marriage? Abida, I am only twenty years old. I can't be married. God, I can't even think of being a father.'

Abida also rose to her feet, her heart quickening with rage, her breath coming out in pants. She forgot that her *dupatta* had slid off, leaving her stark naked. 'You think I want to be in this condition? This is something that the two of us did together. This thing inside me, it didn't sprout on its own.'

Kalim, fully clothed, reddened. 'At least put on some clothes. Then, we can talk.'

Abida let out a cackle, she couldn't help it. 'You men are all the same. Minutes ago you couldn't wait to get me out of my clothes, and now my body disgusts you?' She crossed her arms over her chest. 'Happy now?' She resisted the urge to hit him.

He held up his hands. 'Okay, okay. You just took me by surprise. Of course, I will marry you, but first I need to know—'

'Kalim, I swear to God, if you ask me who the father is, I will kill you right this second.'

'Hold your horses, Abida. I only wanted to ask if there was a way to, you know, get rid of it.'

Abida didn't dignify that with an answer. She started pulling on her clothes.

'Abida, please.'

She took a deep breath, trying to calm her racing heart. A headache of epic proportions seemed to be settling in her forehead. 'Listen, Kalim, I have known about this for months. Do you think I haven't tried? I know better than you how difficult life can be in this village for an unwed mother. Come to think of it, there is no life, is there? They'll just kill me in the name of honour, leaving my body for the crows to peck at. Your baby's too.'

'Abida, for God's sake, I didn't mean it like that. Of course I will marry you if it comes to that.'

If it comes to that. 'That's just it, Kalim. I don't want you to do it out of duty. Don't you love me? Did you ever plan on marrying me?' She gestured around their love nest. 'What was all this about? Fun?'

Now fully clothed, she waved his protests aside and pushed past him, into the mustard fields, her body rigid with fear. What if he didn't follow her and instead just gave up on her? How would she ever manage without a husband? She pictured herself married to the fat, sweating Khalil, sharing his bed every night, but as distasteful as that prospect was, even that was no longer open to her.

She was too far along now to marry him. By the time the ceremony took place, she would be showing.

She listened for Kalim's voice calling after her, but he was silent, as if someone had padlocked his mouth. She knew that the only reasonable solution was for Kalim to marry her immediately. But would he? Judging by his silence, he might already be coming up with an escape plan for himself. Would he turn her over to the *jirga*? Would she be stoned to death or drowned or whatever the pir persuaded the *jirga* to do? The weeds scratched the bare skin of her ankles, but she didn't slow her pace. If she could, she would have kicked herself for her stupidity.

'Abida, you fool,' she whispered to herself, furious that she had to rely on a man to keep her alive.

Just as she was reaching the end of the field, her heart threatening to break into a thousand pieces, she thought she heard something. She paused, straining to listen, but all she could hear was the wind combing through the mustard stalks.

And then: 'Abida, wait. Just wait, will you?'

He was panting by the time he caught up with her. With his hands on his knees, he doubled over, trying to catch his breath.

'All this smoking is going to kill you one day,' she said, unable to conceal her glee. 'I hardly walked a few yards away from you.'

He looked up, smiling, a droplet of sweat gleaming on that crooked nose of his. 'You call that a few yards, do you? Are you an Olympics medallist?'

'What is Olympics?'

He burst out laughing and threw his arms around her. 'This is why I love you so much. Even in ignorance, your confidence is staggering.' Kissing the nape of her neck, he added, 'I will talk to my parents tonight. Come what may, we will be married by the end of this month. After all, it isn't just about us any more. There is a third life we need to think about now.'

Abida smiled as he spread his hands over her belly. Now all she had to do was speak to her parents and everything would be fine.

⁂

One day turned into a week, and a week turned into a month, and still there was no word about marriage from Kalim. Not a single word. Sure, he would send her the occasional note through a trusted child in the village square, and then they would meet in the fields, but that was only to satisfy his desire. When she brought up the baby, Kalim simply averted his eyes, busying himself with his clothes.

'My Abbu is not doing well. He has just been diagnosed with some awful disease. I don't even want to say it, and you probably won't understand it. Nobody does,' he told her the last time they had met behind the towering chicken coops Kalim's father owned. Although the wire mesh shielded them from prying eyes, the chicken coops were in full view of Kalim's house, which made it risky to meet like that. It smelled awful with months' worth of shit lining the floor, the broiler hens pecking at it along with their feed. Abida didn't care. Kalim had been avoiding her for days, and she was desperate. She hung on to his every word, watching him closely. She could see nothing but honesty and distress in his grey eyes as he spoke. *Why won't you marry me, then?*

'My parents are struggling to make ends meet, Abida. Even with all my education, I haven't been able to help them out with the business. They are losing all the cattle and chickens to some mysterious disease.'

'The chickens look healthy enough to me.'

Kalim rolled his eyes. 'Abida—'

Abida hadn't meant to come off as insensitive, but she couldn't help blurting out, 'What does this have to do with me? Why haven't you told them about us yet?'

'They need me right now, Abida.' Tears pooled in his eyes. 'My father's daily medicine costs over one thousand rupees. He is desperately trying to sell his remaining cattle before they die. I can't go up to them and tell them about my sins. They'll kill me; or worse – they'll fall dead themselves.'

'Kalim, I am not your sin.'

Kalim closed his eyes. 'That was a bad choice of words. I'm sorry, Abida.'

'They only have to marry us. Or we can do that ourselves. And I'll work. I won't be a burden on them.'

'I need some time. I've put out feelers for a job in the city. I need to be free of my parents before I can even think of raising a family.' The frown between his eyebrows deepened. 'I should never have returned to the village. At least, I'd have spared you the shame of being with child out of wedlock.'

She should have slapped him, but she let him take her hands. They were softer than hers. It was obvious that Kalim had never worked a day in his life. 'Tell them, Kalim. Your excuses will not make this baby go away.'

What he said next chilled her to the bone.

'It's not like you're showing yet, Abida. We have time.'

That's what he didn't understand. They did not have time. He wasn't the one carrying a baby inside him like a ticking bomb. And now she was starting to show, almost without her realising. The change was so subtle at first, just a bump developing in her lower abdomen. She ignored it, thinking she had a few more months before it became obvious, but then things sped up. It was as if the child was growing at an accelerated rate. In a matter of days, she saw that her belly had hardened, assuming a rounded shape. She starved herself, hoping that would starve the baby, but it only served to make her belly look rounder than ever.

She could still hide it under her clothes, but she didn't know for how much longer. Thankfully, she had never been too skinny so any changes in her body might be passed off as weight gain. She bet her life that her mother, despite having given birth to seven children, still didn't know about her condition, which was astonishing to say the least. Her father was another story. While he didn't know about the baby – not yet, at least – she noticed the way his eyes swivelled in her direction whenever she appeared.

His moustache would quiver as if he was getting ready to say something, but then he would shake his head and turn his gaze away from her. She felt she was breaking away from her family, the baby isolating her, first from them and then from the world. She knew what her fate would be if she remained unmarried, and the prospect terrified her. The lipstick she had traded to buy bangles from a roadside pedlar, for Kalim's benefit, felt like a sin now.

Jamil

If living at a distance from the village had benefits, it had its drawbacks too. Except for Farida's soft snores and the occasional shuffle from the kids' room, the house was quiet. The cool breeze that had picked up sometime in the evening had died down again, and even the trees didn't rustle. It was hot in the room. Jamil wanted to get up to turn the fan on, but it was as if he was paralysed. He couldn't summon the energy to lift his head, let alone rise from the *charpai*.

He knew the cause of his weakness. There was only one – Abida. This was the third night in a row that she had been absent from the house. She thought he didn't know that she jumped out of the window of the other room after dinner, leaving her bed padded with clothing and covered with a sheet to fool them. Farida pretended to be knowledgeable about things related to women, but seeing her now, sleeping with her mouth wide open, he had a sudden urge to laugh. She could be clueless about things that actually mattered. Abida fed her lies about visiting some expecting mother called Safiya, and Farida swallowed them whole. But he knew better.

And yet here he was, pretending to be paralysed so that he wouldn't have to go out and discover the reason his daughter was absent every night. He wasn't a fool. He knew it was something to do with a boy, but could his daughter really be that foolish?

He shook his head, attempting to rouse himself. She was his responsibility, and the least he could do was steer her towards the right path. But what path was that? he wondered. The path that led to a lifetime of toil, a gradual death of confidence and freedom, qualities that his daughter possessed in abundance – that was, if one could quantify freedom. In this village, Jamil thought, you could. One point for managing to save your baby daughter from being 'accidentally' killed by someone in the family, just because she was female. Another point to the woman if she managed to roam the village without a male escort. Ten points for marrying for love, which rarely, if ever, happened.

The list went on and on – small freedoms that women had gradually gained from the men in the village. But there was a long way to go, and Jamil knew that it would be well after Abida's time that true freedom for women would come to Khan Wala village. In the meantime, Abida had to be controlled. For all their sakes.

Despite trying to remain alert, his brain was surrendering to his body's demands for rest. His eyes were closing when the door creaked – the insufferable, termite-infested plywood door that never ceased to scream the latest arrival. Jamil almost smiled. While the window was easy for jumping down, the same wasn't the case if the person wanted to climb back up. It was too high. It seemed that even Abida had limitations.

The familiar rustle of her clothing filled the air as she tiptoed towards the other room. She was almost at the doorway when Jamil spoke.

'Where were you all night?' He tried to pack as much authority into his voice as he could. It still sounded weak.

'Safiya took ill,' Abida replied, without a trace of hesitation. 'She will be having her baby any day now. She needs all the help she can get.'

'She's been with child for as long as I can remember. Birthing an elephant, is she?'

'That's hardly something to joke about, Abbu. Carrying a child isn't easy, as you should know. You have seven.' Abida's reply was terse, clipped. His own daughter was talking back to him. *What a girl you are*, he thought, not knowing whether to feel angry or impressed.

What a liar *you are*, Abida, he thought then.

'The streets at night are no place for a girl your age. Why didn't you just sleep there? Safiya's place is quite big from what I've heard.'

Ha, he thought. *Answer that*. It was foolish of him, but he couldn't help feeling a hint of triumph as Abida hesitated for the first time.

'I ... I just didn't want to disturb the family.'

'And yet they have no problem with disturbing you. I will have some words with Safiya's father-in-law tomorrow.'

'No!' It was a command. Jamil physically shook at her tone.

Farida was still sleeping next to him, unaware of the conversation.

Jamil raised himself onto his elbows. 'What did you just say?'

The moonlight fell across the fabric of her kameez, making her seem like a pink shadow in the darkness. She took a step forward. 'I'm sorry. I won't be late again. I promise.'

He knew he should be firm with her, that this was the moment to drive the point home that there would be no violations of his house rules. But it had been a long day, he was tired and, most of all, he was a coward. A coward afraid of his own daughter.

He let his head fall back on the hard pillow. 'Go to sleep,' he told her.

'What was that all about?' Farida murmured, rousing only now.

❧

The next morning, Abida had left before he even woke up. If anything, he was impressed at his daughter's ability to survive on so little sleep. The question that loomed over him, though, was where had she gone? It wasn't like she went to school. Her responsibilities were limited to assisting her mother with household tasks, and later she would have a husband who could command her. And control her, he hoped.

He didn't ask Farida – there really wasn't any point.

Even at the shop, all he could think about was Abida. How could he put a stop to this affair he was sure she was having? Could he even bring himself to challenge her about it? What if he was wrong, and she was innocent?

But what if he was right? He felt the throb of blood beneath the feathers of the chicken he held. For a moment, just one, he imagined himself holding his daughter's neck between his hands. His thoughts took him to the fields, to his daughter in the embrace of her lover, ruining and condemning not just herself but her entire family. His knife came down hard against the neck of the unsuspecting chicken, severing it completely. The chicken crumpled in his hand. He threw it into the waiting barrel without a second thought.

The other chickens had witnessed the carnage and now squawked in terror, pushing against the cages to distance them-selves from him. He didn't bother wiping his hands, but reached forward to grab another bird. Provoked perhaps by the blood on his hands, they went berserk.

The racket was so loud that he didn't hear her approach the shop. He saw her only when a shadow loomed over the chopping block. There she stood, bold as brass, holding his lunch tray, her apparently innocent grin looking more like a knowing smirk to him.

She said the customary greeting and laid the tray on a cleaner table away from him. Jamil didn't reply, his ears pounding at the thought of where she had been. He knew she'd only lie if he asked her. But still he couldn't resist. 'Where have you been?' he asked.

'Safiya's house again.' It was as if she had been born a liar.

She removed the chequered cloth with a flourish, revealing yellow lentils in a bowl with a pair of chapattis and half a raw onion. With all the chicken in the world around him, all Jamil could put on his family's table was lentils. He washed his hands in the old steel bucket he kept on the floor. The water turned a deep rosy pink, the colour of his shame for having Abida as a daughter.

He took his time scrubbing the blood from underneath his fingernails, hoping that she would just leave him be, but when he straightened up, she was still there. 'I can sit with you if you don't want to eat alone, Abbu,' she said.

His heart threatened to melt, but he steeled himself. 'And have the entire village call me shameless for having my daughter on display for everyone to see? I think not. Go home this instant. You've done your duty.'

The old Abida would have begged him to let her stay and eat with him, but the girl before him didn't bat an eyelid, and turned on her heel.

Yet more proof that his daughter had changed, and not for the better.

'Cover your head,' he barked after her.

She turned around, that infuriating smirk still in place, and flung over it a flimsy *dupatta*. She looked like a lady of the night.

From the corner of his eye, he caught the pir approaching. He couldn't face him like this: his nerves were far from settled, and a conversation with the pir required every ounce of his concentration. He busied himself with another chicken, hoping against hope that the old man would simply pass him by.

No such luck.

The pir paused right in front of the shop, casually leaning against the corrugated-steel counter. 'I've caught you at a busy time, it seems,' he said.

Jamil was forced to look up. The pir was dressed as usual in a starched white shalwar kameez, his snowy beard combed and oiled, and a light crocheted cap on his head. Jamil greeted him, but he didn't say anything more for fear of making the conversation longer than usual. He tried to busy himself with the chicken.

Another clean swipe against the neck. The bird shuddered in

his hand before he threw it into the waiting barrel with its unfortunate kin. The pir watched him transfixed.

'Does the blood ever wash off?' he asked. 'I've noticed your fingernails are always encrusted with it.'

What a silly question for someone so supposedly intelligent. 'With the soap they are making these days, everything washes off, Pir Sahab. It's just that you usually see me in my butcher's clothing.'

The pir sniffed the air. 'The stench of this place. Ah, I expect one gets used to it. Already, the smell of dead birds seems to be receding. I guess it must be the same for people who clean the open drains.'

Jamil was sure the comment was meant to upset him, but over the years, he had armoured himself against such insults. The pir's intended arrow just bounced off him.

'Rukhsana and I have been thinking,' the pir began.

Ah, so now he gets to the point. It had been weeks since the lunch he had hosted for the pir and, after a few encouraging remarks, there had been silence from him. After a point, Jamil had simply given up. His only regret was that he had wasted good money on all that food – money he could have used elsewhere.

'Abida has grown into a young woman,' the pir remarked, shaking Jamil out of his thoughts. 'I wonder why she doesn't have a female chaperone with her.'

'Chaperone?'

'A female companion.'

'We didn't hear from you for so long, Pir Sahab,' Jamil began. 'We assumed that there was nothing left to hope for.'

The pir stroked his beard. 'Well, I like your daughter. I think she would be perfect for my son.' Before Jamil could reply, he raised his hand. 'But something has been bothering me.'

The happiness that had suddenly bloomed inside Jamil shrivelled. 'Bothering you, sir?'

'Just the other day, I was out in the village at one in the

morning. Not that I usually have any business strolling about at such a late hour, but you know Safiya, the carpenter's wife? She gave birth recently and I was there to witness the baby's circumcision.'

Jamil's heart rate picked up. His fingers went numb. He put down the knife, straining to hear the pir's voice over the rushing noise in his ears.

The pir, sensing Jamil's tension, leaned closer. 'As I was coming out of the house, guess what I saw?'

Jamil didn't dare utter a word. He knew what the pir would say next. His vision was interrupted by black dots.

'Abida,' the pir whispered. 'Your daughter, running down the back alleys at such a late hour. I couldn't believe my eyes. How could such an honourable man's daughter be running around at this time of the night? What could she possibly be *doing*?'

Jamil murmured something.

'Eh? I didn't catch you there, I'm sorry.'

The pir leaned in further, close enough that Jamil could smell the bitter scent of his oil and his rancid breath. A network of deep wrinkles, almost like ridges, spread around his eyes.

Jamil cleared his throat. 'Abida never goes out of the house after six in the evening.'

The pir raised his eyes. 'But are you sure, my dear man?'

This time, Jamil met the pir's gaze. 'Of course. None of my children go out after dark.'

'Well, then my eyes must be deceiving me.'

'They must indeed.'

The pir sighed. 'Oh, what a sad business growing old is. I wouldn't wish it on anyone. To think my eyes could deceive me like that.' He straightened up and patted Jamil's shoulder. The old fingers felt like knives. It took all his strength not to recoil.

'Rukhsana will be most pleased to hear that it wasn't Abida I saw, although I shall be making an appointment to see a doctor in the city soon. These eyes of mine need testing.'

He left shortly after that, and it wasn't until Jamil saw his back vanish that he realised he had been holding his breath.

Abida, you fool.

༜

True to her nature, Farida started nagging him the moment he set foot inside the house.

'I've heard that the pir came to see you at the shop today. What did he say? Does Rukhsana like our daughter? Has she forgiven her?' She wrung her hands. 'Why won't you say anything?'

The beginnings of a headache began to set into his temples. 'Let me be, Farida. I've had a long day.' Farida opened her mouth to speak, but Jamil held up a hand. 'Not now.' She pursed her lips, giving him an icy glare.

He sighed. He couldn't meet Farida's gaze for the rest of the evening. All he could do was hold his head in his hands as the pain sharpened in his forehead. The days were getting warmer with May upon them, and rivulets of sweat ran down his back, soaking his kameez. He often thought that his other children were too young to understand anything, but Yousaf and Abbas surprised him by coming to sit beside him on either side of the *charpai*. He still had his head in his hands, but he knew it was the boys who had come to him. He could recognise people by their scent.

'Like a dog,' his teacher, Hashmi Sahab, had said to him once, slapping him hard across the face. 'Always inhaling people's scent like a stray dog. What is wrong with you? Hasn't your mother taught you any manners?' As if the slap wasn't enough, he proceeded to beat Jamil with a stick, hitting him behind the knees, where it hurt the most. 'If I catch you smelling people again, I'll have your hide, *kuttay ki aulad.*'

Jamil remembered his mother striding into school the next day, lifting her burka to confront Hashmi Sahab head on. Her eyes had blazed.

'How dare you call him a dog, *haramzaday*?'

Hashmi Sahab had actually clutched his chest at the insult. For a few moments, he was lost for words, and his mother used this to her advantage.

'I am taking him out of this school now. He will go to school in the next village, he will walk a mile, but he will not return to a place where he is not respected, where he is beaten to within an inch of his life. I almost died while having him. Do you think I'll let a disgusting little man like you kill him for fun?' With that, she had spat on his face.

His dear mother. How could he ever forget all she had done for him, and how badly he was failing her now. His family was spiralling out of his control.

'What's wrong, Abbu? Do you need anything? Water?'

Yousaf placed a tentative hand on Jamil's knee. Jamil removed his hands from his face and covered his boy's little hand with his own. He must be having a growth spurt because he'd been tiny the last time he'd checked. Jamil shook his head. His mind had been so preoccupied with putting food on the table and with Abida that he hadn't had time for the other children. Sometimes he couldn't even recall their names, there were so many.

Before he could say anything, Farida swooped in and shooed the boys away. 'Abbu needs rest. Don't be bothering him with silly stuff now. He has more important things to worry about.'

'I was just offering him water.' Yousaf's tone was sullen, but he turned away to join the rest of his siblings in the other room.

Now that they were alone, Farida threw a fresh sheet over the charpai and smoothed it over the jute. While she worked, she let out several sighs, which he knew were aimed at him. Still, he didn't say anything – he couldn't unless he knew for certain what Abida was up to.

'Why is she getting so fat?' he asked her, finally.

Farida blinked. 'What? Who?' He could tell that this was the last thing she had expected him to say.

Jamil repeated the question, his voice slow and measured.

Farida's eyes widened just a little. 'I don't know what you mean. She hardly eats anything. Whatever little I do manage to feed her, she brings up. It's almost as if...' She laughed, shaking her head.

'As if what?'

'Forgive me. All this worry over the pir and Rukhsana has addled my mind.'

'I asked you a question, Farida. Almost as if what?'

Farida narrowed her eyes. 'Why are you being like this?' Only when he leaned forward, preparing to rise did Farida add, 'I meant that it's almost as if she were with child, the way she's vomiting all the time. Happy?'

Jamil sank back into the charpai. All of a sudden, his knees began to shake. He held them steady with his hands.

'What's brought this on?' Farida asked him, but he ignored her.

Could Abida truly be with child? The weight gain could be attributed to too many of those oily jalebis she was fond of, but something told him that wasn't the case. Of course, it wasn't. She had never gained weight before. Jamil pulled at his hair, shaking his head when Farida offered him a cup of tea. It reeked of cow dung.

'Can you at least make my tea over a wood fire, Farida?'

'There isn't enough wood, Jamil,' Farida whispered with a stricken expression. 'You were supposed to fetch some a week ago.'

Jamil closed his eyes. 'When will she return? Did she say anything?'

Farida didn't reply, and he groaned. He was just going to have to wait.

By the time Abida finally arrived, the rage he had built up had cooled. Exhaustion had set in. It was all he could do to keep his head upright. He didn't even have the energy to question her. He closed his eyes, relishing the darkness. If only he could sit like that for a few more minutes, he was sure that the pain pounding in his head would go away.

It was Farida who spoke first. 'And where have you been, my girl? Do you have any idea how worried your father has been?'

Abida's laugh was bright, almost musical. 'But why? It isn't even dinner time yet. Besides, I would have stayed with poor Safiya but Abbu has been acting strange and I didn't want to risk his wrath.'

It was the lie, so easily spoken, that did it. The energy that had ebbed away during the wait for Abida coursed back. His head cleared. He leapt out of his seat, finally confronting his daughter over something that had eaten away at him for far too long. He cast one look at the other room and, satisfied by the chatter of the children that they would not hear, he advanced at Abida.

Fear twisted her features for a second before she assumed an amused expression. 'Abbu, what's going on?' She looked at both her parents. 'Ever since the pir came for lunch, both of you have been acting weird.'

'Where were you?' Jamil asked. *Lie*, he thought. *Lie this time and see what I do to you.*

'I was with Safiya. Where else would I be?'

Farida exhaled. 'Oh, Abida, how many times do I have to tell you not to overwork yourself for others?'

How easily Farida swallowed her daughter's lies. As had he.

Abida's smile was bordering on smug, but then her gaze landed on Jamil. The smile faded instantly.

'Safiya had her baby weeks ago,' he said. 'Rumour has it that she is doing quite well, so what exactly are you doing at her house all day long?'

Abida stepped back from Jamil till her back touched the cheap, whitewashed wall, which shed flakes of paint all the time.

'There goes your beautiful kameez,' Farida said. 'Silly girl.'

'Shut up!' barked Jamil, not caring now if the other children heard. They might as well, he thought. It would serve as a lesson. He rounded on Abida again, moving close to her. 'So, my dear daughter, who have you been meeting?'

'She doesn't have any friends,' said Farida. 'Who would she be meeting?'

To his horror, Abida spread her hands across her belly. He tried to blink back the tears. He was disgusted to find himself sobbing like a girl. 'Abida, you have ruined us. You have ruined yourself.'

'Oh,' Farida said. Jamil wasn't certain if the full horror of their situation had dawned on her. For all he knew, her mind could still be fixed on the ruined kameez.

Abida stared back at him, her mouth slightly open. There wasn't a trace of guilt in those clear features. On the contrary, she looked triumphant. 'I love him, Abbu. We are getting married.'

Jamil was so close to his daughter he could have swung an arm and hit her squarely across the face. God knows, he wanted to. 'Abida, you are such a fool. Stop lying to yourself. Whoever he is, he will never marry you.' His sobbing had stopped. He wiped at the snot with the cuff of his kameez.

'He will,' Abida replied, unfazed. 'If you knew who he was, you wouldn't be so frightened.'

Her response shocked him so much that, for a moment, he just stood there, his arms at his sides.

'I don't want to know who he is. Don't tell me.'

Abida's face softened. 'It's all been decided, Abbu. So, there really is no need to worry.'

That spurred him into action once again. 'No need to worry? You have been seen. By the pir, no less.'

Behind him, he heard Farida collapse to the floor. 'Who with?'

The fear he had glimpsed earlier returned to her face. Now she looked puzzled, vulnerable, her eyes lowered. 'What will he do to me?'

Jamil tapped his chin. 'Hmm, well, let me think. How about drowning you in a river? Or, even better, burning you at a pyre? How does that sound?'

Abida's face had turned the colour of sour milk, but she shrugged. 'Who cares about the pir? He won't be able to do anything once we are married. He's just a sad old man who is of no use to anyone.'

That was when he struck her across the face. His hand stung, but he didn't pause to draw breath. With his other hand, he pushed Abida's face into the wall.

Abida's scream sounded like music to his ears, but only for an instant.

Farida cried herself to sleep that night, but Jamil was wide awake. He felt as if he would never sleep again. He looked at the spot on the wall where he had pushed Abida's face. In the darkness, he covered his own with one hand, waiting for the traitorous sobs to pass.

Abida

Her head felt sore but, remarkably, her face showed no sign of the assault. It was as if her father had had training in causing pain without leaving a trace. He would occasionally shake her mother, but he had never hit his children, so the slap to her cheek had come as a great shock. And then he had shoved her face into the wall. It was the shock more than the pain that had caused her to burst into tears and retreat to her room, if it could be called a room. It reeked of wet earth and unwashed clothes, of disease and neglect. Abida had lost count of the number of times one of her siblings had caught malaria in there, the days that had streamed past as she had helped her mother nurse them. It was as if she had been born to be a slave, to work without any reward. She didn't dare admit it to herself, but there were times when she wished her family dead, just so she could finally be free.

Abida's gaze fell on her sleeping siblings. They looked like pretty angels. Was she really that evil? Was her father right to beat her as he had? The questions swirled inside her head until she rose from the *charpai*. A brief moment of dizziness as pain seared through her head, but then her vision cleared and, clutching her belly, she moved towards the wall, away from the doorway. Her mother had left some *imli* in a bowl for her. Abida snatched it up, sucking on the tamarind greedily.

None of it mattered now, the pain or her family. The decision had been made, for better or worse. Her return to the house last night had been only to say goodbye. Having retreated to the far corner of the room, she pulled out the cell phone she had stowed inside the strap of her undershirt.

'This is only meant for emergencies, Abida,' Kalim had told her last night, as he passed it to her. 'Don't use it in front of anyone in case they get suspicious.'

Her joy had been difficult to contain. She felt as if she would burst out laughing at any moment. Even when she was being beaten by her father, she had thought the laugh would come gushing from her mouth.

They were running away. She could hardly believe it. Silly Abida, she thought, reciting an *ayat* and blowing it into the air to protect herself from evil. It was a crazy plan with a good deal of running involved, but it was better than no plan at all. Her heart sank as she thought back to all the sleepless nights she had spent pounding her belly, sometimes lying on the floor, at others cursing the baby inside her. She had even tried to push it out, the way her friend Safiya had done weeks ago. But hers was a grown baby carried to term while Abida's was still developing, stuck to her as if by some invisible glue. And now the same baby was to be her salvation. Kalim didn't have the courage to tell his parents, but at least he was willing to take her away and marry her.

'We can't wait now. You're beginning to show. We'll worry about our families later,' he told her. 'When they see that their grandchild is on his way, they will melt. I just know it.'

His way? Kalim already believed it to be a boy, which annoyed Abida. Why not a girl? Of course, she was in no position to take the moral high ground, considering she had, until recently, been trying to murder that same baby by any means.

'Calm down,' she told herself, as she peeked through the curtain again. It was not yet dawn so everything was shrouded in shadow, the only light coming from an old oil lamp in the far corner. She tiptoed past the doorway and her parents' *charpai*, her heart thudding in her chest. Her father was a light sleeper at the best of times, and after yesterday's events, he would probably be on edge. But she had to look. Kalim's promises were all very well – getting married in secret, then returning proudly with their child to the village – but Abida knew better. She had always been realistic. To evade the suspicions of the village elders, they would need to stay away from the village for several months, years even. It wouldn't be easy to wipe off the stink of running away, not in this village.

She looked at her sleeping parents and swallowed sudden tears. She wondered when she would see them again, those frown lines between his father's eyebrows, now permanently etched on his face, lines she had come to love: worry for his family had caused them. Her mother's face was in shadow, but even if it wasn't, Abida knew she would be unable to see it. Like all good wives, her mother kept her head covered while sleeping, usually covering her entire face. Once or twice, one of the little ones had screamed, thinking she was a corpse.

Abida choked at the memory, but then clamped her hand over her mouth.

His father stirred, mumbling something in his sleep.

She drew closer.

'Abida,' he said, before his words dissolved into an incoherent mutter.

It was time to leave. Any moment now, Kalim would call her on the cell phone, and Abida didn't want the noise waking up the entire household.

'Forgive me,' she murmured, before turning away.

Jamil

'Wake up! You must wake up!'

His mind registered the words, but refused to act on them, instead pulling him deeper into a dark abyss of sleep, so peaceful that it wasn't until he felt the sting of a slap on his face that his eyes opened.

Sudden rage filled him, and he raised his hand to strike whoever had dared raise their hand on him. His eyes met Farida's panic-stricken gaze, and his hand lowered itself.

His throat was too dry to form words. He sputtered at her.

She sputtered back. It would have been funny if he hadn't seen the terror dancing in her eyes.

He grabbed her by the shoulders and shook her. Thankfully, his voice came to him then. 'What's happened?'

The command in his voice only made her break into tears.

For the second time in twenty-four hours, he raised his hand to a woman. The slap sent Farida reeling to the ground.

'Please forgive me, Farida. I don't know why I did that.' His hands were trembling. He bent down to help her up, and it was then that the words came spilling out of her. What she said shook the earth beneath his feet.

He took her hand and together they rushed outside, the children following them out.

'Abbu, what's happened?' Yousaf shouted.

'They shouldn't come with us,' he told his wife, but she was in another world. A deep fear gripped him when he saw the expression on her face.

He shook his head to get rid of the dark thoughts that seemed to swarm all over him. He knew the children were following them, but he had no strength to scold them; he didn't even have the strength to look back. If he did, he didn't know if he would be able to keep moving forward. Despite all the sleep he had had, his legs felt drained and brittle, as if one gust of wind would break them. One step at a time, he told himself.

There was an eerie silence in the village square. Only a few children moved around the empty stalls, their plastic flip-flops clapping against their heels as they chased each other. The tall shisham tree in the middle of the square loomed like a sentry.

A child's face brightened on seeing Jamil. He pointed at him. 'They've taken your daughter to the riverbank,' he said, glee written all over his features. 'All the village is there. It's going to be so much fun. Die, Abida, die!'

He didn't know how he covered the distance between the square and the river. It was only when he stepped on a thorn that he realised he was barefoot. He didn't care if he was bleeding. After everything that had happened, he deserved it. He had failed his daughter.

He heard them before he saw them – a loud unified noise, like the roar of an angry lion. When he did see the people, his knees buckled. The crowd was like a huge wave of anger, a sea of black heads aimed towards the riverbank.

He raised himself, took Farida's icy hand again, and pushed through the throng, driving his shoulder into people's backs to get past them. They sprang out of his way. A few hissed at him. When they reached the riverbank, Jamil noticed the men in starched turbans standing on a mound of earth with Abida in the middle. Her shirt had been torn all the way to her chest revealing her nakedness. He was shocked to see how far along she was: her belly stood out, as if someone had thrust a watermelon inside her. He felt a surge of affection for the thing – his grandchild. Abida's hair flew in the wind like the black sails of a sinking ship. When she saw them, she shouted one word: 'Abbu!'

It was like a whip across his back. Farida sank to the ground with a groan of pure terror.

'Let her go,' Jamil shouted over the din.

The pir, standing triumphant in his starched white turban, his eyes blazing, raised a hand to silence the crowd. The roar died down. 'Too late, Jamil. You have failed in your duty as a father. Your daughter was discovered trying to escape the village this morning with a boy. She let the boy go, and now refuses to divulge his identity. But no matter, we will find him. Nothing stays hidden in this village for long.'

Jamil closed his eyes. *Abida, you fool*, he thought. *Who escapes in broad daylight?*

'They are going to be married,' he said out loud.

'Liar,' the pir shot back. 'Liar, liar, liar. You were going to bring this *kanjari* to my house, thrust her at my honourable son if I hadn't caught her in the act. This product of lust and sin inside her bears testament to your daughter's character, the *kanjari* that she is.'

'They had my permission.'

'Another lie. Since you have so obviously taken leave of your senses, dear Jamil, allow us to sentence your daughter for you. You can do the honours, of course. So what should it be? Love or honour?'

Jamil began to protest, but someone grabbed his hand. He looked down to see that it was his wife.

'Let her go,' she said. She was still sitting on the ground, the scarf having slid from her head.

Jamil pulled his hand away. 'You have lost your mind.'

'Can't you see that we have lost her? Please, husband, don't lose the others. Look at them.'

Jamil shut his eyes, the tears tracking down his cheeks.

'Look at them!'

He glanced back and saw his children trembling in the wind. How could it be so cold in late summer? He saw the life they had in front of them if Abida survived. He saw their expulsion from the local school, their inability to find jobs, even as apprentices. He saw them being kicked and shoved wherever they went. He saw the end.

'No.'

His gaze moved towards Abida again but, to his surprise, she was smiling. 'Think of the little ones,' she called.

My poor fool, he thought.

'Love or honour?' the pir shouted. 'Tell us.'

The crowd followed his cue and started shouting too: 'Love or honour?'

'Come now, I am asking the father to choose the fate of his daughter. At least meet me halfway.'

Love or honour?

Farida was weeping now. 'Go and do it – save your other children. Let them have a chance at life. She is lost to us.'

Abida's smile faltered. He saw the effort it cost her to keep smiling. She nodded. 'It's alright,' she mouthed. Only for him to hear.

He remembered protecting her from Farida's slaps, how she would wrap her arms around him, and they'd dance out of Farida's grasp until she collapsed on the *charpai* with her head in her hands. 'You have spoiled her beyond recognition.'

Had he?

Without knowing how, he somehow arrived in front of his daughter.

Gently, the pir guided his hand to rest atop Abida's head. 'You're doing the right thing,' he murmured. 'You cannot burden yourself with the sins of this creature. She ceased being your daughter when she fornicated with her lover. She deserves to die.'

Jamil was numb. He heard the pir's words, but they didn't make sense.

Abida turned around and waded into the water. 'Do it.'

The current wasn't strong, but if someone were to venture

further in, it would be hard to get them out. The water slapped against the riverbank, soaking Jamil's shalwar. He followed Abida in the water.

It was cold.

'Do it,' the pir urged him.

And, just like that, he applied more pressure on her neck until her head vanished into the murky brown water.

No bubbles rose to the surface. Abida was as limp as a fish.

Why won't you fight back?

He saw the girl in front of him and remembered her birth, when the people around him were praying for a son, but he had secretly prayed for a daughter.

Love or honour?

He thought of her first steps, taken with his finger in her little hand. He remembered giving her the first tour of the village, how she had squealed at the sight of cotton candy, her chubby face smeared with sugar as she attempted to lick it clean.

Love or honour?

He saw the husband she would never have, the children she would never give birth to, the home where she would never live.

He saw the end.

He saw his daughter, just another girl in the river.

His daughter? A girl in the river?

In a split second he had kicked the pir aside and pulled out Abida's head from the water.

She gasped like a newborn baby, then spluttered as the water emptied out of her lungs.

The crowd was like a wave of red-hot anger, of hostility.

The pir's eyes widened as he pulled himself up from the ground. Jamil saw with some satisfaction that his brilliant white clothes dripped with mud. 'Why you *haramkhor*...'

Jamil pulled Abida close to his chest. He would never let anybody hurt her again. 'Stay back!'

The pir opened his mouth to scream something, but then his

face drained of colour. In the distance, the sound of police sirens was growing louder.

Abida

Abida clung to her father, a scared child, wet and whimpering. His grip around her was so tight, she thought he might fracture her ribs. It was as if he would never let her go.

'Who called the police?' the pir demanded.

'Kill her before they arrive,' someone screamed from the crowd. 'Drown her. Burn her.'

She clamped her eyes shut in the face of the villagers' rising anger, but the sirens were now drowning their shouts.

'Abida, look,' her father whispered. 'We are safe.'

She opened her eyes and the flashing lights nearly blinded her.

It wasn't just a small police car: a huge convoy had arrived, complete with female police officers who were stepping out of the jeeps, their olive-green *dupattas* swirling in the wind. The expression on their faces was murderous. They tore Abida from her father.

'You are safe now, girl,' one of them whispered in her ear. 'You are safe from these animals.'

The pir was livid. Abida had never seen him like this – saliva shot from his mouth as he screamed, his eyes wide and bulging, his hands held high. He raised a shaking finger in the air. 'This girl's fate has already been decided by the *jirga*. You cannot do this. She is bound by our laws, and we have sentenced her to death.'

'Shut up, old man,' the police inspector said. 'Anything you say may be used against you in a court of law.'

'You have no authority here.'

The police inspector stared at him. In the flashing lights, his face was blank. 'Tell me again that I have no authority here. Contrary to what you might believe, killing for honour is a crime now.'

Everyone, including Abida, gasped.

'Is the girl even related to you?' the policeman scoffed. 'If not, I fail to understand how her honour is any of your business. I mean, what are you even trying to protect?'

The pir opened his mouth, then thought better of it, but when the female constable attempted to steer Abida into one of the jeeps, he leapt into their path. 'You are interfering in matters of the *jirga*. She ... she is pregnant out of wedlock!'

The officer glanced at Abida. 'She doesn't look pregnant to me.'

'Look at that bulging belly of hers, you fool!'

The inspector seemed to be enjoying the pir's distress. 'I don't see anything.'

The pir seemed close to tears. 'Don't you realise how much evil this will unleash?. Do you know how many girls could follow suit? Do you want them all to taste freedom? From your accent, you seem like an honourable man from south Punjab. Would you want that on your conscience?'

The inspector laughed. 'You're telling me that you'll kill every last girl who raises her head?' He shook his head and turned away.

He didn't notice the pir mouth, 'Yes.'

It sent a chill down Abida's spine.

'Get out of the way, old man, and go home. Constable Rabbiya, it's time to take the girl to the neighbouring village. Her future husband awaits.'

'This isn't over,' the pir whispered, his eyes fixed on Abida's belly. 'You have ruined the name of your family, girl, and the reputation of this village. These crimes don't go unpunished. Remember that.'

'Don't listen to him,' Constable Rabbiya said, as she gently pushed her into the waiting jeep. 'Get in quickly before he tries anything else.'

It dawned on Abida that the police would never intervene in village business ... unless they were paid to do so. They wouldn't think to take on a village elder like the pir just to save her – not because they couldn't, but because they simply didn't care. They had to have come from the city. They had more important matters to deal with than saving a girl from being killed for honour. Honour killings happened every day. Kalim must have spent all he had to save her. The constable's pity seemed fake now, but Abida still clung to her. She had to.

Her mother was weeping openly, but nobody stepped forward to comfort her. Finally her father stumbled towards her and took her in his arms. Her siblings stood in a tight group, hugging each other, tears and snot running down their dirty faces. Abida knew she had condemned them all. She buried her face in the constable's shoulder and sobbed.

Jamil

'Do you accept Kalim Nawaz as your lawfully wedded husband?'
Abida nodded.

The *maulvi* asked her the same question thrice, and each time, Abida nodded. Jamil felt his chest swell. His beautiful daughter, married at last. There would be no killing for honour now. Even the pir couldn't dare suggest they murder a newlywed couple.

'He may not be able to do anything openly,' Farida whispered in his ear, 'but that doesn't mean he cannot harm our daughter secretly. He has the entire village at his disposal.' She wiped at her tears, which left the kohl streaked across her eyes. Despite her attempt to make herself presentable in a starched cotton shalwar kameez, she looked like a ghost.

She was right, though, and listening to her, Jamil felt the strength drain from his body. He didn't feel capable even of opening his mouth to reassure her. He collapsed into a nearby chair as the *maulvi* invited the witnesses to sign the marriage documents. The pir could take his daughter away from him at any moment. She had only to venture out of her home for something bad to happen. And looking at the expression on the face of Kalim's mother, he could tell she would be happy to see the last of Abida.

Apart from them and Kalim's parents, nobody from Khan Wala village had plucked up the courage to attend the *nikkah* ceremony. The village of Chauns Shah was bigger than Khan Wala, but the people here were equally suspicious and judgmental. It was a miracle a *maulvi* had agreed to wed the couple. There was a large pot of chicken curry bubbling outside with freshly baked naan to go with it, but fear of the pir had kept everyone away. Even beyond Khan Wala the name Pir Sadiq commanded fear.

'I'll just distribute the food door to door,' Jamil told his wife. 'It is a sin to let good food go to waste.'

'Especially given how much you've spent on it. This might be the last chicken we see for a while now. Let the children have some first.' Farida's face was lined with premature wrinkles, and the frown between her eyebrows never seemed to leave her. 'I can't imagine what our lives will be like from now on. With the pir as our enemy, we may have to beg in the streets.'

'Don't be silly, Farida. Give thanks that our daughter is alive.'

'For now.'

Her words pierced his heart. He rose to his feet and stepped away from her. He had more pressing matters to think of without the added burden of Farida's fear.

The *maulvi* cleared his throat and everyone went silent. He bunched his white beard in one hand. 'You should leave this area,' he murmured. His watery gaze landed on Kalim, before travelling to Abida whose head was bowed, an embellished net *dupatta* covering her hair. 'I know Pir Sahab very well. He will never forget this humiliation. Every day you stay in the village, alive, will be a slight to him. Even Chauns Shah is not safe. Pir Sahab's influence extends far and wide. Your baby will be his sworn enemy. He will go to any lengths to take his revenge. The moment the police leave, he will make sure you are killed, Abida.'

He was right. The police inspector had left immediately after yesterday's events, leaving only a couple of constables behind. With their batons and aged rifles, which didn't even look like they worked, the protection they afforded seemed flimsy.

Kalim's parents didn't seem particularly shocked by what the *maulvi* said, but, then, it wasn't their daughter's life on the line.

Jamil was wondering what he would have to sell so that he could afford to send his daughter out of the village when Kalim spoke up.

'We are moving to Lahore. I have a friend who has arranged a job for me in the city. We will be very well settled there.'

Farida gasped. '*MashAllah* – how wonderful. Praise be to God.'

Jamil felt a mixture of relief and dread. Lahore was far away. The pir would never find Abida there. But it was a different world to the village. She wouldn't know what'd hit her. But then, if she stayed here, she would most certainly be killed, one way or another.

He glanced at Abida, expecting tears, but she was smiling. Her eyes were locked with Kalim's. 'It's all I ever wanted,' she said.

If you're happy, then I'm happy, Jamil thought as he smiled, but the dread remained in the pit of his stomach.

Abida

God. Miracles. Fate.

Abida believed in everything now. After what had happened to her, who wouldn't? Every bump in the dirt road caused her intense discomfort, but somehow she managed to ignore it. Nothing could come in the way of her happiness today. Her arms encircled her husband's waist, and even in broad daylight, on a motorbike, she could feel his desire for her.

'I'm almost six months along,' she chided him. 'Mind yourself.'

Kalim didn't look back at her, but she knew he was grinning. 'Can you blame a man for desiring his wife? Should I desire someone else?'

She tightened her arms around him. 'Never.'

She had spent her entire life in the village, so when the lush green fields gave way to thatched houses and proper metalled roads, she sat a bit straighter on the motorcycle. The more they ventured into the town proper, the noisier it became. A cacophony of car horns, street hawkers and screaming ambulances made her cover her ears. Was Lahore going to be like this? She couldn't find a single tree in this concrete jungle. It was a sea of grey and brown, with beggars parading the tight streets, men selling caged parakeets, while others sat around shops, staring at her, their feet dangling over the open drains. Unlike the village, where women were very much a fixture of street life, the city was strangely empty of them. Maybe it was the dirty stares from the pot-bellied men that kept them indoors. Abida's stomach grumbled at the smell of fried fish, but she dared not say anything to Kalim. So many men made her nervous. She would wait until they were in an open area. She nibbled a sad little strip of dried beef that her mother had packed for her. 'Cost your father a fortune, so make sure you finish it all.'

Her dear mother, always worried about money. Sometimes, Abida wondered whether she even loved her, but then she thought of the moments when she was being drowned and she'd seen the despair on her mother's face, and she chided herself. Of course she loved her. Her love was just different from Abbu's. Nobody could love her like her father did. She knew that now.

Before she could fall deeper into her reverie, Kalim said, 'Look around, Abida. We've arrived in Khanewal and soon we'll be on the train to Lahore.'

Abida sniffed. Khanewal wasn't what she had expected. For a city that was supposed to be huge, everything seemed to be packed pretty close together. Still, when they emerged into the wider, tree-lined boulevards with large houses painted in shades of grey and beige, her jaw fell. Unlike the village, a city had many faces. If Khanewal was like this, what would Lahore be like?

Lahore ... the word still sent shivers down her spine. If someone had told her a month ago that she would soon be married to the man of her dreams, that she would be allowed to live while being with child out of wedlock, she would have laughed. And yet, somehow, it had all come true. Every single thing she had dreamed of.

It was strange, now that she thought of it. She had been so close to death, close enough to embrace it and feel its spindly fingers reach into her throat to extract her soul, before her father had given her life again. A child was brought into the world by a woman, but she had been given life again by a man. Her father. If it hadn't been for him, she would have been dead. The police would have arrived too late. After everything she had put her father through, his love for her hadn't dimmed. She remembered how Shabnam, and countless girls before her, had been thrown without mercy into the river, how some of the elderly women said that they saw their souls wandering in distress, some searching for the babies that had been drowned in milk and left for the crows. Yet here she was, heading to Lahore.

She ran a hand over her swollen belly, and felt a kick from the baby. The quickening had happened some weeks ago, but it still surprised her. If it hadn't been for her father, her baby would be dead along with her. They had signed the official documents that declared them husband and wife a day later, Abida putting her thumb impression on the papers, as she was declared illiterate. She couldn't bear to tell anyone that she had committed yet another transgression in secretly learning to read and write from Yousaf. Besides, it was better if everyone thought she was illiterate. They'd returned to Khan Wala village, and then made the short journey from her parents' house to that of Kalim's.

Kalim's father had gone home ahead of time to prepare a proper welcome for them, but his mother's mouth had thinned when her gaze met Abida's, then slid down to her belly. A cruel smile spread across that thin mouth. 'I would leave you alone for your first night together ... if only it were your first night together.' And then she had laughed – an unpleasant sound in a woman on such a day.

Despite Kalim's repeated requests, his mother hadn't let them take the jeep.

'Your father is a sick man. He seems fine right now, but that wretched cancer can return at any minute. You may be running away to Lahore, but I'll still be here, taking care of him. Do you want me to carry him to the doctor on my shoulders?' She was a small woman with a slight build, but her eyes blazed with hatred for her new daughter-in-law. Abida had shrank back from her gaze. Kalim's father had given her a small smile before busying himself with food. He didn't hate her, at least, but he also didn't like her enough to take a stand in front of his wife. In the end, Kalim had borrowed a motorbike from a friend.

She shook her head. Now was not the time to think of that.

It was obvious that they couldn't stay in the village, not after what the *maulvi* had said. They had escaped the pir once, but there was no telling what he would do once the fear of the police had passed. And so, the very next day, Kalim and Abida had climbed onto the motorbike bound for the railway station in Khanewal.

As they approached station, Kalim spoke to someone on his cell. 'Cover your face, Abida,' he told her when he ended the call. 'We're not in the village anymore. Respectable women in Khanewal hide their faces from strangers.' Maybe he felt Abida stiffen, for he stopped the bike beneath the shade of a towering shisham tree and sighed. 'It's only till Lahore. After that, I promise you can do whatever you want.' He climbed off the motorbike, holding it steady until Abida slid off as well. 'Here comes the man I was talking to. He'll take the keys of the bike from me.'

A shot of panic hit her. 'What will we do in Lahore? We won't have any way to get around.'

'We will have each other, Abida. Now, you make a start for the station entrance while I deal with this man here, but don't go too far. Khanewal isn't safe for a woman on her own.'

Abida wasn't entirely convinced by Kalim's answer, but she forced herself to stay calm. There was no point in panicking. It wasn't as if they could return to Khan Wala village again.

Her new life was ahead of her and she had to face it.

The station was a low building that seemed to have been freshly painted white and green. It gleamed in the sun, the small minarets catching the light and casting their dappled shadows on the cement floor. As they made their way towards the platform through the multitude of people, she marvelled at the rail tracks crisscrossing everywhere. The smell of petrol and damp clothes was heavy in the air. Before Abida could so much as look around, a strange hum filled the air. She froze. It steadily grew louder, and in a blink of an eye, a beige train rushed past the platform. A gust of wind accompanied the roar of the engine, which seemed to consume everything for a moment.

'Was that a train?' Abida asked, her eyes watering from having kept them open for so long. She never wanted to close them again. She had just witnessed a marvel.

'Khanewal is a major stop for trains heading north or south. Sort of like a pit stop.'

'What's a pit stop?' Abida asked him, but Kalim simply laughed.

The wooden benches were all occupied by older women who held their heads in their hands as infants cried on the floor. Abida stood next to Kalim as trains arrived and departed. Without Kalim, she thought, she would be lost. She didn't know anything. She tried to take his hand, but he shook her off.

'Not here, Abida. Nobody holds hands in public.'

'But we're in a big city now.' She hated the whine in her voice. 'Surely people don't care.'

Kalim shook his head, but didn't reply.

'Is that fried fish I smell?'

A man was eating it out of a polythene bag, peeling away the bits of newspaper that clung to the crusted fish before biting into it. The juice dribbled down his beard. Abida should have been nauseated by the sight, but her stomach surprised her by groaning in response. 'Can we get some?' she asked Kalim, but he had already wandered ahead, his gaze fixed on the tracks. Abida reached into the pocket she had sewn in the waist of her shalwar, but then thought better of it. This precious money that her father had given her could be put to better use elsewhere. Kalim had to buy her something to eat. What was wrong with him? It was lucky that their train arrived at that moment as Abida felt she would burst into tears. Why did everything always have to be so difficult?

Inside, the train hummed with life. After the bumpy ride into Khanewal, the torn leather seats in the compartments looked inviting. She collapsed into the one Kalim indicated with her hand held over her belly. They had barely seated themselves in the carriage before she felt her eyes closing, and it was a small mercy that Kalim let her rest her head on his shoulder.

'This feels nice,' she murmured, before falling into a dreamless sleep.

It wasn't until they were arriving into Lahore that her eyes fluttered open.

'Wake up, my love,' Kalim whispered in her ear. 'See the city you have dreamed of with your own eyes.'

She gripped the steel railings across the window and peered out, her eyes watering as she struggled to keep herself from blinking. She took in the smell of potato fritters and rotten fruit coming from afar, mixed with a noxious chemical vapour that seemed to blanket the very air. It left a bitter taste in her mouth. Was this what the people of Lahore had to put up with? It wasn't at all like Khan Wala village, where she could see miles in the distance and the only smell was that of open drains and cooking fires. Here, she couldn't see beyond the slate grey roofs of the small houses that squatted near the tracks. Young children hovered dangerously close, some mere inches away from the train. The driver sounded the horn several times, but nobody seemed to care. There were too many people and the mountains of garbage were unlike anything she had ever seen. Back in the village, most of their garbage was food waste which in turn helped the crops thrive, but here, there was plastic everywhere. Plastic bags flew in the air, some snagging into the barbed wire lining the walls. For Kalim, Abida made the appropriate noises to demonstrate her wonder, but deep down, she couldn't wait to cover her nose and mouth and double down. As far as first impressions went, Lahore had disappointed her. The train continued to whizz through the sprawling city, the tracks lined with fruit vendors and shanty towns now, before it slowed into what looked like a vast hall full of people. It had a certain grandness to it with its red-bricked walls and polished, cement floor. A large yellow sign hanging from the ceiling read *LAHORE*.

'The great railway station of Lahore,' Kalim announced. 'It has existed for hundreds of years.'

Abida watched the crowds of people milling about, most holding their luggage over their heads as they jostled for space on the narrow concrete platform. All of them were making a beeline for the main hall, and judging by Kalim's frown, they had to as well. Abida held her *dupatta* over her nose as the smell of human sweat and excrement assaulted her. Unlike Khanewal, though, she could see plenty of women here, their colourful shalwar kameez a welcome relief in the otherwise drab station. Even the sky looked grey and unforgiving.

For better or worse, she had arrived.

Jamil

It was warm inside the hut even with all the windows thrown open. The overhead electric fan hung defeated, cobwebs dangling from its wings. Farida sat on the *charpai*, trying to finish embroidering the shirt she had been working on for weeks. By now, the white cotton fabric was stained brown in places. Farida sighed, putting her needle down again.

'I can't work in this heat,' she announced. 'June is supposed to be hot, but not this hot, surely? I feel as if I will suffocate any second. And this will need to be washed before I can hope to sell it.'

'Why don't you go and join the children at the tube well? The water is always cool there.'

'And risk someone seeing me with my head uncovered? I'd rather die in here.'

'No one goes there now since it's so close to our home. It's as if we own it.'

Farida fanned her face with her *dupatta*, the rivulets of sweat streaming down to her chest. For some reason the sight aroused him. He was just about to rise from his seat when Farida rose from hers with a huff. 'I might as well go down there. Any people who watch me, be damned. It's not as if our family is free from scandal anyway.'

Jamil leaned back on his chair, ignoring the sweat rolling down his own face. 'Farida, be thankful that she is alive and away from this place. They would have killed her otherwise ... they almost did. *I* almost did.'

Farida gave him a cold look. 'You think I don't care about my daughter. I can see it in your eyes. You relish the fact that nobody loves Abida more than you. Unlike you, I love all my children equally. Just because I don't put Abida above everything and everyone else doesn't mean I don't love her.'

'Oh, come now, I didn't mean that. You know I love you more than anything.'

Usually, the effect of words such as these was immediate, but today Farida was having none of it. 'You're just saying that because you're bored and you need me in bed with you.'

'Would it be too bad if I did? I am your husband after all.' He winked at her, but she shook her head.

'I wish I could, but I don't think I'd survive it in this heat.' With that, she threw the *dupatta* over her head and walked out of the hut.

Jamil stared after her. This was probably one of the few times she had talked back to him. Despite what she had just said, he felt he couldn't understand her love. One minute she would be as protective as a lioness of her cubs, but the next, Jamil wondered whether she loved Abida at all. He still couldn't forget how she had advised him to kill Abida to save the other children from ruin. Her own daughter. How could she? He knew he was being harsh in judging her, the mother of his children, but he couldn't help it.

At last, he gave in and wiped the sweat off his face with the back of his hand. It had been two weeks since their electricity had been cut off. Their house being at the far end of the village, it really didn't take much effort to slice through a single dangling wire. Jamil was surprised it had taken the pir so long. He sighed. One more thing on his list. If he didn't get the electricity fixed today, Farida would most likely kill him. The thought made him chuckle. His mother would have been proud to see Farida today, a daughter-in-law who possessed a spine.

'We outnumber men in this country,' she used to say to Jamil. 'If we could all just band together and raise our heads and fists, we could rule. And I know just what we can do with the men of this village.' The language she used for men brought tears of laughter to his father's eyes. Jamil missed her. Not a single day went by when he didn't think of her.

'Till we meet again, Ama Jaan,' he murmured.

It had been more than a month since Abida had left the village with Kalim. Once a week, he would dial her mobile-phone number and talk to her. His throat would constrict when he heard her voice, his first instinct being to reach out and protect her. But there was no need. She was happy – happier than she had ever been. The date of delivery was approaching and Kalim was spoiling her.

I've put on a ton in weight, she told him, *the way Kalim feeds me. The day isn't far off when I won't fit through a doorframe, and the doorframes in the city are wider than in the village.*

Jamil couldn't help laughing. How could such a child have made it across Punjab, all the way to Lahore, carrying a child in her belly? His very own Abida. When a mysterious letter arrived from the city some weeks ago, Jamil had thought it must be a summary of the police report, but he was shocked to see the uneven, messy scrawl of a person who had recently learned to write. His Abida. The words were fuzzy and barely legible, but they were words, telling him her news as well as her phone number. Abida now qualified among those who could read and write in Pakistan. His chest swelled with pride at the thought, and made him forget his worries.

I learned it from Yousaf, but Kalim helped.

Jamil wasn't surprised. The boy would burst into tears if he saw a goat being slaughtered. He had a kind heart, most unsuited for life in this village. Perhaps, in time, he could join his sister in Lahore for his higher studies. The village would destroy his dear little boy. He deserved better.

Yousaf and Abbas were back in school, now, but there was still the issue of the pir. He hadn't killed another girl yet, but he had

had one lashed in public. Jamil had watched in horror as the scene unfolded, the anger from the onlookers erupting like lava. This time, no police arrived. Everyone wanted a piece of the girl as she was led down the dirt track. Some of them tore at her clothes while others pulled at her hair, and threw rotten eggs and tomatoes at her face. Some, however, held back. It was a subtle shift from the unanimous hatred such events brought on. Jamil noticed the unease on their faces, the way some of the women covered their faces with their *dupattas* and turned away, the men averting their gaze as the girl was paraded in front of them. He watched a few of them take their wives by the elbow and steer them back home.

'Nothing to watch here,' one of them whispered to his wife. 'This has become the norm, and frankly, it terrifies me. We have daughters at home too.'

It almost made Jamil want to intervene, but he held back. Maybe, just maybe, the pir would let the girl off with a warning. After all, it was only alleged by a child that she had been having sex in the fields. Even the pir couldn't make a case out of nothing. He couldn't kill her. By the time she arrived at the village square, her kameez had been ripped to shreds. That, too, was then stripped off, leaving her in a bra and shalwar.

'You didn't feel any shame when you removed all your clothes for that boy, so why should you feel any now? The whole world should see you for what you are. Corrupt and evil. A monster.'

The girl hadn't tried to cover herself with her hands. Her eyes just stared in the distance.

Jamil had been shaking so hard that he had had to wrap his arms around himself. Beside him, Farida had put a hand on his shoulder.

'Don't even think about intervening,' she had whispered. 'Remember your own kids at home.'

They had all watched as the girl's brothers spat on her first, followed by her mother, sisters and finally her father, who allowed the pir to do the honours. Jamil liked to think that some sudden burst of fatherly love had stopped the man lashing his own daughter, but from his erect posture and stony gaze, he soon realised how mistaken he was. The poor girl, accused of falling in love and giving herself to the wrong sort of boy, was made to face the shisham tree as the pir lashed her back. She didn't lift a finger to save herself. It would have been futile, anyway, but Jamil knew that she was so completely exhausted, she would have welcomed the lashes.

As soon as Kalim and I have saved enough, I am going to have you all move to Lahore with us. The village is toxic.

Sitting in his chair, with fresh sweat dotting his forehead, Jamil realised how right she was. The village was no longer a safe place for them. But they didn't have any money to move somewhere else. Unless a miracle occurred, Jamil knew he would die in this village. His only consolation was that he didn't have his daughter's blood on his hands.

Abida

Abida was happy. There was no other word for it. It felt different, surreal even, to be married to the love of her life. She never thought she would settle in Lahore so easily, but she had taken to it like a duck to water. Kalim was kind and considerate, just as he always had been, only now she could fully appreciate it. They'd been here for a month, and he already had a job at an airline office, the salary from which landed in her palm.

'You're the lady of the house,' he told her when he got his first pay packet. 'You make all the decisions.' Abida thought he was joking, but when she saw the honesty in his eyes, the smile that she had come to love, she knew she had struck gold.

Despite her condition, they made love everyday without fail. Kalim loved her, and that's why she didn't let a moment of doubt cloud her mind. So what if this month the salary was half what it had been previously? It was still plenty, and if he kept earning that much, they could think of moving away from Anarkali. She was blooming. She saw it on her face every day, that pink, healthy glow.

'That's the glow of pregnancy,' Saima, her next-door neighbour, told her. 'Pregnancy looks pretty now, but wait until you've got to lose all the weight again. That's torture.' She kissed her eight-year-old son on the forehead. 'Still, all worth it in the end.'

Saima was the only woman in their building who didn't have a husband.

'Naa, *Ji*, I don't need no man in my life,' she would say. 'I've seen enough of them to last me a lifetime.'

When Abida asked her what she meant by that, Saima just brushed her off. 'You're better off not knowing, *meri jaan*. It might be too much for your delicate little ears.'

'She used to work as an escort, Abida,' Kalim told her later that evening. 'Surely, you must have picked up on that? I'm surprised you're associating with people like her. Saima has a bad reputation.'

'She is good to me, Kalim,' Abida replied, her back turned to him as she made him another chapatti. 'She's my only friend.'

'It's because she is your friend that you don't have other friends. Still, do what you will.' He held up a hand when she brought him the chapatti. 'No more. I'm just tired. I think I'll go rest.'

'Is everything alright?' Abida didn't want to admit it, but Kalim was losing weight. His face had assumed a yellowish pallor and his hands trembled sometimes. 'Is the job proving too stressful? We can survive with less money, Kalim. You don't need to work so hard.'

Abida hated the one-bedroom flat they rented in noisy Anarkali, but if staying here meant that Kalim could remain healthy, she was prepared to do that. She took his hand in hers. It shook a little, but she ignored it. 'You're going to be a father soon. You have to be at your full strength.'

Instead of smiling, Kalim burst into tears.

'Kalim, I – I didn't mean to...'

He surprised her by wrapping his arms around her. 'You'll stay with me, no matter what, right?'

'Kalim, come on. Where else would I go? What's the matter with you?'

'Just promise me you won't give up on me.'

She tried to free herself, but his grip was strong. She looked back at the chapatti she had left on the *tawwa*. It was going to burn and stink up the whole flat. Even the baby kicked in protest. 'Stop, you're pressing too hard on my stomach. The baby...'

'Abida, please promise me.'

'Of course, I promise.'

Abida
One Month Later

They called Lahore a city of contradictions. Abida knew now how true it was. On the surface it appeared that everyone was devout, that not a drop of alcohol was consumed in this city, but she had discovered its seething underbelly. Sometimes she wondered what the pir would think of this place but maybe he already knew, and it was fear that the village might turn into a place like Lahore that compelled him to send innocent young girls to their deaths. What a load of rubbish, she thought. There was no excuse for what the pir did. She knew that with all her heart. Any place was better than Khan Wala village. Besides, Lahore was a large city, fairly well policed, so it would be impossible to kill someone for honour here, and that alone made everything seem worthwhile to Abida. She pretended not to hear the snippets of gossip that reached her ears, about girls being murdered in their sleep and buried near the River Ravi. Surely, Lahore couldn't be like the village she had left behind. Surely not.

People in the city knew that honour killings took place, but they talked about them as if they happened in a different country, a different world, not right under their noses. No one knew that Abida had nearly suffered that fate. Perhaps the city was just so big, people had other things to gossip about. All she knew was Lahore was one place where the pir couldn't follow her. Nobody would let him get away with slicing her throat here. She, a respectable married woman, expecting her first child. He would never survive the mob, let alone the police, who seemed to be stationed at every intersection. Some young policemen would leer at her, she had noticed, but for the most part, they stepped forward to help, sometimes even stopping the traffic so that she could pass. If only she could talk to them about all that went on in her village.

Unfortunately, parties and gambling were the norm in their block. Kalim saw this as a chance to indulge himself, and he began to invite friends to the flat for parties and gambling. Abida wouldn't have minded them if she hadn't had to stand in front of the stove for hours, preparing food for his friends. She clutched her bulging belly in one hand as she stirred the chicken broth that would go into the pulao rice. In the heat of the kitchenette, she felt lightheaded. Their one-bedroom flat was in the heart of Anarkali bazaar, which meant that little, if any, light or air entered through the windows. All around their home were other concrete buildings, most of them crumbling or in varying degrees of disrepair. At night, they had to keep the windows open to lure in a breeze, which invariably meant that the noise from their rowdy neighbours reached them, almost as if they were screaming right in her ears. Anarkali was a colourful place with streets spilling over with shops, and clientele that ranged from local people to posh women who came in their air-conditioned cars, sunglasses on top of their heads, as they looked for designer-bag knock-offs. Once, Abida had caught a whiff of conversation from one of these ladies as she asked the shopkeeper about the origin of the designer bags.

'What are designer bags?' she'd asked Kalim, but he had just laughed.

'God, Abida, you've got so much to learn. I just love your innocence. These bags are carried for style and a proper original bag probably costs as much as this flat.'

Abida's eyes had nearly popped out of their sockets. 'For a simple bag?'

Kalim had laughed again. 'For a simple bag.'

Most of what she saw and heard went right over her head,

which meant that sometimes she felt out of her depth, claustro-
phobic even, and found herself longing to return to her village, to
her family. Today was one of those days.

Pouring water into the half-cooked rice, she covered the pot
and collapsed into the chair by the window, her head craning out
to catch the whisper of a breeze. Their concrete flat trapped heat
like a furnace. Even the floor underneath the rug was warm. Abida
flapped her *dupatta* over her sweating face, but no respite was to
be had. She thought of her family eating their afternoon meal in
the airy courtyard, her mother ladling the lentils into the waiting
plates while her father distributed the chapattis. She couldn't tell
if the droplets falling down her kameez were tears or sweat. And
to think Kalim expected her to be fully made up before the party
started. Even in her dehydrated state, Abida couldn't help but
wonder why it was necessary for her to dress up. It wasn't as if any
of Kalim's friends brought their wives with them. They said
Lahore's monsoon was a thing to behold. Where was it now? All
Abida could see was the punishing sun, the white sky, and all she
felt was the heat that bore down on them from above and rose up
from the ground in equal measure.

Saima said that men changed after marriage.

'Once they have you for life, your value in their eyes starts to
disappear,' she told her once as she applied kohl to her almond-
shaped eyes, her forehead erupting into a mass of wrinkles as she
raised her brows, making her seem much older than she claimed
to be, which was twenty-five. 'It begins with a whisper at first, and
then, before you know it, you are worth less than even your
children. You're a mother not only to them, but to the man-child
you've married as well. Believe me, I know.'

Abida didn't believe her. What did she know about marriage?
Kalim had told her that Saima was no better than a prostitute and
that she should stay away from her. Saima had raised her eyebrows
when Abida told her about Kalim's instruction, but then she'd just
shrugged. 'I'm moving anyway. What do I need you for? You'll

learn your lesson soon in any case. Now leave.' She'd closed the door in Abida's face.

My husband treats me like a queen, Abida had wanted to scream at her, but instead she'd just returned to her flat with a strange emptiness inside her. In a weird way, she had liked Saima. She was the closest thing she had to a friend in this sprawling city. Who would teach her about etiquette and manners now? Whatever Kalim claimed she was, nobody could deny that Saima had style.

It didn't matter, though. Not really. She knew Kalim loved her.

Or did he? Would a loving husband purposefully force his wife to abandon her only friend? He was very expressive in the bedroom, gently holding her belly as he kissed her on the neck and whispered sweet nothings to her. The fact that they were still intimate despite her advanced pregnancy explained his lust, but she could feel the respect in his eyes waning. Perhaps it was the stressful job, but his face was transforming. Gone was the healthy pink pallor, replaced by a yellowish gauntness that scared her. The fact that this transformation had happened within a couple of months was even more worrying.

'If you get a call from my parents, tell them you're ready to give birth,' he had told her last week, scratching his neck. 'We could do with the money.'

'Don't you earn enough from your job?' Abida had asked innocently.

His expression hardened. She could see him taking deep breaths, but she didn't understand why he had taken offence. After all, how could any income from the villages match what people earned in the city? Even a semi-educated person like her knew that.

'Just do it, Abida,' Kalim said finally, putting on a bright smile for her. She noticed then that his teeth were yellowing. 'You might need to stay in the hospital for a few days. We need to be able to get our hands on money easily. I can't borrow any more from my friends.'

'You've borrowed money?' Abida's shock was complete, but Kalim pretended not to have heard her and had simply left for work.

She still wouldn't have minded all of this had it not been for the dismissive remarks he seemed to have started making towards her. If she didn't know any better, she would think he was becoming a whole new person, and there was only one thing that could change a person so completely.

Her heart fell just thinking about it.

'Drugs,' she whispered. She may be from the village, but even she had seen how they could ravage men and women, reducing them to mere shadows of their former selves.

It couldn't be Kalim, though. She refused to believe that. He was just going through a phase. This was the man who was madly in love with her, who had dared to stand up against the pir and call the police. This was her Kalim. She shook her head, wiping away the tears, but bad thoughts were like weeds. No matter how many you pulled out, they kept multiplying.

Just like Saima had warned her, it had started with a passing remark about Abida's dishevelled state, back when the parties and dinners first started. Kalim had asked her to come out of her room and help with the food. Without thinking, Abida had followed him in her sweaty clothes and grimy *dupatta*.

'*Tauba*, your wife smells,' one of Kalim's friends had said, wrinkling his nose. 'Don't you villagers know the concept of showering?'

Abida wanted to tell him that she was eight months pregnant and had stood all day in front of the stove, but she ignored the remark. She shouldn't have. She should have set the record straight and told him it was none of his business, especially not where someone else's wife was concerned.

'You need to learn the ways of the city,' Kalim had whispered to her that night, while he ran his hands over her belly. 'You can't let them think we're savages.'

'They shouldn't be commenting on the appearance or smell of

another man's wife,' Abida replied, careful not to chide him. Kalim had treated her well that week, handing his entire weekly earnings from the airline office to her, but she had noticed a mean streak emerging in him. Whether it was due to the company he kept, or something else, she didn't know. All she knew was that she didn't want to cross him. 'Perhaps you should meet them elsewhere. I don't feel comfortable moving around in a room full of strange men.'

'Spoken like a true villager.' There was an undercurrent of anger in Kalim's voice, and Abida froze. He removed his hands from her belly and turned away. 'They're right. You smell. Don't let me see you in this state ever again. This is Lahore, not your father's old hovel. We have a shower in the bathroom. Learn to use it.' Then he had pretended he couldn't hear her sobs. Now, something offended him every night.

She didn't know where he had amassed all these friends. Apart from a few, she didn't even know their names. Every night seemed to bring different people. She had no idea what they did after dinner, but from the stench and smoke that filled the flat, she guessed it wasn't something healthy. She feared for her baby, but voicing her anxiety would only infuriate Kalim.

A few hours later, she was clean and showered, wearing a tiny amount of the deodorant they had bought a couple of months ago, back when they had enough money. For the past week, she had received a pittance, which meant that there was no more money for things like deodorant and makeup. The little money she had saved was for the baby, all of it stuffed into a pile of her underclothes in the wardrobe, a place where Kalim's eyes never ventured. She wondered when *he* had last taken a shower. She feared the look on his face when she asked him for money, so she didn't. But she would have to very soon.

She opened the lid of the pot and steam billowed out, bringing with it the aroma of cinnamon, cloves and basmati rice. She pulled out the few pieces of chicken from the bottom of the pot, arranging them on the side for Kalim. His friends could go without chicken for a day, she thought.

It turned out that they couldn't.

She had just retreated to bed when she heard Kalim call her name. Although she was exhausted, she sprayed a little deodorant over her clothes before covering her head with a *dupatta*.

'*Ji*, Kalim,' she said, as she emerged into the living area. All she could do was stare. There were even more people than usual today, most of whom she didn't recognise. They were all gazing at her. Abida tried to cover her belly with her hands.

'How many times do I have to tell you not to call me by my name? This isn't something respectable wives do.' Kalim was slouched on the sofa, with his two best friends, Fareed and Liaquat, sitting on either side of him while the rest of the men were crowded on the floor or in chairs.

Abida lowered her head, but not before she had rolled her eyes. 'Yes, husband.'

'Such a subservient wife you've got, Kalim,' Fareed said. 'Find me a wife like that. I'll even settle for someone from the village.'

'There wasn't enough chicken in the rice,' Kalim growled. 'Don't I give you enough money? Are you sending it all to that useless family of yours?'

Abida didn't lift her gaze, but fear pierced her. Kalim sounded different. There was an edge to his voice, a seething dislike for her. She cleared her throat. 'You are under the influence of the home-made alcohol and whatever it is you smoke, husband. If you just come and rest for the night, everything will be better in the morning.'

'How about we send him to sleep, and you can come and sit with us, Bhabhi?' Fareed called.

Abida looked up at the impish grin on his face. 'No, thank you. And if you are calling me your sister-in-law, then treat me as such.'

'Come and sit with us, Abida.' She could see that her husband was under the influence of something, she didn't know what, but his words still came as a blow. What were these *kanjars* giving him?

She shook her head. 'No.'

'I said, come now!'

Without a backward glance, Abida lifted the flap and returned to the small space that served as their bedroom. Her heart was pounding somewhere in her throat, her sweaty hands massaging her belly. Any moment now, Kalim would storm in and drag her back into that room full of men. She wanted to lock herself in the adjoining bathroom, but it was too hot there. She would die of heatstroke. These cemented walls heated up in the summer, and the humidity only added to the discomfort. No, she had to face her fate right here. There wasn't a lot of space in the bedroom, just enough for a double bed, a bedside table and a wardrobe, the tatty rug on the floor the only decoration.

Kalim never came, and as the noise outside ebbed, so did her heart rate. When the last guest had left, Kalim finally lifted the flap and came in. Abida was sitting on the bed, the *dupatta* still covering her head. Whatever he had said, she couldn't help but feel relief that he hadn't sunk as low as to drag her back to those men. He was still better than most husbands.

She smiled as she rose to meet him. He had a strange, lopsided grin on his face that she couldn't quite place. She was about to comment on it when he struck her across the face. The force of his slap sent her crashing onto the bed. She let out a cry as pain shot through her belly. She froze for a moment. She was fine. Shaken, but fine.

'When I order you to do something, you obey me. You get it? As my wife, it is your duty.'

'Does that include parading around a room full of strange men?' The words were out of her mouth before she could stop herself. She squeezed her eyes shut, waiting for the blow.

But it didn't come.

Instead, Kalim sat heavily on the bed beside her. 'Fareed and

Liaquat are my friends. They are investing in my new business venture. If I don't keep them happy, they will withdraw their investment.'

Abida didn't turn to look at him. Her eyes were fixed on the floral pattern of the bedsheet. 'What happened to your job with the airline?'

'I quit. The pay was shit. I was not born to be a secretary's assistant and work long hours in offices. I was born to be a leader, and Fareed will make it a reality. Soon, we will be rich.'

'This is the first time you've ever raised your hand at me.' Abida's voice caught in her throat as she swallowed a sob. 'Do whatever you want with your life, but don't treat me like this.'

If she was expecting him to console her, she was mistaken. There was steel in his voice as he stood up and headed for the living area. 'Husbands hit their wives all the time. It's normal. And if you had obeyed me, it wouldn't have happened. No wonder your parents were desperate to get rid of you. You can be quite a handful, Abida, but you would do well to remember that you are not in the village any more. This is Lahore. And I paid good money to the police to save your skin from the pir. Don't you ever forget that.'

Abida recoiled from his words. There wasn't a trace of the Kalim she had fallen in love with in this man. Not for the first time, she wondered how he had gotten involved in alcohol and drugs. Her blood boiled when she thought of the person who had turned her innocent Kalim into this monster. But as she looked at him now, the way he was shrinking into a husk right before her eyes, she knew she couldn't blame anyone else. This was all Kalim's fault. And hers. She should have stopped him.

'This is the alcohol or whatever they gave you talking. This isn't you. This isn't the man I married.'

Kalim paused in the doorway. He didn't look back, but when he spoke, his voice broke. 'You're right. I don't know what comes over me. I'm sorry.'

'No, you're not. You're just desperate for your next fix. Whatever it is you're taking, it's slowly killing the person you used to be. It probably already has. Now go,' she said, a sob breaking into her voice. 'Go wherever it is you go.'

He didn't come to bed for a long time afterwards. Abida wished she hadn't risen to investigate what he was doing. She wished she hadn't peeked through the gap between the flaps in the doorway to see Kalim sitting in front of the coffee table arranging lines of white powder. She wished she hadn't seen him snorting that powder, then producing a syringe from his pocket and injecting himself with something.

After that, she obeyed him whenever he called her outside.

Abida

'You are nearing birth,' the doctor told her as she removed the stethoscope from her belly. 'From the way your belly is distended, you could go into labour any day. Just make sure you tell your husband to bring you here when the contractions become very frequent.' She held up a finger. 'When they are coming at intervals of one minute or less. Don't come before that or you'll just be wasting your time and your husband's money.'

If only he gave me any, Abida thought, rummaging in her bra for cash – the only place that felt safe to her nowadays. Kalim was desperate enough to search the wardrobe now. His eyes showed terror, the look of a person on the precipice of losing everything, including himself. No matter how much he demanded that she hand over any cash she had saved, Abida didn't. She denied its existence. She no longer felt scared of him. Instead she pitied him. She knew what her plan was. As soon as the baby came, she would wait a few months before returning to her village for good. From what her father had said over the phone, things had settled down. Surely the pir wouldn't object. Even if he did, she had no choice. Each day here brought its own challenges, and the longer Kalim remained unemployed, the more precarious their situation became. Besides, she had had enough of him and his unpleasant friends.

'That will be two hundred rupees, please,' the doctor said, holding out an open palm. The yellow chiffon *dupatta* on her head looked to be worth at least a thousand. Still, Abida couldn't begrudge her the money. She was doing her job.

Abida counted out two hundred rupees and laid them in the doctor's waiting hand.

The doctor's gaze softened, and she put the money on the table. 'Listen, why don't you keep this money for now? Just come back when you start getting those frequent contractions, and we'll take it from there.'

When Abida objected, the doctor simply shook her head, and called, 'Next.'

Abida picked up the money and left.

Her happiness over the money was short-lived, as that night a strange thing happened. For the first time ever, Abida heard the tinkling laughter of women in her flat.

Kalim had been looking increasingly strained, to the point that Abida was afraid to speak to him. So, when he called her name, Abida pushed aside the flap hanging in the doorway and stepped outside.

Her eyes found the girls in an instant. Their skimpy dresses sparkled in the harsh glare of the yellow bulbs overhead. Their faces were powdered a pasty shade, their lips coloured blood red. They reminded her of the women she had seen once in a neighbouring village, the ones who traded their flesh for money.

'*Aye haye*,' one said. 'Where have you been hiding this pregnant gem? Look at the glow on her face. Come and sit with us, darling.'

'Come, Abida,' Kalim said, his smile tight, his yellow teeth bared. Abida averted her gaze and lowered herself onto the sofa next to him. Her condition meant she had to sit with her legs spread apart.

The girl in the black dress laughed. 'Ah, look at her airs and manners. What a proper little lady you've got, Kalim, but look at how she spreads her legs. You could almost mistake her for one of us.'

Abida felt the sharp jab of Kalim's elbow in her arm. 'Sit properly. Close your legs.'

'Kalim, I can't.'

'Do it!'

She was about to retort when Fareed leaned over Kalim and took her hand. 'Don't mind these girls, Bhabhi Ji. These scarlet women wouldn't know a diamond even if it stared them in the face.'

Abida was so taken aback that she froze. Fareed's hands were warm as he rubbed her knuckles.

'You've got a beautiful wife, Kalim,' he murmured, his amber eyes on Abida. 'I wonder whether you know her true worth.'

Abida snatched back her hand.

Kalim snorted. 'I wouldn't have married her if I didn't know her true worth. I paid a fortune to the police to save her from a pir. Her own father would have drowned her if I hadn't intervened.' He shrugged. 'You know, that's what illiterate parents are like in villages. Wish I could have that money back now. I could really use it.'

Laughter rang out in the room.

Abida drew herself to her full height even though it put pressure on her belly. 'My father would never have killed me. And he wouldn't have let the pir do it either.'

Kalim put a hand on his chest in mock concern. 'Is that so? Then why don't you go back to your village and see how long he can save you from the pir?'

Fareed wagged his finger at Kalim. 'Oh, my dear man, this isn't how you speak to beautiful women. You treat them with kindness. With *love*.'

'Once she's had the baby, send her over to us. She'd earn a pretty penny in the market,' the girl in black said. 'Uptight Abida would make the madam really happy.'

'She'll never mix with the likes of you.' Fareed's authoritative tone immediately silenced the girl.

Abida's heart was pounding. Fareed's gaze lingered on her chest. She tried to wrench herself out of the sofa. 'I don't like this, Kalim. Why have you asked me to come in here?'

Kalim wasn't listening. All his attention was focused on the pouch of white powder that Fareed was brandishing in front of him. 'Because Fareed wanted to see you,' he gasped, his eyes following the progress of the pouch as it hovered over his waiting palms.

'It's called cocaine,' Fareed whispered. 'Your husband has spent every last rupee he has on it. In fact, he has spent the money I'd lent him for investment too. He owes me more than you could possibly imagine. He's also into heroin.'

Abida had vaguely heard her father talk about the harmful effects of heroin, but she had never paid attention then. She made a mental note to ask Saima and then realised she was no longer friends with her, and that it was too late to make amends. Saima had disappeared in the night, almost as if she had never existed. Tears sprang to Abida's eyes.

Kalim's eyes shone. 'Come on, Fareed, give it to me.'

It dangled inches from his fingers. 'What will you give me in return?' Fareed's words were like icy droplets down her back. She shivered.

'Kalim, please,' she said. 'I need to go.' She pulled hard on his sleeve. 'Don't you see what you are doing? Are these people and their drugs more important to you than your wife and unborn child? Was this why you brought me to Lahore, so that you could make my life even more miserable? Where is the Kalim I fell in love with?'

For a moment, Kalim turned his gaze towards her, recognition flickering in them. 'Abida,' he murmured. 'My Abida.'

Before Abida could say anything, Fareed had thrust the pouch in Kalim's lap. 'There, take it. But, I ask you again, what will you give me in return?'

Abida shook her head. *No, Kalim. Please come back to me. I know you're in there somewhere.*

'Anything,' Kalim said, as his fingers closed around the pouch. He sighed. 'Take anything you want.'

Abida

Her first thought when her eyes fluttered open wasn't about the baby, but how drenched she was in sweat. She lay in a pool of it on the floor, so slick that her hands slipped when she tried to raise herself into a sitting position. She crumpled. And noticed there was blood too, dotting the chipped marble, maroon and congealing. Summoning her entire strength, she pushed herself up, and ran a hand down her shalwar. It came away bright red. A cry escaped her lips.

Her baby...

She didn't know where she found the determination, but she scrambled to her feet, and made for the bedroom, where she knew Kalim would be, drugged unconscious but, as the father of the baby, she hoped he would help her.

Pain shot through her as she walked, and it took her a moment to realise that she wasn't in her own home. It was a room of some kind, dark and full of shadows, with only a single dangling bulb illuminating the floor she had lain on. She didn't know where the room ended; the corners were shrouded in darkness. It took her a moment longer to feel the sudden lightness of her body, as if a heavy weight had been lifted. With trembling hands, not daring to look down at what had been a round belly yesterday, she touched it.

The baby was gone.

Her stomach was still swollen, but she knew it was empty. Someone had taken her baby. For the second time since waking, she let out a cry, despair creeping into her from all sides, like the darkness. She fell to the floor, allowing the darkness to engulf her again.

The next time her eyes fluttered open, she was in a well-appointed room. A thick quilt enveloped her in a cocoon of warmth, and her head rested on the softest pillows she had ever felt. The comfort almost allowed her to drift into sleep again, but then a thought sliced through her mind.

The baby.

And just like that, the comfortable warmth of the bed transformed into a radiating heat. She flung off the covers, surprised at her strength, but before she could raise her head, dizziness compelled her to lie still.

'Shh,' a voice whispered. 'Don't get worked up, my dear.'

A straw was thrust into her mouth. She sipped at the water, feeling its coolness spread through her body.

'The baby,' she whispered. 'What did you do with my baby?'

The dizziness refused to let her open her eyes, so she had no idea who she was talking to.

'Hush, little dove,' the voice whispered again. 'You've spent a long time in confinement. It's time for you to rest now.'

'But the baby...'

'All in good time, my dear. Rest, recover, and face this new chapter in your life.'

'Chapter...' she said. 'What chapter?'

'Hush,' the voice said again, and Abida slipped into unconsciousness.

※

After a few days her strength had returned, but the betrayal stood fresh in her mind even weeks after she had arrived in this ... place. For what else could she call it? She had heard the sounds coming from the other rooms. Unless her ears betrayed her, this was a pleasure house – a brothel. Her eyes wandered around the well-appointed room, complete with expensive furnishings and brocade drapes. Her bed was the softest she had ever lain on, yet it all felt wrong.

Sold. That was the first answer that was given to her constant questions. 'You've been sold by your husband for a few cheap shots of heroin.' As if being sold for an extravagant price would have made her feel better. Sold. She still couldn't get the word out of her mind. Kalim, to whom she had given everything, had betrayed her in the worst possible way, and for what? A few days' worth of drugs.

'He verbally divorced you first, though. You were conscious then, and you acknowledged his words even if you don't remember them now. It happens.' It was true. Abida had no recollection of Kalim divorcing her, but she did remember him hovering over her, whispering something in her ear. That was before he'd coaxed her into eating food from his plate. She thought – she'd hoped – he was contrite, was trying to make amends, and she'd happily eaten the pulao rice from his hands, even playfully biting his finger, but when she started feeling sleepy and felt the feeling leave her legs, she realised he'd drugged her. *Haramzada*. It didn't matter. He had given up on them, on their unborn baby. Abida closed her eyes, tears leaking out of them. It was too much to stand.

And where was he now, the wretch? She hoped he was lying dead in a ditch somewhere. How could he have gone from the innocent, loving Kalim she had known to that savage, heartless beast? She knew the answer: she had seen his gradual transformation, but refused to believe it. Saima had warned her, but what had she done? Cast her aside on Kalim's insistence. She had hidden the truth about Kalim's descent into drugs from everyone, even her own father, and what had he done to repay her? She could still see the glimmer in Fareed's eyes as he had stared at her: 'You've got a beautiful wife, Kalim.'

The words still rang in her head. She should have run for the hills when she had heard that, but where could a pregnant woman on the verge of giving birth go? She had done the only thing she could think of: she had snatched the pouch of cocaine from Kalim and flushed it down the toilet. Initially Kalim had thought she was interested in it, just wanted to look at it, but when she went into the bathroom, he rushed after her. She still remembered his scream when she had pulled the flush on the white powder.

The feeling of triumph was short-lived, though, because one of Kalim's slaps had sent her crashing to the floor, her head hitting the hot concrete. The next thing she remembered was being tricked into eating the drugged food and waking up in that god-forsaken room.

Sold. Like livestock.

She almost welcomed the knock on her door now.

It was the same woman who had delivered her the news that she had been sold. She was the one who had 'bought' her.

'Feeling better, my dear?' she asked, walking into the room, an expensive leather bag hanging on one arm like a piece of jewellery. Behind her trailed a young girl who couldn't stop smiling at Abida.

'*Salam*, I am Muniba.'

'Quiet,' the older woman said. 'Where are your manners, Muniba? Allow me to introduce you first. This is exactly the kind of behaviour that stops you having any exclusive clients. Your big mouth puts them off.'

Muniba bowed her head, a cascade of silky brown hair hiding her face.

The older woman pulled a small wooden chair over to Abida and sat down on it. From her face, it was evident that she was in her mid-fifties but she had kept herself in excellent shape. There wasn't an ounce of fat on her toned arms, which were bare of any fabric. Her *dupatta* was carelessly thrown across her neck in the classic style of the elite women of Lahore, whom Abida had sometimes seen. She smelled of flowers and something heavy, like sandalwood. Abida wanted to vomit.

'Now, dear, my name is Amna, but you may call me Apa Ji. Everyone else does. You may not remember me from the last time we met as you weren't quite in your senses, but I hope that now that we know each other, we will be good friends.'

She leaned forward and cupped Abida's chin. 'Consider me as your mother. I will always be here for you. This is now your home. Don't mistake it for a cheap *kotha*, dear. They no longer exist and might as well be the stuff of fairy tales. This is a place of merriment for men with refined tastes and deep pockets.' She winked at her. 'It is up to you how far you can persuade them to loosen those pockets, though. And if you're lucky, you may even become a second or third wife. How wonderful would that be? The wife of a rich man.'

Abida was watching her in disbelief. The thought of entertaining other men, allowing them to touch her, made her feel sick. She opened her mouth to protest, but before she could, Muniba shook her head at her. Once.

'What was that, my dear?' Apa Ji asked, her voice like honey.

Abida closed her mouth.

'Lovely. Now, Muniba, make sure she is beautiful to meet her first client tonight. His identity is a secret,' she added, in a conspiratorial tone. With a small laugh, which she covered with a bejewelled hand, she glided out of the room.

Abida gaped. Her first client? Tonight? She was shaking.

'Miserable old cow,' Muniba muttered. 'The day I think of her as a mother is the day I'm buried in the ground. Maybe not even then.' She sat down on the chair Apa Ji had vacated. Up close, Abida noticed that Muniba was not as young as she had first thought. Late twenties or early thirties, perhaps. Her face was free of lines but, despite the warmth in her expression, there was a deep sadness in her eyes. Her hair was possibly her greatest beauty. Long and thick, the colour of chestnuts. 'I dyed it,' Muniba said, as if reading her thoughts. 'I came into this world with a mane of jet-black hair, rough and tangled.' She clutched at a strand. 'This is all thanks to Apa Ji.'

Abida was only half listening. She couldn't stop trembling. How could she let someone touch her? Thoughts of escape flitted in her mind, but one look around, and she knew she wouldn't be going anywhere anytime soon. Behind the beautiful raw-silk curtains, the window was padlocked with thick iron bars crisscrossing it. The only other way out was through the door, which would, no doubt, be under heavy guard. Besides, she didn't have the strength to run.

Muniba clucked. 'I was once in the same position, my dear. I would advise you not to contemplate escape. The result is never good.'

Something in her tone made Abida look at her. 'What do you mean?'

Muniba lifted her shirt. Her stomach was riddled with silvery scars from what must have been deep gashes. In some places, small chunks of flesh were missing. 'After I tried to escape, she gave me to one of her more demanding clients. He had a penchant for violence. Obviously she regrets letting him have his fun as he's left me permanently scarred and I am forced to cover my stomach when I am with clients. Maybe Apa Ji didn't intend for it to go that far, but it's always best to be careful.'

Abida moaned. 'I can't be here. My baby ... I need to go to the baby. Will you help me?'

Muniba looked at her sadly. 'You didn't take in a word I said, did you? Your baby is gone. You were in a pretty bad shape when you came to us. I've never seen Apa Ji so happy. She negotiated a very low price for you from that husband you had. She delivered your baby herself.'

Abida's breath caught in her throat. 'And then? What happened then? Why don't I remember any of this?'

'You were delirious with pain.' Muniba picked at a zit on her forehead. Her lack of emotion scared Abida. 'I'm not surprised you don't remember. But, don't worry, it will all come back to you.' She sighed. 'It always does.'

'And my baby?' Abida didn't dare breathe. 'Please tell me it survived.'

'Of course it did. There is nothing Apa Ji can't do. She takes great pride in her midwifery skills. A strong healthy baby girl. Taken straight to the orphanage.'

When Abida let out a cry of despair, Muniba just looked at her, impassive, but there was also kindness in her eyes. 'Don't cry. When has it ever done anyone any good? Besides, it all happened days ago. Just be thankful your baby is alive and well. Maybe someday, when you get out of this place, you can reclaim her from the orphanage. I can tell you she won't be going anywhere.'

Abida buried her face in the pillows. 'I want to be alone.' In a matter of a few days, she had lost everything. She thought back to how brave her father had been in saving her life, her baby's life. It had all been for nothing. The mere thought of him made her scream into the pillow. Her poor father. He'd probably die from the shame of having a daughter in a pleasure house. 'Kalim, you *haramzaday,*' she wailed. He had ruined her life. For good.

Muniba tutted. 'Are you using these fond words for the man who sold you? Listen, you can't escape. For better or worse, this is your life now.' Suddenly she laughed, which made Abida look up. 'But that doesn't mean you can't have any fun. You have me. We have each other and the other girls. I'm friends with them all.' She began counting them on her fingers. 'Rabia, Naghma, Bano, Neelma and ... yes, Nargis. How could I forget to mention her? Although I'm not really friends with her.'

'Nargis?' For some reason she wanted Muniba to keep talking. What a strange creature she was. Something about her energy soothed her. For just a second, it made her forget the injustice she had suffered, the injustice that was to come.

Muniba rolled her eyes. '*Arre baba*, you know nothing, do you? Nargis is our queen bee. The reigning courtesan in this house.' She leaned forward to cover Abida's hand with hers. 'She's Apa Ji's pet. Just like you can't cross Apa Ji, you can't cross Nargis either. She has the best clients, the best room, the best food, but there is one thing she doesn't have any more.' Muniba broke into a toothy grin. 'Youth. Our dear Nargis is older now. Past her prime, only surviving on the countless expensive creams and treatments Apa Ji lavishes on her. You'd think she was the sole breadwinner of the house. But it's not Nargis who has to deal with needy, demanding clients who ask for everything under the sun. Like, for example—'

Abida pulled her hand from Muniba's grip and held it up. 'Please. I don't want to know. I don't want anything to do with this life.'

Muniba blinked at her. 'But you have to get ready for your client or Apa Ji will be very angry.'

'You seem educated, Muniba. How can you even think of doing this?'

Muniba's face hardened. 'Sometimes we don't have a choice. Yes, I am educated, but that didn't save me.'

Abida burst into tears. 'I can't. Please don't make me.'

'But you must, Abida.' Muniba lowered her voice to a whisper. 'You see, your first client is a senior policeman.'

Jamil

The old bus was a gas-guzzling wreck, spouting noxious fumes as it shuddered on to its destination. It was sweltering inside, with dozens of people packed close together, some even sitting on the floor. The conductor sat sweating in one corner, attempting to cool himself with a Chinese paper fan. The sight would have brought laughter if Jamil's nerves weren't already on edge.

Abida had vanished. There hadn't been a single letter from her for more than a month. Her cell phone was constantly switched off. When he had mentioned it to Farida, she had snapped at him.

'She's happy in her life. Let her be. Just because she's your first-born doesn't mean you forget the others. You need to think of your boys.'

It was true. Things were very bad in the village with nobody ready to buy any meat from him. They'd all shifted their loyalties to drunk, lazy Shabbir, who wouldn't know a good cut of lamb if it stared him in the face. Jamil couldn't say he was surprised though. The pir's influence extended far and wide.

Jamil wiped the sweat from his forehead with the back of his hand. Farida was secretly selling her embroidery and making ends meet by offering to do cleaning and washing for some of the richer people in the village. Apparently, that wasn't something the pir objected to. Jamil sighed. At least she was making ends meet. Not like him – unemployed and good for nothing. He had sold the last of his chickens, for far less than they were worth, to Shabbir and used that money to come to Lahore.

Farida had screamed and cried, but in the end she had understood. She was Abida's mother after all. 'Do what you have to do,' she had said. 'Make sure she is fine. Do not come back without news of her.'

'Will you be fine with the other kids?'

At this, Yousaf had risen from where he was doing his homework and thrust out his little chest. 'I will protect the family, Abbu. You go and find Abida Apa.'

The sight of his ten-year-old son standing in his stained shalwar kameez, a solemn expression on his face, had tugged at Jamil and for a moment he wondered whether he was doing the right thing, abandoning his family at such a crucial time. But his love for Abida trumped everything else. Most parents pretended to love each child equally, but Jamil knew it was all a farce. Of course there were favourites, and it was the love of his favourite that made Jamil turn his back on his wife and the rest of his children.

With Abida's last-known address written on a piece of paper, Jamil had hopped onto the first bus to Lahore. A train would have gotten him to Lahore sooner, but he couldn't afford to waste any money. He knew he had to brave the fourteen-hour journey with its countless stops along the way. The piece of paper containing Abida's address was nestled deep inside the chest pocket of his kameez, but he had already committed it to memory.

Anarkali Bazar.

He had been to Lahore just once, as a child. Anarkali Bazar was named after a famous courtesan who had been buried alive in a small concrete chamber. Her only crime was falling in love with the Mughal emperor's son. *Love*, he thought. Wasn't it the root of all the evils of the world?

Despite the heat in the bus, Jamil shivered. He sent up a silent prayer for Abida's safety. What if she had died in childbirth, and Kalim's parents were saving him from the pain? But then he thought of the savage expression Kalim's mother had worn when he had confirmed the address with her. She blamed Abida for snatching away her only son, and he realised that, no matter what fate Abida had met, she wouldn't think twice about telling him. He jerked his head from side to side. *Stop it*, he told himself. Abida was fine. She had to be.

The mud-brick huts had given way to concrete buildings, both small and large. Grey seemed to dominate the streets of Lahore. Most of the squat buildings were either undecorated or their paint was peeling. The bus then groaned through a fashionable part of the city; Jamil marvelled at the steel-and-glass towers, the neat, grassy parks, the towering trees that seemed so green, as if they had been washed by rain, yet the sky was a hazy grey with not a cloud in sight. In contrast to the less savoury parts of the city, everything here gleamed. There were hardly any people on the street, most of them travelling in shiny luxury cars. There were even workers in uniform sweeping the roads. Who swept roads? he thought. Wouldn't they simply get dirty again? What was the point? Jamil shook his head. He would never be able to fathom the lives of the rich. He tightened his grip on the bundle of clothes he had in his lap. Stashed deep inside his underpants were the few thousand rupees that would have to sustain him during his stay in Lahore.

After what seemed like an eternity of watching grand bunga-lows with their large lawns and armies of gardeners, they finally entered the older part of the city, where the sparkle dimmed. As the bus drove on, the surroundings became increasingly rundown, with more and more people milling about the roads, most block-ing the way of incoming traffic. The bus driver's hand didn't leave the horn their whole journey through the old city, until at last Jamil and his fellow passengers were dumped on the pavement when the bus ran out of fuel and was unable to complete its journey to terminus.

A roar of angry voices rose over the din of the bustling city, but the bus conductor waved his hand. 'Get off while you still can. As soon as we refuel, we head back to Okara. If you don't want to end up there, better get off now.'

Jamil stepped off the bus. The smell of the city was an assault on the senses. Underneath the heavy stench of the gutter, there was the scent of *jalebis* frying in oil, mixed with the unmistakable stench of burning garbage, with an undercurrent of raw meat from the butchers. Some were familiar, but in this strange environment, everything seemed foreign to him. Jamil's eyes watered.

'Need a hand, Chacha?'

A boy, probably in his early teens, was smiling at him, his open mouth revealing blackened teeth. Jamil saw him pick up a discarded cigarette from the road and take a heavy drag. A weak spiral of smoke emerged from his lips. That made him smile again. 'Not from around here, are you, Chacha?'

Jamil looked down at the bundle he was carrying. Apart from that, he had no baggage, but there was a bigger problem. He didn't know where he was.

'Can you guide me to Anarkali Bazar, son?'

The boy laughed. 'Chacha, you are standing in Anarkali Bazar.' He gestured towards the rundown buildings around them. 'Anarkali is as big as a city. Tell me where exactly you want to go, and I'll take you. For a small charge, of course.'

When Jamil showed him the address on the piece of paper, and the boy grinned again. 'Easy. Follow me.'

Trust came naturally in the village, where everyone knew each other. But in a city that was home to millions, Jamil didn't know whom to trust. The gleam in the boy's eyes didn't betray any greed, and it seemed he genuinely wanted to help – for a small charge, of course – so Jamil didn't think twice. He needed to get to Abida.

'Lead the way,' he said.

'Call me Saleem.'

Despite his worry for Abida, he couldn't resist taking in the sights of the city as Saleem led him down a twisting alley, past a potbellied man who sat naked above the waist, kneading mounds of flour. Sweat dripped down his forehead and into the pile.

'Adds a nice saltiness to the naan,' Saleem remarked.

Jamil's stomach turned.

They emerged into a wider lane that boasted shops of every kind, and for a moment, Jamil forgot why he had even come to Lahore. People glanced at him and laughed at his wide-open mouth, but he didn't care. He was too busy taking everything in.

It wasn't until they ducked into a narrow alley and Jamil felt a tug at his kameez that he realised they had stopped. Dusk had fallen, and in this deserted street, the sounds from the main road seemed very far away. 'This is the place?'

Before Saleem could reply, three burly men emerged from the shadows, grim purpose in their eyes. One stood in front of him while the other two stood behind. Jamil could have laughed at his own stupidity. And he did. His laugh rang out in the empty alley. Alarm crossed Saleem's features, and he bolted, leaving the men to deal with Jamil.

A thick fist connecting with his cheek was the last thing he remembered before he passed out.

Abida

Abida was the first to wake. The sound of steady snores by her side reassured her. He was still asleep. These were the few precious moments she had to herself, before Majeed woke and demanded her full attention. She ached everywhere, even in places she never knew she could ache. She'd been with Kalim before, but the violence with which the men here treated her was beyond anything she could have imagined. Still, she was thankful that Majeed had come into her life. His brand of violence inflicted pain too, but at least she knew how to respond to him. She was one of the lucky ones – not many of the girls here had exclusives. Lifting the sheet off her naked body, she pushed her feet into the fluffy slippers Apa Ji had given her and proceeded to rise from the bed. As she did so, it let out a loud creak.

Abida closed her eyes and cursed herself as the snoring stopped, and a giant hairy arm shot towards her, encircling her waist.

'Where do you think you're going?'

Forcing herself to smile, Abida sank back into the bed. She tried not to turn away when his moustache grazed her face. Instead she lay there like a statue, letting him run his face all over her. After the garlic naan he had eaten last night, his morning breath was worse than anything she had ever smelled. She almost threw up.

'May I take a shower?' she asked. 'I also need to brush my teeth,' she added, hoping he would catch her meaning, but Majeed's grip on her upper arms tightened. She let out a cry, but that only seemed to encourage him, to make him feel more than the man he already was.

And so it began again. Abida pretended it wasn't her who was being subjected to this treatment. She had long since assumed this role, once it had become clear that she was here to stay.

'Screaming and resisting won't get you out of this place, my dear,' Apa Ji had told her. 'Wrap these men around your little finger and they will gladly lift you and take you out of here as their bride.'

'But, Apa Ji, what if I don't want a lifetime of beatings from that same man?' she had asked.

That had earned her a tight slap across the cheek, which Apa Ji had later nursed with lime water and honey. 'You mustn't test me, my dear. Look at you, I almost left a mark on your beautiful face.'

She had never been taught the art of seduction – a word she had picked up from Muniba – and she didn't know what Majeed saw in her, unless he loved the very idea of control, for domineering he certainly was. Although she knew that he was a policeman, Abida hadn't been able to broach the topic of her imprisonment until their third meeting, when he had made the deal to become her exclusive, thankfully shutting out worse clients. Better one than a hundred, Abida had thought. During that third night she spent with him, she had told him timidly about what had happened to her.

He pretended not to have heard.

When she repeated her story, he clapped a hand over her mouth, silencing her. A coldness had crept into his eyes as he watched her, and Abida knew that it was a lost cause before he even said the words.

'Every slut I've ever met has said the same thing. Just because you look innocent doesn't mean you really are. If you think I would betray someone like Apa Ji, you have another think coming.' His fingers lingered over her neck before he closed them around it. Abida remembered the air leaving her lungs, her chest heaving as she struggled to breathe. 'Be grateful I'm your exclusive.'

Now, the deed done, Majeed rolled off her, and Abida opened her eyes again to the world. Surprisingly, she hadn't felt anything this time. She had blocked him out completely. From the stiffness in his posture, it appeared that Majeed knew. Although policemen in general were fat, Majeed had kept himself in good shape, even though he was in his mid-fifties. He glanced sideways without turning to meet her gaze.

'Learn to enjoy this, my dear. Try not to fall out of my favour.'

It was a mistake blocking him out. Time to put on her mask, Abida thought, as she slid out of the bed and put on her gown with a flourish. 'Oh, Majeed Sahab, you know how much I look forward to your visits. They brighten my day.' She knelt in front of him and laid her head on his knee.

'It doesn't seem like it,' Majeed muttered, but without conviction. 'At times, it seems as if I'm making love to a wooden doll.'

'You got the doll part right.' Abida raised her head to give him a smile, which she hoped looked playful.

That seemed to cheer him up. 'Well, good, because I have been going over something in my mind, and I think it's time.'

Abida's heart leapt. Could he really mean that? She dared not show the slightest hope in her eyes. She struggled to keep her expression blank. 'And what is it that's been occupying your thoughts, my love?'

'Shahid.'

Abida frowned. 'Shahid?'

'My son.'

'What about him?'

'You see, Abida, my son is almost twenty-three years old and he's still, you know ... not very comfortable around girls. Very inexperienced. Very shy. God knows why he doesn't have a girlfriend yet. I don't trust the other girls here ... Most of them could be carrying nasty diseases - you never really know, despite whatever Apa Ji might say. So, I was hoping that you could, you know...'

Abida stared at him, her mouth falling open, the excitement

draining from her body, replaced by anger and a wave of despair so deep, she wished she could just sink into it and never emerge. 'And you thought what?' she said, unable to keep the coldness out of her voice. 'That the father's plaything can be the son's plaything?'

Anger flashed in his eyes. 'Don't pretend you're a *shareef* girl, now. Do you think I don't know that this is all an act? This is what I pay you for.'

'What you pay Apa Ji for. I've never seen a single rupee.'

She stood up and withdrew to the armchair by the barred window. This was her lot in life, being a prisoner, losing her child. She wondered what her family was doing. Perhaps they were happy to be rid of her. Served her right for having lofty dreams of love and independence.

'It's not like you need to have sex with him,' Majeed said, and Abida was relieved to hear guilt in his voice. She had feared she had pushed him too far. 'You just need to talk to him ... maybe show him how to interact with a woman.'

'You could ask Nargis,' Abida ventured. 'She's Apa Ji's favourite.'

'I don't trust Nargis. I trust you. Besides, Nargis is as old as the bloody hills.'

Abida pretended to sigh, but deep down, a glimmer of hope was raising its head. Perhaps all was not lost yet. Trust was the first step in the journey to love, wasn't it? Maybe one day Majeed would marry her and take her out of this place. And then she would run away.

She forced cheer into her voice, as she looked back at him with a huge smile. 'Of course I'd be happy to entertain him.'

'That's my girl.' Majeed took her in his arms, and for a moment she leaned into the safety of his embrace, the sound of his steady heart. Briefly, she let her guard down.

Maybe the moment was profound for Majeed as well, for he pulled away and began busying himself with the heap of clothes on the floor. 'My boys at the station tell me that crime is on the rise in the city. People getting robbed in broad daylight. They picked up some guys near Heera Mandi last night and have been unable to get a single intelligible word out of them. Apparently, they speak Urdu in a weird accent.'

'Like what?' Abida asked absently, her mind struggling to construct an image of Shahid. How did one entertain a twenty-three-year-old? How did one entertain anyone?

'How would I know? I've not met them yet, but they probably talk like you, in a mix of Saraiki and God knows what else. Very nasal. They're from Khanewal. Is that where you're from?'

What use was it to tell him where she was from? It wasn't like he was going to rescue her. Abida pretended to swat him on the arm. '*Haye jee*, you mean you can't understand what I say, hmm?'

Majeed laughed, and Abida was glad they had cleared up any misunderstanding. 'It's just that your accent is endearing. I didn't mean it in a bad sense.'

Abida rolled her eyes, and collapsed into the bed again. 'I'm going to sleep now.'

Abida rose again at midday and proceeded to tidy her room. Other than the bed and the armchair, there was precious little to put away. The few clothes she owned – most of them gifts from Majeed – hung in the small closet in the far corner of the room, and her toiletries and makeup all fitted into a single drawer. She hadn't known things like sanitary pads had even existed.

'This is a woman's curse,' her mother had said. 'Do not under any circumstances let your father or any man see the blood. They don't like it. If they spot even a little bit of it on your shalwar, they will blame me, possibly brand us whores and your father a pimp.' She had pointed to the rag. 'Use it well and keep it hidden. Wash it in the darkness yourself.'

Abida took a deep breath now as her hand clasped the door handle. Time to face the real world.

'Abida darling,' Apa Ji called from the living room, as soon as she arrived downstairs. No matter how quiet she was, Abida could never escape the woman's notice. It hadn't occurred to her that Apa Ji might have cameras installed in the corridors and on the staircases – perhaps even in the bedrooms. Who could tell? Abida was hungry, but she knew by now that to ignore Apa Ji was like playing with fire. With a sigh, she walked into the living room.

Apa Ji sat on her high, wing-backed armchair while a woman with her back turned to Abida sat painting Apa Ji's toenails. With a jolt, Abida realised it was Nargis – Apa Ji's prime property. Catching her gaze, Apa Ji smiled. 'Nargis used to do manicures and pedicures at a beauty parlour when she was a girl. Waif of a thing, but fingers as nimble as any I've ever seen. She was ambitious too, and look how far that ambition has brought her.' She lowered her reading glasses and surveyed Abida with the attention of a hawk. 'I see you've lured Majeed into your web.'

Her web? Abida knew enough to stay silent. She lowered her gaze.

'He's very happy. Happy enough to pay double to remain your exclusive. Keep going like this, my dear, and the day isn't far off when you'll be his wife.'

Abida was careful not to grimace.

Apa Ji laughed. 'Of course, he'll need to come up with a dowry first. If he wants my daughter, he must pay the right price for her.'

'A dowry?' Abida asked innocently. 'How much does he need to pay?'

'Clever girl,' said Apa Ji. 'Isn't she, Nargis? You'd better pray she gets married to the old policeman, or I can see her taking your place.'

For the first time during that conversation, Nargis turned around to look at her. Abida's breath caught in her throat. Even though she had seen Nargis many times, her beauty never failed to amaze her. With her delicate features, green eyes, and the long chestnut hair of which she took meticulous care, Nargis was stunning. Her eyes blazed, but she didn't say a single word. Nargis was beautiful, but she wasn't that young any more, and that could soon make her a liability in a place that preyed on the young.

'Fading beauty,' Muniba had remarked. 'As her beauty dulls, her claws become sharper. No matter what you do, never get on Nargis's bad side.'

Abida took a step back. 'May I go and eat something with the girls?'

Apa Ji waved her away. 'Of course you may eat something, but take your food up to your room. I don't want you to associate with the others. You're still new. However, make sure you eat plenty. We wouldn't want you losing these beautiful curves, now, would we, Nargis? What will old Majeed hold her by then?'

'Indeed,' Nargis said. The chill in her voice could have frozen oceans.

'Now hurry along, dear. Don't forget you have another visitor coming.'

All thoughts of food left her then. 'Who?' Abida stuttered. 'I – I thought I was Majeed's exclusive.'

'Of course you are. It's his son who is visiting you this evening. They're of the same blood, so it doesn't really matter whose exclusive you are. You can be used by both.'

Nargis shook with repressed laughter.

'Now, go,' Apa Ji commanded.

✻

Abida paced around the tiny room. She couldn't sit still. How low had she fallen? Was the pir right? Had she always been a 'little slut'?

Her hands clenched into fists as she thought of the baby she had been robbed of, the promise of life. Not for the first time, she wondered where Kalim was, whether he felt any regret at what he had done. Despite herself, she gave a loud bark of laughter. Regret? Kalim? She was dreaming with open eyes now. The moment he had touched those drugs, he had given up on her, on them. He didn't even think of her as a person. In those last few days she had spent with him, he had looked like a walking corpse. He had scared her. She had seen addicts back in the village, but their descent had been gradual. Kalim, on the other hand, had withered right in front of her eyes, quickly turning into a monster. Perhaps deep down, he had always been a monster, and the drugs had simply helped expose it. Tears trickled down her cheeks as she thought back to her life in the village, her siblings, her mother and, most of all, her dear father. She still remembered the unease in his eyes as she had left for the city, his body stiff and upright as he saw her climbing on the motorcycle. He had been smiling, but his eyes had given him away. They always did.

'Come and find me, Abbu,' she murmured now, and sobbed at her stupidity.

'You mustn't beat yourself over this,' Muniba told her later, once Abida's thoughts had settled. She was sacrificing her precious time between clients to sit with Abida, but Abida couldn't bring herself to thank her. Not yet. She couldn't trust what might emerge from her mouth. What would Majeed's son be like? If his father was anything to go by, violence would be the first thing she was subjected to. She shivered.

'Quit worrying,' Muniba continued. 'You're doing so well. I was a snivelling wreck during my first six months.'

Perhaps I am a little slut, Abida thought. It had been only a few weeks, and here she was, the comfortable mistress of Majeed. She folded her arms across her chest to stop herself clawing her skin. She deserved to die.

'Maybe he won't be too bad,' Muniba said hopefully. 'He's young, isn't he, and didn't you say you only had to talk to him?'

'That's what they all say,' Abida shot back. 'He can't be coming all this way just for a chat. I know what he wants.'

The words rang in the room.

'Can you keep a secret?' Muniba murmured.

'Why?' She could see Muniba was dying to tell her.

'We are planning an escape.'

Now she had Abida's full attention. 'What? How? And who's "we"?'

Muniba gulped, tucking a stray lock of hair behind an ear. 'Well, we've been planning it for a couple of weeks.'

Abida didn't know what to be shocked about – the fact that there was an escape plan or that Muniba had been keeping a secret for all this time. Usually whatever she was thinking about spilled straight from her lips.

'I don't believe you.' Abida rose from the bed and began pacing around the room.

'Well, that's up to you, but we thought we should include you in it, seeing how miserable you are. The only reason I didn't tell you earlier was because Nargis thought you were content in your life. Smug, even.'

'Nargis?'

Muniba looked down. 'Those were her words, not mine.'

'Nargis?' Abida repeated. She plopped back on the bed. 'She hates me. And she was laughing at me while Apa Ji made me look a fool.'

Muniba was smiling. 'You're clever, Abida, but apparently not clever enough to see that Nargis behaves like she does to trick Apa Ji. Nargis can be kind. I only found that out recently.'

'You told me never to get on her bad side.'

Muniba pulled out a pocket mirror and checked her appearance. 'I did, and I believed that to be true ... I kind of still do, which is why I warned you, but then I found out about the escape and was invited to join it.'

'Then why not tell me herself?'

'We had to know whether we could trust you. For all we know, Apa Ji could have planted you among us as a spy.' She reached into a bag of potato crisps and put one in her mouth. The crunch pierced the still air.

Abida snorted. 'That's pushing it. Even for Apa Ji.'

'Would you believe me if I told you she killed someone just to save her reputation?' She held out the crisps. 'Care for some?'

Before Abida could reply, there was a soft knock on the door. 'May I come in?'

It was a man's voice.

Muniba's eyes widened. 'That must be Majeed's son.' She leapt from the bed, stowing the bag of crisps in her purse. 'If someone sees me eating crisps, I'll get such a dressing down from Apa Ji. I'll see you later, and, remember, not a word about any of this. Believe me, in spite of everything I've told you, you still don't want to get on Nargis's bad side.'

With that, she crept away, leaving Abida in a mess of nerves. She hadn't even had time to put on some makeup. She was bare-faced and in the shalwar kameez she wore for bed. Apa Ji would be furious. But it was too late. The door clicked open and a brief exchange of pleasantries followed between Muniba and the man. Then it closed. There was silence, but Abida knew that she wasn't alone in the room. She shifted to the head of the bed and wrapped her arms around her knees.

She heard footsteps and, in those few seconds, Abida's heart raced. She grabbed a comb from the bedside table and ran it through her hair. She hoped that in the soft light, he wouldn't notice her bare face.

She could hardly hear anything over the roar of blood in her ears. If it wasn't for the way she gripped her legs, she was sure her knees would be shaking. Disrespect wasn't tolerated by Apa Ji, and Abida had already broken one of the most important rules: being ready for her visitor.

'Who's there?' she called, hating the fear in her voice.

The man had stopped near the bathroom door so that from where Abida sat she couldn't see him.

A throat was cleared. 'My name is Shahid. I am Majeed's son.'

The voice was soft, respectful, very unlike the rudeness with which his father spoke. It couldn't be too bad, could it? 'Come inside,' she said, hoping he'd inherited his father's good looks. No matter how violent his behaviour was with her, she couldn't deny that Majeed was a handsome man. The shadow on the floor short-ened as Shahid stepped forward. Abida didn't even realise she was holding her breath until she saw him.

'You aren't at all like a prostitute,' he blurted out.

Abida stared at him. 'Excuse me?'

He reddened. 'I'm sorry. I didn't mean it like that.' He didn't seem to know what to do with his hands so he held them behind his back. 'I've never done this before, you know, talk to a ... a...'

'A prostitute,' Abida finished for him. Despite herself, she wanted to laugh. 'They're people too, you know.'

He held up his hands. 'Of course. I didn't mean anything by it.'

This man was probably Kalim's age, but he had none of his con-fidence. His forehead was creased in anxiety as the weight of those eyes fell on her. He had beautiful features, a straight nose, piercing black eyes that seemed to stare right into her soul, but there was nothing overly masculine about him. He was shrouded in a mist of shyness.

She adjusted her *dupatta* to cover her chest, but Shahid wasn't looking there. His eyes were glued to her face.

Abida decided to give him the benefit of doubt.

He paused before the bed, his lips parting as he drew a breath. 'I was told your name is Abida,' he croaked. 'You're beautiful.' He groaned. 'Sorry, I didn't mean to say it like that.'

To her surprise, the hint of a smile stretched her lips. She looked up, and there were those eyes again. Abida felt as if she could lose herself in them for days. What a silly thought, she mused. The mind really was a funny place. Instead of feeling dislike for this person who was the son of that hateful Majeed, she was contem-plating his eyes. She watched as he stared at her hungrily, taking in as much as he could. 'You're kind to say so, Sahab,' she replied finally.

'You can call me Shahid.' He tried and failed to add gruffness to his voice.

'Shahid,' she repeated. Her voice caught as she tried to make sense of the tumult inside her. In the meantime, he lowered himself onto the bed, watching her the entire time, careful not to make any sudden movements.

'You have a beautiful voice.'

Despite herself, Abida scoffed. 'Majeed Sahab makes fun of my voice, you know. Has a lot of special names reserved for me. He speaks very highly of you, though. But then, you're his son.'

Shame seemed to hit him like an arrow. The blush rose from his neck and spread all over his face. Good, Abida thought to herself. She couldn't humiliate a person like Majeed, but she could at least make do with Shahid. It was her turn to blush. She was changing. This place was transforming her into something she was not.

'He thinks I need to act like a man,' he began haltingly. 'To Abba Jaan, I am not man enough.'

She drew in a breath. What a thing to say to one's son. She decided to take pity. 'I have always wondered at Majeed Sahab's eyesight. He wouldn't see a man if he danced naked in front of him. He has eyes only for women.'

Shahid laughed, and when he saw her smile, his eyes lit up. 'You're beautiful,' he said again.

It was the wrong thing to say. Whatever good humour that had blossomed between them evaporated, and she lowered her gaze. 'If you say so.' Her voice was devoid of any warmth.

Shahid held up his hands again. 'I meant no harm. It was a foolish thing to say to someone I've barely met. I'm sorry if I offended you. Please don't be sad. It's just that I haven't had the chance to talk to a lot of girls. Everyone makes fun of me, and that makes me more awkward.'

'You needn't apologise to a whore. This is what you all do. You call us beautiful and then treat us as if we were no more than a stuffed toy. Do whatever you want, but please don't call me beautiful. I am anything but beautiful.'

Shahid watched her spellbound. He attempted to reach for her hand, but thought better of it. 'Do you really hate it here?' he whispered.

'Should I love it? Men barging in to have their fun, then leaving without a word of comfort. All the while I stay here, imprisoned in this room. Oh, yes it is very enjoyable. I'm having the time of my life.' Her voice broke, but she blinked back the tears that threatened to roll down her cheeks. She would not cry in front of someone she was meeting for the first time, and definitely not in front of the son of Majeed. 'Why am I telling you this? You'll just tell Apa Ji, and she'll make life worse for me.' She pulled her *dupatta* from her chest. 'Let's begin, shall we?'

Shahid averted his gaze, focusing instead on the tiled floor. 'You don't have to do this,' he said quietly. 'You may cover yourself.'

Abida felt some of the venom leave her. 'When your father told me you were coming, and you would want just to talk, I didn't believe him. In the weeks I've been here, I have learned never to trust the word of a man. Never. If you want to talk to me, talk, but don't expect me to answer every question. My body may be freely available, but my secrets are not.'

With that she turned away from him, but not before she caught one more look at those black eyes.

Jamil

Jamil woke up with the afternoon sun beating down on him. He was drenched in sweat, his entire body aching from sleeping on the pavement. He blinked and looked around. He had no idea where he was. All around him, the city bustled with life. Cars, rickshaws and motorcycles whizzed past him, their drivers so intent on reaching their destinations it was as if demons pursued them. Nobody had the time to spare him a single thought. People just walked past him as if he was invisible. There was a lot of honking, a great deal of dust and grit, but there was also life. Women in colourful shalwar kameezes emerged with bulging bags from boutiques that sold clothes. Where he came from, fabrics were sold in shops to be sewn at home, not modelled by dummies in shop windows.

Someone had covered him with an old blanket that stank of rot and smelly feet. He threw it off and stood up. His head spun. How long had he been lying there? And then he remembered the young boy who had lured him into that dark street. Jamil must have crawled his way to the main road. He felt his pockets. Empty. And the money he had hidden in his underpants as a precaution? A cry of despair rose from his lips when he discovered that that had gone too. They had fleeced him. His small bundle of clothes was lying on the road next to him, evidently too useless to steal. He thanked God for small mercies.

There was one thing on his person that the robbers hadn't taken. He fished out the piece of paper from his pocket and smoothed it. There was only one thing to do – catch a ride. But how? Jamil looked at the stampede of vehicles and felt light-headed again. How would he bring himself to a cab's notice, let alone get it to stop? And there was the issue of payment. Jamil sat down again and put his head into his hands. If this was how he was going to navigate the city, there was little chance of him finding Abida.

He didn't know how long he sat like that, with the merciless sun on his back, streams of sweat gathering in his palms while he closed his eyes to the world. There had to be some way he could get to his destination.

A rustle of fabric accompanied by a rush of air alerted him to a presence. He lifted his head out of his hands and stared upwards, blinking against the temporary blindness.

A kindly woman was looking down at him, a crisp hundred-rupee note in her fist. 'Here,' she said. 'Buy yourself a decent meal.' She dropped the crimson note into his lap and walked away, leaving behind the scent of tuberoses. Jamil looked down and cried in surprise. There wasn't just one note, but several, all lying in front of him, dropped by passers-by. They must have thought him a beggar. He could count a few hundred – at least – which would be enough to take him to Abida's home. Before he could pick up the notes, he paused. Had he fallen so low as to accept charity now? A stronger voice immediately killed the small voice in his head. Yes: if charity was going to reunite him with his daughter, he was not above accepting it. He gathered the notes in his fist, his heart lifting. Money meant power, especially in this city.

He discovered that if one waved a hundred-rupee note in front of a rickshaw, it immediately ground to a halt. The driver poked his head out. 'Where to?'

For the first time since he had arrived in Lahore, Jamil smiled.

❧

Kalim's flat wasn't in the sort of building Abida had described. Jamil had looked up apartment buildings on the village computer, but the building in front of him was nothing like them. It was a couple of storeys high and poorly built, the cement falling off in places to reveal the red brick and concrete underneath. The entire area smelled of crime and neglect. And waste, both animal and human. Jamil had always been able to tell the difference. 'Not the best part of the old city,' the driver muttered, as he shoved the hundred-rupee note deep into his pocket. 'I would advise you not to linger. There are thieves and pickpockets everywhere.'

Jamil could have laughed. He had already been robbed, and had nothing else to give, apart from his own life, which he didn't think held much value in the eyes of robbers. 'Let them do their best,' he replied.

The driver shrugged and drove away, the rickshaw sputtering out black smoke in its wake.

Inside, it was very hot. Jamil wiped the sweat from his brow as he climbed the narrow stairs to the second floor, his hand gripping the rickety banister for he feared he would pass out from dehydration. He didn't see any people. It was late afternoon, so he assumed everyone was still at work. The second-floor landing had just two doors. Both were made of cheap plywood, crudely painted to hide their flimsiness. The paint was already peeling, the once-whitewashed walls dirty from passing hands. The floor was matted with what looked like the accumulated filth of centuries. The door to Kalim's home was ajar. That didn't bode well. His heart was hammering as he drew closer. Somehow he had known he wouldn't find Abida here, but still his breath caught when he looked inside. He let the tears flow freely as he took in the tiny living room that also served as the kitchen. This was what his daughter had been reduced to. There was a single sofa that was turned upside down, the table in front of it littered with plastic bags and food wrappers. It smelled of oil and rotten meat. Jamil swallowed the bile rising in his throat and proceeded towards the curtain that separated the bedroom from this space.

'Abida?' he called out cautiously. 'Abida, my child. Look who is here.'

Even as the words rolled off his tongue, he realised they would achieve nothing. Abida was not here. His daughter was gone.

A sound behind the curtain piqued his curiosity. He moved towards it, a mixture of a moan and a snore. It could be only one person. His blood pounded in his ears as he pulled the curtain aside and entered the pitiful space that was supposed to be the bedroom. Despite the rage he felt, he was rooted to the spot as he saw the filthy cement floor, the stained mattress on the rickety bed frame, the single light bulb casting deep shadows across the room. There was nobody in the bed. Before Jamil could wonder at the sound, he heard it again, and this time, he knew where it was coming from.

His son-in-law was lying in a pool of vomit in the space between the bed and the wall. The smell was harsh and acrid, and Jamil had to hold a hand over his nose and mouth to stop himself gagging.

With all the strength he possessed, he grabbed Kalim by the back of his neck and pulled him upright, shoving him into a sitting position beside the bed.

'Who's there?' Kalim moaned, without opening his eyes. 'I'll return your money tomorrow. Leave me be.'

Jamil waited, but when he heard a snore, and felt Kalim's body slackening in his grip, he slapped him across the face. Hard. Harder than he had ever slapped anyone before. 'You *Haramkhor*,' he said.

Kalim's eyes flew open. 'Uncle ... oh, Uncle is that you? Why, this is such a pleasant surprise. Why didn't you tell me you were coming?'

'Where is my daughter?' Jamil said quietly.

Kalim blinked several times, green snot running from his nose.

'She's gone to the market to get some groceries.' He tried to scramble to his feet. 'Let me go and find her. She will be so happy to know that you are here in Lahore.'

Jamil slapped him again, and this time Kalim hit the bed frame. He yelped, covering his head. 'Why are you hitting me, Uncle? Is this any way to treat your son-in-law? Wait till I tell my parents. They will have your hide for this.'

Jamil closed his eyes, struggling to calm his racing heart. If he wasn't careful, he would kill the boy, and where would that leave him? 'Your parents haven't heard from you in months. Neither have I heard from my daughter.' Jamil advanced towards the cowering figure on the bed, his fists clenched. 'Tell me what you did with my daughter or I swear I will kill you.'

As if on cue, Kalim started beating his chest with his fists, his eyes streaming. 'She left me, the little *kanjari*. I gave her a home, happiness, stability, and she ran away with the first person she met. I should have known. If she could forget her honour with me, she could forget it with anyone.' He looked up at Jamil. 'I didn't want to tell you as it would have broken your heart, but now you know. You just can't trust women, especially not in a place like Lahore.' After a moment, he added, 'You must have brought some money with you.'

Jamil didn't believe his story, not for a second. He looked his son-in-law up and down, then he went straight for the bulge in Kalim's front pocket. He withdrew a small plastic pouch. It was filled with white powder. Genuine fear now entered Kalim's eyes.

'Give that back to me, Uncle, if you know what's good for you.'

'Give this back?' Jamil breathed. He sped towards the adjoining bathroom, not caring that it smelled like an open *nullah*, the toilet covered with excrement. Kalim followed him in, this time wailing for real. 'Give me the pouch, Uncle. It's medicine. I am suffering from a life-threatening illness and I need it to recover.'

Jamil held the pouch over the toilet. 'Where is Abida?'

Kalim sank to his knees, his hands joined together. 'Please, Uncle. If I tell you, will you give me my medicine back?'

'For the last time, Kalim,' Jamil lowered the pouch into the toilet despite Kalim's vehement protests, 'if you don't tell me what you did to my daughter, the loss of this will be the least of your worries.' He sounded braver than he felt. His knees were shaking. He gulped. 'Tell me.'

With a final whimper, Kalim told him. He told him every last bit of what he had done to his daughter, his firstborn, the girl Jamil had saved from the village mob.

Jamil dropped the pouch into the toilet and flushed it.

Abida

Shahid was falling for her. She could see it in his eyes, something she had once seen in Kalim's. Maybe it was love, but by now Abida knew better than to trust men. Even men like Shahid. He hadn't made any advances on her yet. They just ... talked, but she knew that this little interlude could end any day, and then she would once again be Majeed's mistress. At least, he hadn't bothered her since Shahid had begun visiting.

Thank God for small mercies, she thought. It had been a couple of weeks since Shahid had been coming, maybe more. Cooped up in Apa Ji's brothel – she refused to call it anything else – she had lost track of time entirely. Only when Muniba told her that they were in the middle of October did she realise that the intensity of heat had lessened. In fact, when she opened her window at night, the breeze was cool. She didn't need it with the air conditioners, but it felt good to feel the fresh air on her face, as polluted as it was. It reminded her of home. Just the other day, she had caught a herder leading a group of buffaloes down the street, and her heart had almost leapt out of her chest. She used to despise these big, clumsy creatures back in the village, but this time, she had watched them with her mouth open, desperate to reach out and feel the hair on their hides.

She hated the city.

Shahid described his life as if it was the most normal in the world. It had been mostly about gaining education. At twenty-three he was older than her and was fresh out of university. Abida knew what a university was, but she always pretended to be ignorant of everything. She had found it to be a useful tool in her arsenal. She was careful not to let her guard down with Apa Ji or even Muniba, but with Shahid, she sometimes became careless. Once she had blurted out, 'Which university?'

He had looked at her oddly, but then he had smiled, the skin around his eyes crinkling. 'Do you know a lot about universities?'

'Just that you go there after finishing matric,' she replied, kicking herself for sounding so knowledgeable. When had that ever helped her?

Shahid looked thoughtful. 'More than that, actually. After class twelve. Then it's university for four years.'

Abida whistled at that. 'Four years of higher studies. Like Pir Sahab's son. You must be the most brilliant man in the world.'

Those crinkles had made a return then, along with a dimple in his right cheek. 'Hardly. I'm not especially smart.'

Abida listened to his stories with wide eyes, holding her face in her hands as she propped herself up on her elbows. It seemed that talking about their past lives was difficult for both of them, so instead, Shahid told her about the different places in Pakistan, the countries he had visited around the world, the things he had seen and eaten.

Abida's favourite topic was outer space, and it was to that she returned now. They sat facing each other on the bed, Abida leaning against the headboard, while Shahid sat in front of her, the sleeves of his white linen shirt pulled back, his brown hair gently tousled as if he had just got out of bed. Sometimes, when the sunlight caught his face, Abida thought she saw a bit of brown in his eyes. Right now, they were jet black, like the fierce monsoon clouds that came in July.

'If we went to the moon all these decades ago, why haven't we managed to land on Mars?'

Shahid laughed. 'It's much further than the moon, Abida. Unlike the moon, it's actually a planet.'

Abida stuck out her lip. 'How far could it be? America is far and people go there every day.'

'It's different in outer space.'

'And I used to think America was further than the moon. At least we can see the moon.'

He laughed again, this time throwing his head back so that his Adam's apple bobbed up and down. For a split second Abida wanted to lean forward and kiss that vulnerable part of him. What was wrong with her? Her mind just hadn't been the same for the past few weeks. Ever since Muniba had brought her news from Nargis of an escape plan.

'Still in the early stages,' Muniba had promised her. 'But be ready for any action that may be required. With Nargis, things move fast.'

With Nargis being Apa Ji's pet, Abida couldn't take this seriously. It might be a trap, and she said as much to Muniba, who rolled her eyes.

'Nargis doesn't work like that. Everyone in this house knows that age is fast catching up with her, and Apa Ji thinks it's high time to get her settled. Otherwise she'll soon be a deadweight for her. Too young to be a madam and too old to serve the clients.'

At that Abida's stomach had churned, but such was their life. 'Why would she risk including us, though?' she had whispered, even though they'd been alone in her room.

'Because she cannot manage alone, and she knows how much we want to escape. She cannot trust Naghma and Reshma, who hate her more than anything in the world.'

Abida didn't think she could endure any more of Majeed's violence. If she could only show Shahid the marks his father had left on her body, but she knew she wouldn't. Shahid was just a boy: she couldn't trust him. Not yet, at least.

Muniba had taken her to see Nargis in her room a few days ago. Compared to the modesty of Abida's room, Nargis lived like a rich woman. Velvet drapes hung over the windows while her bedspread was made of gold brocade with Egyptian cotton sheets underneath.

'A hefty thread count to these sheets,' Nargis had remarked, but then her face had fallen. 'So much luxury, and yet I feel like a talking parrot trapped in a gold cage. I could preen myself all day, but the only people who would see me are my clients, who have to pay their way into this golden prison.' Her piercing black gaze had met Abida's. 'Do you want to rot in this place for your entire life? Do you want midwives pulling half-formed babies out of you, without anything to dull the pain?' She had shuddered. 'I have long planned to escape, but there wasn't anyone I could trust, anyone who had the urge to get away.' Smiling, she added, 'Except Muniba, of course.' Patting the velvet cushion on the bed next to her, she beckoned Abida. Leaning forward so that only Abida would hear her, she whispered, 'I know where Apa Ji sent your baby, where she sends all the babies born here.' She wasn't lying. Abida could see the knowledge glittering in her eyes. Of course, she had said yes to the escape plan.

Shahid snapped his fingers in front of her. 'Hey. I lost you for a minute.'

Abida plastered a smile on her face. 'Tell me, if I was outside, a free woman, would you still like to know me?'

Shahid blinked, and Abida could have hit herself. Why had she said that? What had possessed her? Now he wouldn't want anything to do with her.

But then his expression softened. 'I'd love to know you anywhere, Abida, but I'm not sure you'd want to know me.' He wrung his hands. 'My father is paying you to associate with me. I don't know any woman who would willingly talk to me.'

His honesty broke her heart. She leaned forward and threw her arms around him. His body tensed for a moment, then relaxed, and when his cheek touched her shoulder, the dampness seeped through her shirt. She tightened her grip, realising that this was their first physical contact. Until now, Shahid hadn't touched her, and here she was, willingly taking him into her arms. After Kalim's betrayal, she'd thought that a part of her had died, that she would be damaged forever, but as she felt the lean muscles of his back shift as he returned her embrace, something in her quickened, something that felt like pleasure. She thought of her escape and the possibility that she might never set eyes on Shahid again. She was surprised that she cared.

'You're like a breath of fresh air in this room,' she said.

He shook at this, his chest rumbling with laughter. 'You really think so?'

'I know so.'

'Wherever did you even learn this phrase?'

'Muniba reads to me sometimes.'

She was aware that his cheek was no longer resting on her shoulder, but closer, his warm breath tickling the nape of her neck. She resisted the urge to tell him to hurry. Whatever this was, love or lust, she wanted it. For the first time in many months, her mind was clear. Unlike Kalim's selfish way of handling her, Shahid was gentle, as if he was holding a feather. She increased the pressure on his back, digging her nails into his shirt.

His hands travelled down to the small of her back and then back up.

'Is this okay?' he whispered.

She wanted to scream her assent, but of course she didn't. No point in alerting Apa Ji. A tumult of feelings played through her body. While Shahid's breathing came out in short pants, hers was completely still. She released the air in her lungs.

'Yes,' she said, tugging at his shirt, and she meant it. 'Yes.'

❧

He'd left her so much money, she was sure she'd be able to buy tickets to Khanewal and then onwards to the village. She knew it from the thickness of the bundle of cash.

'My father takes so many bribes, he wouldn't even notice this going missing,' Shahid had whispered in her ear before leaving.

'Just make sure that old hag doesn't find it. She takes enough money from you as it is.'

Abida had no plans to tell Apa Ji about the money. She shoved it deep inside her shalwar where it wouldn't be visible and lay down on the sweat-drenched sheets. She drank in the scent of him. Shahid was a sweet young man, but they had no future. Despite his whispers of love, he was heavily dependent on his father for money, and no matter how tough he tried to sound, he was still a boy. It would be best for both of them if Abida were to depart from his life. She didn't know why she had asked if he would want to see her outside. No point in fanning those flames, she thought.

Still, if she were to be honest with herself, she would miss Shahid, the feel of his soft hair, the way his fingers travelled down...

She sat bolt upright. She had to focus on the plan, the escape. Muniba assured her that everything had been arranged, that Nargis had never been one to make empty promises. When Nargis decided the time was right, they would go. That could be tomorrow, or ten days hence, perhaps never.

Shahid came back to see her several times after that, and each time his intensity increased. It was as if he couldn't get enough of her. To some extent, the feeling was mutual. Each day he visited, she thought of it as the last time they would see each other, and made love to him with a passion that surprised him.

However, he hadn't brought up the subject of life beyond these walls. He hadn't broached the idea of marriage. The fact that his father had been seeing her before him maddened him.

'I don't want you to see him ever again,' he told her, as they lay among tangled sheets, their breathing heavy. 'I cannot stand the thought of his hands on you.'

'Neither can I,' Abida replied. When he stiffened, she softened her tone. 'I know he's your father, but I don't like him. The fact remains that I am a prisoner here and I have to do whatever I'm told to do. At least he hasn't visited me since your visits began. It seems he really does want to make a man out of you and is willing to give you time.'

'He's not visiting because I won't let him. He knows I'm smitten and he's enjoying it. For the longest time, he thought I couldn't get it up.'

'Get what up?' Abida asked innocently, before collapsing into giggles. That was the thing with Shahid. They could veer from serious topics to crude jokes in seconds.

Shahid reddened. 'Never mind that.' He propped himself up on an elbow, his black eyes piercing into hers. 'Seriously, though, is there no way you could leave this place with me?'

Abida played with the sparse hair on his chest, lowering her gaze. How could she say the words?

'You do know that I love you, Abida, don't you? I'd do anything to get you out of here. Pay any price.'

It was the first time he had told her he loved her. She had known, of course, but now that he had said the words aloud, she had the strength to say the words she had been dying to say.

But before she could speak, he asked, 'Don't you love me, Abida? Don't you want to escape from this prison? Say the words and I'll get you out of here.'

'You could marry me.' The words tumbled out of her mouth. 'That's the only way she would let me go.'

'Marriage?' The change on his face was immediate. It wasn't unease or hesitation. It was alarm and fear. Abida saw it before he turned his face away from her. 'I'm only twenty-three years old, Abida. I'm ... I'm dependent on my father for everything.' He sighed. 'He will never agree. We have to take things slowly. I want you to get out of here first.'

Maybe it wasn't love, then. Maybe it was just lust between them. Abida didn't reply. She couldn't believe she had opened herself up to him and he had rejected her. She wasn't surprised, though. Who would want to marry someone like her – damaged goods?

'When I asked about taking you out of here, I meant somehow paying Apa Ji, and somewhere down the line, once we've had more time together, we could then...'

His words faded. Abida didn't need him to complete the sentence.

'You're a coward, Shahid.' She turned away from him and buried her face in the pillow. 'I would like you to leave.'

'Would you let me explain?'

'Please leave now or I'll scream.'

'Gladly,' he replied, tumbling out of bed.

Good, she thought. He deserved to feel hurt. He deserved all the heartbreak in the world.

'Coward,' she whispered, when he shut the door.

❧

The call to escape came sooner than Abida expected. In fact, it came the night she'd argued with Shahid. She was awakened from a fitful sleep by someone tugging at her sleeve, then shaking her.

Abida's eyes opened to Muniba's stricken expression. 'You must wake up, Abida. Nargis has given the signal for escape.'

Abida propped herself on her elbows. 'Now?'

'Yes. Pack a couple of things and meet us downstairs in five minutes. Don't make any noise or it will wake Apa Ji and the other girls.'

Abida's eyes darted to the clock on the wall: two-fifteen a.m.

It had been barely a couple of hours since she had fallen asleep. She was possessed by a sudden fear. She grabbed Muniba's arm. 'Don't leave me here alone. Let's go downstairs together.'

Muniba freed herself with a tut. 'Don't be silly, Abida. I have to pack some things too.' She stroked Abida's cheek. 'Just get downstairs and I promise I won't let you out of my sight after that.'

'What about the guards?'

'Tch, just worry about yourself. Don't be late.'

As soon as the door clicked shut, Abida launched herself at her wardrobe, shoving the beautiful readymade dresses Apa Ji had bought for her into a plastic shopping bag. It was only later that she realised how useless those fancy clothes and lingerie would be in the village. They wouldn't even be fit for barter since nobody would dare wear them, not even in the privacy of their bedrooms. Wives would rather lose their heads than flaunt the silken garments in front of their husbands. And besides, she could tell from the smell of the clothes that they weren't new at all. Who knew how many bodies had sweated through these fabrics. She almost threw up at the thought.

In the end, Abida left the room with just the clothes on her back and the wad of cash shoved deep into her undergarments, far from any wandering eye, including Muniba's. She had put on the softest *khussas* she possessed, but in the deathly quiet, even her soft tread made sounds. She flinched at every step, half expecting Apa Ji to leap at her from behind. She didn't dare look over her shoulder. She was afraid of what she would see.

At long last, she took the final step down the staircase, but when she rounded the corner to enter the large foyer, she knew something was wrong.

Instead of two people, three were standing in the shadows.

Abida's heart leapt into her throat when she realised that one was a security guard. She felt her legs wobble.

'Come here, Abida,' Muniba squeaked, fear choking her voice, but Abida was rooted to the spot. She could see herself spending the rest of her life locked in that dreadful room, slave to the whims of rich men. She couldn't do it. She couldn't go back to that life. She wouldn't.

It was Nargis who moved first. She was oddly calm. 'This is your chance. You girls go ahead while I entertain Rehman for a bit.' She glanced at the stairs. 'Hurry before someone comes and sees us.'

'No,' Abida whispered. 'You cannot be serious.' Fear clutched her throat. She suddenly felt lightheaded. She took in a deep breath.

'I'll just head into the nearby store room and finish him off there. He never lasts long.'

'But—'

Nargis sighed. 'I've been here a long time, Abida. I know this place like I know my own body. There will be more chances for me. If it hadn't been for Rehman arriving before his shift, we could have made it together, but as it happens, there are a few things he needs me to do and I'm perfectly happy to do them. I promise you, I will follow, but you need to go now.'

There was a wicked grin on Rehman's face, his hand tightening around Nargis's waist.

Abida wanted to throw up. How on earth could they let her make this sacrifice? Besides, Abida didn't know this part of Lahore. How would they manage without Nargis? She shook her head. 'We can't let you do this.'

Nargis waved away her protests. 'Don't be silly. You girls won't survive much longer in this place. I'll be fine. Just go.' She looked lovingly at Rehman. 'This guy won't say a word if he knows what's best for him.'

Rehman responded with a snigger.

She tucked a piece of paper inside Abida's bra. 'This is information on your baby's whereabouts. Open it only when you get out of this area.'

Abida's vision clouded with tears. 'Nargis, I ... I don't know how to thank you. Should we wait for you outside?'

She smiled. 'Don't be silly. Make for the main road, and I'll get in touch with you when I can. Just go. Be free.'

In the end, Nargis had to push them out of the door.

'We don't know how to thank you,' Muniba whispered, as they passed over the threshold.

Nargis's face betrayed no emotion. 'Oh, don't worry, girls. Thanking me will be the last thing on your minds out there. Just promise me you'll be happy for as long as you can.'

With that the door shut on them, and the cool but humid air

of Lahore enveloped them completely. Abida had been in air-conditioned spaces for so long that her body seemed unprepared for the outside. She felt lightheaded and would have pitched forwards if it hadn't been for Muniba.

'What are you doing? Let's run.'

Abida felt as if everything was happening on a stage or screen, like a dream that could end at any moment. Her legs were slow to follow her mind, which screamed at her to hurry. She started after Muniba, who had already disappeared into the darkness. For the first time, Abida had a chance to take a good look around the area. Apart from a few houses on one side of the street, the area was desolate. Not even trees grew there. It was too soon to imagine rescuing her child and returning to the village. She had to focus on putting one foot in front of the other and getting out of this dreadful place.

She looked back and saw Apa Ji's house receding, glittering like the den of evil it was. It was only after her legs had assumed a rhythm and she was hurrying forward that she realised she had no idea where Muniba was, or which area of Lahore she was in.

'Muniba,' she called quietly, but there was no reply. Apart from the sound of her shoes smacking on the road, there was silence. Abida swallowed the lump that was threatening to rise in her throat. Where was Muniba?

And then she heard a scream. It was unmistakably Muniba, and it wasn't a scream of encountering the unknown. It was of one's worst fear realised. Without a second's hesitation, Abida turned back and ran in the opposite direction. She would get help and come back for Muniba. She would rescue them all from this prison. There would be safety in numbers. All she had to do was reach a market of some sort, and help could then be found.

She ran as if her life depended on it. Muniba's screams had lost their shrillness. She was saying something now, pleading, but Abida was too far away to make it out. All her focus was fixed on getting as far away as possible. Her heart thudded in her throat as she passed Apa Ji's house again, but she kept to the shadows – which was exactly what they had expected her to do.

As her foot caught in a snare, her entire body pitched forward, her arms flailing for purchase. She collapsed hard on the ground, her vision blurring, her mind fading, but not before she caught Rehman's cry of delight: 'Little rabbit is back in her hole.'

Jamil

Jamil was standing at a biryani stall when his phone rang. Without even checking the number, he knew it would be Farida. Who else would call him? He almost smiled when he put the phone to his ear and was greeted by his wife's breathless voice.

'*Assalam Alaikum*. Any news of Abida?'

Jamil dropped a fifty-rupee note in the stall owner's waiting hand as he received a plate of hot biryani. The weight of the rice was already weighing down the paper plate, so he rushed to the nearest table. He looked at the steaming rice longingly. He hadn't had any breakfast, but if he didn't talk to Farida now, she would presume the worst. '*Walaikum Salam*, Farida. How are you? How are the kids?'

'Any news of Abida?'

Jamil closed his eyes, wishing the darkness would consume him. What was he supposed to tell her? 'I am working on it,' he replied after a pause.

'Is she alive? Please tell me, husband. I cannot bear it. She's dead isn't she?' The pain in her voice almost broke him. 'We're barely managing here without you. I wish you hadn't bought me this wretched phone. It cost us a fortune. I could have used that money to feed the children.'

'Farida, my dear, if I hadn't bought you this, how would we have been able to speak? Tell me, do you really have no money? What about your embroidery?'

Farida sighed the long, drawn-out sigh of those who have suffered for decades. It broke Jamil's heart a little. 'Oh, we will manage. I don't know what's got into me. I pray day and night that you both return home safe and sound. Please tell me my daughter isn't dead.'

'You do have some money, don't you?'

'We are managing, husband. God will be kind on us. I just worry for you and my Abida. It was so foolish of me to try and stop you from going. I could never have dreamed Kalim was mistreating her. I hope you've had words with him?'

You have no idea, he thought.

It took a few more minutes to convince Farida that all was well and that progress was being made, but it left a burden on his chest. How long could he keep up this charade?

'Typical mother,' he said once he'd disconnected the call. He shovelled the biryani into his mouth ... anything to relieve himself of the despair that had settled in his stomach. What was he supposed to say to Farida when he didn't know anything himself? He had gone to the place Kalim had mentioned, a rather grand bungalow somewhere north of the city, and asked after Abida, but the security guard had just shouted at him. 'This is a house of respectable people, vermin. Why would we know where your daughter is?'

It didn't matter how politely Jamil reasoned with him. Rather than a kind word, he got a kick in the shins. 'Get out before I call the police.' Turning his back on Jamil, the guard muttered, 'Must have run away with someone, the slut. These fathers are all the same. Can't control their daughters, and then come blaming others.' He turned around. 'Off with you!'

As if Jamil was no better than a rat.

He had been in the city for weeks, and was still no closer to finding his daughter. Rather than looking for her, all his energy was spent on survival. A week on the streets had taught him he needed to work. In a city like Lahore, nobody had time for charity, especially not for him as he had no experience in begging. It wasn't as if he could ask Farida to send money. His family needed every rupee Farida had and, besides, his request would only make her panic. With so many little ones to look after, the last thing he needed was Farida panicking.

So, here he was, spending all of his energy on pounding concrete day and night. A building contractor was breaking up the existing road to construct a new one, and he had gladly taken on Jamil for the minimum wage, which was just enough for two square meals a day. Still, after a few weeks of working for the contractor, Jamil had saved up a thousand rupees, enough to take a couple of days off to look for his daughter again.

But look where? The sheer size of Lahore made his head spin.

Patience, he told himself. *Patience*. Good things happened to those who waited for the right time. Back at the construction site, he handed his hammer to the overseer and made his way to the bunch of tents nearby. His was a particularly small one, just enough to hold a skinny mattress and a single change of clothes. He didn't have anything else. He wasn't looking forward to the damp smell inside the tent. No matter how much he beat the mattress in the sun outside, it still smelled of rot and stale sweat. However, instead of going inside and collapsing into a dreamless sleep, he proceeded to the open area at the back and squatted in front of the hand pump. Peeling off his sweaty kameez, he gave it a good beating in the water, and pulled out the small razor blade he had purchased for ten rupees. Using his reflection in the water, he shaved away the week's growth of beard and gave his hair a good wash. The sun had already dried his clothes.

Appearances matter, he thought.

Nobody asked where he was headed as nobody knew him that well. After a long day in the sun, nobody cared.

For the first time in weeks, Jamil felt like himself. His stash of money now hidden deep in his underwear, he walked as far as he could before catching a bus headed north. No matter what the security guard said, he knew that that house had something to do with his daughter. An addict like Kalim could lie, but not when it came to his drugs, and when Jamil had held that pouch over the toilet, he had seen the truth in Kalim's bleary eyes.

He saw the same red-rimmed eyes wherever he looked in Lahore. It seemed like half the city was drugged out of its mind. This time, he wasn't stupid enough to walk up to the security guard. He waited in the shade of a towering *shisham* tree, one of the very few in the area, and observed the house. He breathed a sigh of relief when he saw that the previous guard was nowhere in sight, and his replacement seemed to be a relic from the Partition era. He'd have been a young man in 1947. His face certainly had enough wrinkles. Even the gun hung limp on his shoulder.

What he saw during that hour confirmed his suspicions, and he almost kicked himself for his stupidity. He hadn't handled the situation well before. 'Practice makes perfect,' he whispered to himself.

During the hours he watched the house, he saw several men enter and leave, most of them spending only an hour inside. He could think of a dozen things they might be doing there, but his mind narrowed them down to just one: sex. This wasn't a cheap brothel, though, teeming with disease and death. This was a luxurious home, and the men who visited came in elegant cars with chauffeurs. Was his daughter sitting inside pleasuring one of these rich men?

His stomach twisted at the thought, but he also couldn't help the relief flooding him. At least she was alive. The pir back in the village would probably slit his throat for thinking that, but he couldn't help it. Right now, all that mattered to him was finding his daughter. Alive. He would deal with the rest later.

A plan began to form in his mind – a plan that involved a threat of calling the police on this place. Of course, he would do no such thing - his daughter might end up arrested - but in this country, just the threat of the corrupt police was enough to get people scrambling. He knew that now.

But before he could walk up to the guard, he witnessed something that made him sink into the shadows again. A young man, in his early twenties, if Jamil were to guess, was being dragged out of the house. Jamil had noticed him going in, but hadn't thought anything of it. His heart sank when he saw that the previous security guard was back, holding the young man by the scruff of the neck as he pushed him out.

'Apa Ji doesn't want you here,' he shouted. 'The person you're looking for is gone. It would be in your best interests not to return.'

Although he knew that the guard wouldn't recognise the cleaner version of him, he also knew that he still wouldn't let him in. No matter how much he cleaned up, Jamil would never be able to match the clientele this place attracted.

Abandoning his plan of approaching the guard, he followed the young man as he made his way down the street. He walked with a slight limp as if he had been kicked in the shins. Jamil knew what that felt like, and he knew who was responsible for that kick. His blood boiled, but he took a deep breath and touched the young man's shoulder. He ducked down, hands covering his head.

'I won't hurt you,' Jamil said, as the young man turned. 'I just wanted to ask you something, if you wouldn't mind.'

His large grey eyes shone with tears, and Jamil realised that he wouldn't be much older than his Abida. She would be seventeen now, and standing there, he looked the same age, innocent and vulnerable. Despite everything, Jamil wanted to throw his arms around him. You're going soft, he thought.

'You might be mistaking me for someone else,' the boy said slowly.

Jamil pointed in the direction of the house. 'I saw you coming out from there. That security guard is very rude, isn't he?'

The boy just stared at him, puzzled. Eventually, he shrugged. 'Guards in these establishments tend to be that way.'

Jamil had suspected as much, but still his heart fell as he heard those words. 'What kind of establishment?'

The boy raised an eyebrow. 'You know the guard, but you don't know what kind of establishment it is?'

Jamil shook his head. He needed to hear the words.

The boy laughed. 'I'm not sure who you are, but even if you were an undercover agent, I wouldn't give a damn about telling you. And it's an open secret, anyway. My name is Shahid, by the way. See? I don't care anymore.' And he extended a hand.

Jamil took it, his heart thudding painfully in his chest. 'I am Jamil. What kind of establishment did you say this was?'

'You're persistent, aren't you? What do you want with this place, anyway?'

Jamil took a step forward and the boy shrank back. 'What is this place?' he asked again, hoping it would be for the last time.

Shahid seemed to regain his composure. His eyes narrowed, a shadow of anger passing over his face, distorting his features. He spat on the ground. 'It's a brothel, what else? And they took the one person I cared about from there. I've been coming here every single day since they took her away, but they won't let me see her. That place can burn to the ground for all I care.'

All of a sudden, Jamil felt lightheaded. 'I need to sit,' he said, his legs buckling under him.

'Whoa...' Shahid stepped forward to catch him as he fell, and eased him to the ground. Jamil was panting heavily. He was aware that the boy might have used his poor daughter, but he had to ask. This might be his only chance.

'Did you ever encounter someone called Abida in that place?'

He watched as Shahid's face drained of colour.

'Who are you?'

'I'm her father.'

Abida

She could hear the shouts coming from outside. She knew who it was. He had come back several times. She would hear him threatening them, then begging them to let him see her. 'Abida,' he was saying now. 'Let me see her just once.'

She could never bring herself to ask for him, not that anything she said would have mattered. It was too late. He had wasted his chance. They both had. She was embarrassed – no, humiliated – that she could have fallen into that trap. Apparently life had taught her nothing. She was as naïve as she had been when she was dragged through the village to be murdered in the name of honour. No wonder Kalim had got away with selling her to Apa Ji. And no wonder she'd fallen for Nargis and Apa Ji's scheme. How could she have thought that Nargis had her best interests at heart? How could she have been so stupid

Abida wanted to smash everything in the room – if there had been anything to smash. Apart from the heavy wrought-iron lamp on the bedside table, her room contained only a bed and an arm-chair. Apa Ji had had the decorative pieces cleared away and, to rub salt into Abida's wounds, she had sent Nargis to oversee the removal.

'Not going to be needing these, sweetie,' Nargis had purred. Then she'd hit the maid who was helping, saying it was for dawdling. 'You little bitch. Is this what Apa Ji pays you a salary for? Dilly-dallying? Sweep the floor properly!'

'Why?' Abida asked her. Just one word. Not a request. Not a plea. Just a question.

Nargis looked at her in astonishment. 'Apa Ji was right. For all your beauty, you are quite stupid. Why do you think? You were getting too popular. I saw how that boy returned time and again, looking like a lost puppy. That look in his eyes, I recognised it at once. It's the one that men reserved for me after I'd brought them to their knees. Rich boy like him, he would have married you and taken you out of this place in no time.' She sniffed, examining her manicured nails. 'Do you think I would have stood for it – an ugly thing like you getting out while I still have to service disgusting men? You see, Apa Ji has this little test. She always asks me to bait the new girls with the possibility of freedom. If they refuse to take the bait, Apa Ji proceeds to send them out for overnight stays and what not. If they're enticed by freedom ... well, I'd rather not describe what happens to them. Needless to say, when Apa Ji discussed the possibility of the test with me, I pounced on it. I had to end you. And just like I predicted, you failed that little test of trustworthiness, and now Apa Ji hates you. At least you'll take this lesson to your grave. Never trust anyone.'

Abida was shaking. 'What will happen to me now?' She hated the fear in her voice. 'What did you do with Muniba? Why did you trick her?'

Nargis's expression soured. 'Worry about yourself. That waste of space will be dealt with in due course. To be honest, she irritated me. I convinced Apa Ji to test both of you together. Genius idea of mine, really. She reached out to flick a strand of hair from Abida's face. 'Apa Ji has already made plans for you.'

'What do you mean?'

Nargis cackled again. 'If I tell you, where's the fun? I shall let Apa Ji do the honours. Little Miss Abida. Who would have known you had not one but two people on the go? The policeman and his little boy? I underestimated you, *larki*. But no matter. Once Apa Ji has dealt with you, I shall reign supreme again.'

Abida would have smashed her face, had she had the strength. She didn't like lying there with Nargis hovering over her. She didn't like displaying weakness, but her head was heavy and so was her body. Apa Ji must have drugged her. She could barely lift her hand.

'Nusrat!' Nargis cried suddenly, freezing the maid mid-sweep. 'Stop sweeping and tell Apa Ji that little Abida is awake. How many times have I told you to use the bloody vacuum cleaner?'

Nusrat squeaked and darted out of the room. Abida's head sank back into the pillows.

'How I wished that I'd be the one to take you down when the time came,' Nargis whispered. 'And now I have. All thanks to Apa Ji.' She must have been a real beauty once, but now she just looked evil – her eyes thinned in hatred, her face resembling that of a wax doll. 'When you came prancing in, stealing my Majeed with your innocent doe eyes, that was when I decided to end you. Who better to rope into the scheme than that idiot Muniba? Sure, the idea was Apa Ji's, but I'll have you know that I executed it all. Gladly.' She'd laughed again, and kept laughing until tears streamed from her eyes. 'You sluts deserve what's coming to you. Now all you can do is repent.' And with a swish of her perfumed *dupatta*, Nargis had swept out of the room without a backward glance.

She was right, Abida thought now. This was a lesson she would never forget. She looked around her prison cell. The air conditioner was turned on, and the room was cleaned every day. She should have been grateful, but fear pierced her whenever she thought about her future. Her baby. She had been so close to her – to escape. Would she remain like this forever? Would no one come looking for her? Not even her father?

Before she could think about anything else, Apa Ji sashayed into the room with Nusrat at her heels. She looked triumphant.

Abida tried to shrink into the bed, holding up the sheet to her chin. 'What do you want?'

Apa Ji's face took on an expression of mock sadness. 'Is that any way to treat your mother? After all I have done for you?' She glanced at Nusrat in the corner. 'Get out of this place or I will have your hide, you eavesdropping good-for-nothing woman.'

Nusrat scampered away, letting the broom clatter to the floor.

Apa Ji smiled. 'Now that we are alone, tell me what's troubling you, my honey bee?' She sat on the edge of the bed, her hand reaching for Abida. Abida screwed her eyes shut against the woman's touch. Apa Ji began massaging her leg in circular motions. 'Since you won't say a word, allow me to tell you where things stand.' The same hand now gripped her calf.

'Apa Ji,' Abida murmured, ashamed at the note of pleading in her voice. 'I promise I won't try to run away again. I promise to do your bidding.'

Apa Ji scoffed. 'My bidding? If you weren't so pretty, Abida, I would have gouged out your eyes for trying to run away. My prima donna. Tell me, *larki*, do you know nothing of this world? I could have expected that of foolish Muniba, but I had thought you more intelligent, despite your ... ah ... humble beginnings. Nargis had warned me that you were a flighty creature, but you seemed like you were enjoying yourself. But then I thought, the best way to find out is to test you. If you'd passed, I'd have sent you for overnight stays without a chaperone. I send out Nargis and the other girls all the time, and they always return. They value this establishment. But you failed, my honey bee. And I don't like people who fail me.' She released Abida's leg and rose. 'It's a pity. I had such great expectations of you. You disappoint me, my child.'

'What do you intend to do with me?'

Apa Ji sighed. 'For now, nothing. Your lover has been camped outside for the past few days. I knew when I bought you that you had something special in you, a certain brand of magic that drives men crazy. Now, I've had a call from his dear father, and you know I cannot say no to him, so I shall allow the boy to see you just this once before you embrace your fate.'

'Do you mean to kill me?' Abida blurted out.

Apa Ji laughed, a loud throaty sound. 'And waste my investment? Honestly, girl, you make me laugh.' Her face hardened. 'Make sure you enjoy seeing your lover. The way he was fighting with me to see you, he might as well be your husband. Dug your claws in nice and deep in the boy, didn't you? It will be the last pleasurable thing you'll do for a while. If it wasn't for his father, I would have had him hanged by the balls for the way he has distressed me.'

Abida hardly heard what Apa Ji was saying. All she knew was that she would be seeing Shahid. Despite her terror, some warmth crept into her heart, and the shadow that had hung over her lifted, not entirely but enough for her to breathe.

And before she could fully process her feelings, Shahid walked into the room, and her world exploded. The warmth turned into joy as a sob escaped her throat. She couldn't believe she was feeling like this towards someone who had so recently rejected her.

Shahid just gazed at her. 'Abida,' he murmured. 'I am so, so sorry.'

'No talking!' Apa Ji shouted. 'I am warning you, Shahid, I don't care who your father is. If you say one word to Abida, I will see you arrested for assault.'

Shahid glared at her. 'Can I at least embrace her one last time?'

'No.'

'Then let me touch her. Just a handshake.'

To Abida's surprise, Apa Ji burst out laughing. 'Ah, the things we're prepared to do for the ones we love.' Her expression turned severe. 'Go on, then. One handshake, and then off with you. Dear old Abida is off to a new home soon.'

'Where are you sending her?' Shahid asked her, his face a mask of worry.

Apa Ji held a finger to her mouth. 'It's a secret.'

Shahid looked from Apa Ji to Abida and then back again. 'You can't do this. When my father finds out—'

Apa Ji laughed. 'Your father wouldn't care a jot about someone like Abida. He's had plenty of women in the past who were far better than her. And besides, do you think he's the only police officer that frequents this place? Don't make me laugh. He may be an important client, but he's starting to piss me off with the way he hogs my girls. I need them to be able to service everyone. I need to make money. The rent doesn't pay itself.'

'You're such a liar. You own the place.'

Apa Ji bared her teeth. 'The girls need to be able to earn their keep, and they can't do that with just one client.'

'But—'

'Don't test me, boy.'

Abida's heart sank, but she knew it was pointless arguing with Apa Ji. 'Shahid, it's okay. I'll be okay.' She knew she wouldn't be okay, not by a long shot, but what else could she say? She was done playing the martyr. That's exactly what had brought her to this point. If she had exerted her will on Kalim, this wouldn't have happened in the first place.

She lifted herself from the bed and staggered towards Shahid. It was strange to feel such affection for someone who had paid to spend time with her, but as they moved closer, she realised that what she felt for him was more than affection, more than friendship.

She was expecting to hold on to his hand for as long as she could, but she froze when Shahid threw his arms around her. 'No matter what happens, Abida, I will not give up. I will come to find you. I promise.'

For someone older than her, Shahid could be very childish at times. Did he really think Apa Ji would wilfully tell him her whereabouts?

Before Apa Ji could object, Abida pushed him away. A glance into his eyes told her he had spoken the truth.

Apa Ji screeched with laughter. 'It seems that she isn't quite as keen on you as you expected, Shahid. Look at how quickly she pushed you off. She can't get away from you fast enough. She's probably more used to a man's touch than a little boy's.'

Shahid still had his eyes locked on Abida's. 'This isn't goodbye,' he whispered. 'I promise you that. You are not alone.'

'But, it is, Shahid,' she whispered back. 'It is goodbye.'

'Enough,' Apa Ji said. 'Now get out.'

Jamil

The boy was useless.

Jamil paced the length of the small patch of ground near the open drain. 'You should have told Abida that I was here in the city looking for her,' he fumed. 'You had one chance and you ruined it. Now she's lost forever.'

His daughter was gone. Before they could come up with a plan, she had been moved. In the flurry of cars that entered and exited the brothel, Jamil couldn't even tell which one had taken his daughter away. He let out a groan and kicked a large rock, earning himself a shooting pain in his toe.

There was little chance of being overheard. The place was rank with human excrement and the labourers only ever came there to relieve themselves. Apart from the sound of his footsteps, there was dead silence. It was the middle of the night. Even the water in the drain, thick with refuse, oozed to the nearby River Ravi silently.

Shahid had his head in his hands as he sat on a log. 'It was too risky. You don't know Apa Ji the way I do. She is like a rat that always sniffs out the food. It was hard enough to whisper the words in Abida's ear. I had to keep the hope alive in her.'

'You met my daughter, the apple of my eye, yet you failed to tell her about her father. What must she be thinking? That her father has deserted her.'

'She doesn't think that.'

'You haven't seen the place we come from,' Jamil scoffed. 'Fathers have killed their daughters for far less. According to the pir, I'm one of nature's mistakes.'

Shahid sighed. 'There's nothing we can do about it now. At least she has hope.'

'What hope? A fool's hope. She doesn't even know her father is here looking for her. How could you fail her like this? What good is the empty water tray to the thirsty bird?'

'We will find her, Jamil. That woman can't have taken her far.'

'It's the fact that we didn't even see her leaving that worries me. She is gone.' Jamil wrung his hands. 'I'll never find her now.'

There was a nip in the air, now that winter was approaching, and Jamil saw that the poor boy was shivering. His heart softened slightly. It wasn't the first time he'd wondered why Shahid was helping him. It was obvious that the boy was madly in love with his daughter, but that went against everything Jamil had believed in. Nobody married for love in his village. Marriages were always arrangements. But, then, wasn't he an exception to the rule as well? He could imagine what the pir would say if he knew what Jamil was up to. 'Snuggling up with your daughter's lover? You're the scum of the earth.' That was what the pir would say.

But why should he care about the pir's views? He was his mother's son. He had to remember that. He thought of the day when she had finally revealed why she had run away from her village, why their family still drew stares from passers-by. Jamil had been caught holding hands with a young girl, Pashmina. She was the daughter of the butcher Jamil apprenticed with, and they'd been exchanging secret glances for weeks until Jamil had plucked up the courage to hold her hand behind the butcher shop. Unfortunately for them, somebody saw, and poor Pashmina had been whipped. Just for holding his hand. Jamil wasn't one to cry easily, but that was the one time he had wept, with loud gut-wrenching sobs. More out of guilt than pity. That was when his mother had sat him down.

'I promised to myself that I would never speak of my past life again, but you need to know something, Jamil.' Her eyes had been earnest, her tone measured. She was not at all angry that Jamil had been caught in a compromising position. 'Love is not a sin. I had fallen in love too,' she had told him matter-of-factly, as if falling in love was the most natural thing in the world. As if she'd read his thoughts, she'd added, 'It's only natural, my son, and I regret nothing. Had it not been for that love, I would never have had you. Your father, God bless his soul, is gone now, but my love for him still remains.'

Jamil listened to her, rapt. He dared not move while his mother talked.

'It was a scandal. Things were worse back then. It was decided that I would have to die for honour. There really was no other way. I hadn't been caught holding hands, you see. I'd been caught in the act of love, in the throes of passion.'

When Jamil reddened, his mother looked at him sharply. 'I'm not embarrassed by it, Jamil, so why are you? Have the villagers been filling your head with stupid thoughts again? And you let them?' Her sharp eyes turned away as if she was disappointed in him. 'My father gave me every last rupee he had and sent me away with your father. When the villagers couldn't find me, their anger was so great that they hanged my father. In full view of his remaining family. He died for honour so I wouldn't have to. My mother never forgave me, but he saved me. He saved our love.'

Tears dripped down her face, and she didn't wipe them away. Jamil had never seen her like that. It was the first and last time he had seen his mother weep. 'I wish I could change our culture. I wish I could go back to my village, see my family again, but I know they blame me for everything.' She'd met his eyes, then, a fire burning in them. 'I gave up everything for love, Jamil, and no son of mine will sit here weeping because he feels embarrassed about something as pure as love. If you want to blame someone, blame Pashmina's family for being so weak. Remember, my son, love trumps everything.'

Love, Jamil thought now. His mother was right. He couldn't give up on his daughter just because he had had a setback. Nothing was more important to him than Abida's safety. But then, he thought back to his latest conversation with Farida. The lies he was telling her about their daughter being alive and well, and that he was just scouting the city for work before he returned. He couldn't bring himself to tell her that he still hadn't found her.

'Why don't you put her on the phone, then?' she complained. 'Safiya's mother has a fancy new phone that has something called WhatsApp on it. Rumour has it that you can get pictures there all the way from Lahore in the blink of an eye. Won't you send a picture of yourself with our daughter and grandchild? The little ones here are desperate to see you all. As am I.'

What was he to say to that? That their daughter had been sold to a brothel, not once but twice? How would she ever bear it? No, he thought. He couldn't subject his wife to that. 'Your phone doesn't support WhatsApp, Farida,' he'd told her instead. 'It is a simple model. Thank your lucky stars that you can at least talk to me. That's enough. Besides, WhatsApp doesn't work in our village. Where would one even get a signal?'

Coward, his mother would have said to him.

Shahid rose from where he was seated on the log. 'I should get going now.' He patted Jamil's shoulder. 'We found each other, didn't we? Who would have thought that two people with a single purpose would get together like that? If God has helped us thus far, He will not desert us now.'

Jamil blinked back tears. 'Why are you helping me, though? No man I've ever known would go to such lengths.'

Shahid withdrew his hand. 'I'm not helping you. I'm helping Abida. I owe it to her.' He had a faraway look in his eyes that Jamil knew only too well. Like himself, Shahid was also trying to atone for his sins, whatever they might be.

'You really do love her, don't you? Despite everything?'

'Despite everything.' His tone wasn't cold, but it brokered no argument.

Jamil's worry eased a little. He was glad to have someone. He didn't care what had happened between Shahid and his daughter. All he knew was that, right now, Shahid was the only person he had in this city of horrors. 'What do we do now?'

Shahid took a deep breath. 'We wait until I can find out where Apa Ji has sent Abida. I will find out. I owe it to you and I owe it to Abida.'

Abida

It seemed to her that it was her fate to wake up in strange beds, only this time she knew exactly how she had got here. She almost wished she didn't, because then she wouldn't have to relive the horror.

A rogue sob escaped her. Was this what her life was going to be like from now on? From the sunlight streaming in through a gap in the curtains, she could tell it was almost midday. Maybe past. And yet here she was in bed, about to be taken out like a sheep for slaughter.

Her entire body shook as the events of the past day came rushing back to her. Apa Ji hadn't told her where she was going. She was just packed into a car with tinted windows and driven away. She had looked back at the house that had been her prison for months, and had been shocked to see Apa Ji waving, as if she was her mother.

Some mother, she thought. She had tried pleading with the uniformed driver, but he had turned a deaf ear, his eyes fixed on the road. Only once had she caught him glancing at her, but when she met his eye, he looked away. When her pleading turned to silent tears, he had finally relented. 'Sahab has been interested in you for quite some time. Ever since Apa Ji told him about you. If you remain quiet and mind your own business, you can live a good life. Give him no reason to beat you up ... or kill you.'

'He kills women?'

The driver had only laughed. 'Who doesn't? You're in Lahore now, little girl. It isn't some backwater. Here, people mean business. From what I understand, Sahab has paid good money for you. He rarely sends me to collect his girls. Most of them come willingly, in rickshaws. It's only the ones he buys that he's very particular about.'

'You're wrong,' Abida countered. 'This is not the Lahore you think it is. You can't buy and sell people here. It is illegal. Someone is bound to come looking for me soon.'

He smirked in the mirror. 'Has anyone come looking for you yet? You've spent all this time with Apa Ji as her glorified slave.' He laughed at Abida's silence. Drumming his fingers on the steering wheel, he added, 'I can imagine your horror and I want to feel sympathy for you, but I've seen it so many times that I don't really care any more. I don't know what you've been led to believe, but kidnappings and murders happen everywhere, more so in big cities like Lahore. Do you know nothing of this world, *larki*?'

'Monster,' Abida had whispered, but now she realised that the driver had been one of the better ones. At least he had spoken to her as a human being, not an animal. She remembered arriving in some sort of compound after bouncing around for a long time on a rutted road. Outside Anarkali, all the other areas of Lahore seemed the same to her. Colourless houses, a mess of electric cables and cars zigzagging along unmarked roads. They didn't go through the posh part of town this time, the driver taking her through dank alleys and muddy streets.

It wasn't until they arrived in the outskirts and took the unpaved road leading into the compound that she began noticing her surroundings. They passed a beautiful stretch of trees bearing orange flowers before the road grew bumpy and the scene changed from orchards to buffaloes idling in open fields, mounds of dung rising in every direction. As strange as it sounded, the smell reminded her of her village, and she felt almost as if she was returning home.

Nothing could have been further from the truth.

As soon as they passed through the steel double doors, she was struck by the sheer size of the house. It was an ancient structure of brick and concrete with windows that seemed to have short-ened with the passage of time. She could tell where new bricks had been added to reduce their height, and a sense of dread settled deep within her. The car didn't stop in front of the main entrance, but near a kind of annexe, where chickens flocked unchecked and a pair of buffaloes were chewing the cud. A short woman stood there to receive her, pulling her out of the car hastily.

'Late as usual, Hafeez, you scum. You've hardly left me any time to make this little thing presentable.'

'She's a human, Salma,' the driver had replied. 'She's called Abida.'

'She's Sahab's new pet, and that's all there is to it. The begum is most keen to see her, of course, but that will have to wait until Sahab has had his fun.'

'Who's the begum?' Abida asked. 'His wife?'

Salma struck her across the face. 'Don't use her name, you little slut. She's too good for the likes of you.' She pulled her by the sleeve. 'Now, come. It's my job to make you look good. God save me, when I die I'll go to hell for helping with this adultery.'

'Now, Salma, don't let Sahab hear this talk,' said Hafeez. 'You know what he's capable of. Besides, he intends to marry her. He'll have your tongue if you go around calling this adultery.'

Abida felt Salma's grip falter, but she recovered in an instant. 'I am their most trusted servant. I'd like to see him try.'

Hafeez had rolled his eyes and flicked his fingers in farewell as Abida was led away.

She had been in solitary confinement ever since, the picture of her new keeper, Rana Hameed, on the wall the only thing to keep her company. Instead of calming her, it made her more nervous. Rana didn't look as old as the pir, but he wasn't young by any stretch of the imagination. He seemed to be stroking his moustache, a wicked gleam in his eyes, as if he might reach out and grab her. He looked like an old goat. She shuddered. She didn't have it in her to be a slave to another man.

'God damn you, Kalim!' she screamed, falling to her knees, not caring if she grazed them against the concrete floor. Maybe he'd see them bloodied and let her go, she thought, then cursed her stupidity. 'You're a dead fish, Abida,' she said to herself. She bit back tears, swallowing the burning sensation in her throat. It was during times like these that she missed her father the most. She thought of how he had watched her every move, silently pleading with her to mend her ways. She had seen the anger in his eyes when she'd delivered lunch to him at the butcher's shop, how his eyes strayed to her belly, but he had remained quiet, desperate to give her time, or maybe he just wished it was a bad dream. She should have listened to him. Having so many children had addled her mother's mind, she knew that now. Her vacant gaze had passed over her daughter's expanding belly, her thoughts focused solely on feeding the family and getting her daughters married off as soon as possible. It was a wonder Abida had remained unmarried for so long: a girl was usually removed to her husband's home the moment she had her first blood. She had seen children married off to older men, girls whose bodies hadn't even developed yet. Pale and waif-like, they were passed to greedy men who couldn't wait to run their hands all over them.

'Some of the men like their girls like that,' she had once heard her father tell her mother. 'This village is a sick place. I wish we could marry Abida somewhere in the city.'

A whole lot of good that did me, she thought now. The city wasn't any better than the village. Still, she had had some good years with her family, and hadn't had to endure marital rape at the tender age of eleven. Rape, however, was unacceptable at any age. She knew that now. What gave these men the right to use her to their heart's content. Who did they think they were?

Before she could sink any further into depression, the door creaked open. She jerked up her head, wincing as she stood. She sighed when she saw that it was only Salma.

'What do you want?'

'Her tongue works like a pair of scissors,' Salma said to herself, closing the door behind her. She cleared her throat. 'I have to get you made up.' A chuckle escaped her. 'Like a shiny new Barbie doll. The ones I've seen my nieces play with, except theirs were shabby little things with broken legs and featureless faces, handed down from some rich begum's kids. They were kind of like you.' She chuckled again. 'I honestly don't know what Sahab saw in you. Begum Sahiba is keen to see you, but she knows she must wait until Sahab has had his fun.'

Abida's eyes filled with tears, her heart thudding with panic. She ran her hand over her sweat-streaked forehead. 'Why are you so mean to me? What have I ever done to you?'

Salma spat on the ground. 'Sluts deserve to be treated like this, coming in from Apa Ji's dirty hovel, carrying diseases. It's a good thing Sahab hasn't had any intimate relations with Begum Sahiba for many years now, or I would be worrying for her health.'

Abida turned away from her and went to sit in front of the dressing table. In the spotted mirror, she saw the despair in her face. At Apa Ji's there was always that small hope of escape, but how could she ever manage to escape this compound? And there was no Muniba to help pass the time.

She put her face in her hands. 'I don't want to live any more.'

Salma tutted. 'Enough of the theatrics. What's the matter with you? Don't you women love this kind of life?'

'Not me,' Abida cried, between sobs.

'Perhaps you're not the same as the other gold diggers Sahab brings in after all. Well, don't let Sahab see you like this or there'll be hell to pay. Do you know what he does for a living?'

Abida shook her head without turning to look at her.

She felt Salma touching her hair, gently handling it. Maybe she was imagining it, but the woman's manner seemed to have become a little kinder. 'He's very powerful, and you'd be a fool to let him think he made a bad investment in you. Now, let me take a look at you. Yah. We have to get you into the shower first before you can be decked out. You look a fright.'

※

There were only a few people in the sitting room. Salma had drawn an embroidered organza veil over her head, but in spite of it, Abida could make out the room. Her eyes searched for Rana Hameed, but he could be any one of the five or six men in the room who had their backs to her. Only the *maulvi* sat facing her, and he averted his gaze when their eyes met.

'The bride is here, Sahab,' Salma purred, all the rudeness gone from her voice. She sounded like a kitten.

It was then that the man in the middle turned, and their eyes locked. He had to be over sixty but he was built like an ox, and despite the lines on his face, he had a silent strength. Strands of white crossed the black of his hair, and, seeing the shocked expression on her face, he grinned at her, revealing several gold teeth.

'Lower your gaze, you foolish girl,' Salma whispered to her.

Abida looked down, and allowed Salma to guide her to the nearest sofa, onto which she sank gratefully. She didn't think her legs could carry her any further. Her breath came out in short pants as her eyes travelled to Rana Hameed again. He was very different from the men she had been with at Apa Ji's. There was something about him, something she couldn't quite place her finger on. At first glance he looked just like any other middle-aged man with greying hair and a lined face, but upon closer inspection, there was a malice in his eyes – the way they took her in greedily, the tip of his pink tongue slipping out of his mouth like a serpent, as if he couldn't wait to have his way with her. An involuntary shudder ran through her. She thought of Shahid, and tears threatened to break out again, but she swallowed the lump in her throat. She couldn't afford to displease Rana Hameed, not when her life depended on it.

'A souvenir from Apa Ji.' One of the men chuckled. 'I swear that woman is a marvel. You find all the best ones there.'

'The bitch asks for triple the amount when it comes to virgins,' another said.

'This one's no virgin,' the first said, laughing openly now.

Abida shivered.

'Look at her sitting up straight on the sofa, bold as brass. Are you sure she didn't pass you damaged goods, Rana Sahab?'

'Quiet!' One word, a command, and the entire room went silent. 'She is about to become my newest wife. I will not tolerate this talk.'

'But, Rana Sahab, we didn't know. Are you really going to marry her? We thought it was a joke, inviting Maulvi Sahab here and all.'

The *maulvi* rose from his seat. 'Do I look like a joke to you?'

'No, Maulvi Sahab.'

Rana Hameed's voice boomed in the room. 'You fool. Would you have me live in sin? What if I'm stopped on the road? Wouldn't it be something to get caught for adultery, rather than drugs? This woman here will be my wife.'

Beside her, Salma quailed in fear, whispering something unintelligible.

'So, you're one hundred per cent serious about her?' the same person asked Rana Hameed. He had to have a death wish, Abida thought. She didn't dare look up as Rana Hameed considered his answer.

'I am always serious about my wives,' he said finally. 'You may be my first wife's brother, Amjad, but you should remember your place.' He turned to the *maulvi*. 'Shall we get started?'

It seemed ironic to her that she was getting married again, this time without her consent.

Before she knew it, the *maulvi* was asking her, '*Beti*, do you accept Rana Hameed as your lawfully wedded husband?'

Abida glanced up to see Rana Hameed leering at her. She didn't want to say anything.

Salma pinched her arm. 'Think what's good for you,' she whispered. 'Say yes.'

The *maulvi* cleared his throat. '*Beti*, I will ask again. Do you accept Rana Hameed as your lawfully wedded husband?'

Salma pretended to throw a friendly arm around Abida's shoulders, but her nails dug into her flesh. 'You fool. You will take us all down with you. What are you waiting for?'

Abida didn't wince. She had suffered too much pain to feel anything. Her eyes were locked with Rana Hameed's. The grin on his face slowly faded, replaced by a frown.

'The girl is an imbecile, Maulvi Sahab,' one of the men said. 'She probably doesn't understand you.'

The *maulvi* shook his head with force. 'The girl has to agree verbally to the marriage, or there is no marriage.' Glancing at Rana Hameed, he sighed. 'At the very least, I need a nod from her.'

Keep trying, Abida thought. She wanted to laugh. She didn't know where this strength had come from, but she felt as if she was standing at the edge of a cliff, and if the only way of escaping the hounds was jumping off, so be it. She kept her head still.

'Uff, you stupid girl,' Salma hissed into her ear. 'Do you know what he will do to me? You are my responsibility.'

Rana Hameed was turning a bright shade of pink as he sat watching her. Then, all of a sudden, he smiled again. 'What is the punishment for adultery in our villages?'

'Death,' answered all the men in unison. 'Death for honour.'

Abida wanted to laugh in their faces. She didn't care. She was already dead, and she wasn't going to give Rana Hameed any satisfaction. She was not going to become his wife.

'And what do we do to the children of these women?' Rana Hameed continued, an edge to his voice.

'We kill them too. The devil's spawn!'

And just like that, she was back on the riverbank, the chorus of voices calling for her death, the shivering that just wouldn't go away, her poor father, who had stared at her swollen belly, unable to hide his pain. Her baby, whom they had given away to an orphanage. Could Rana Hameed really know about her baby? Would he dare kill her child? Of course he would, she thought. He didn't care about the sham wedding. He just wanted to live in honour. If he had to kill her child to get her assent, he would do it. She knew enough of this world now to believe it.

The life drained out of her and she sagged.

'Yes,' she murmured. 'I accept him as my husband.'

Jamil

Winter wasn't just coming. It was already here. Jamil could feel it in his bones as he woke up in the morning, his heart full of guilt and regret. Why had he ever let her out of his sight? Why had he sent her off with Kalim? The questions circled his head until he got himself out of his tent and walked over to the communal kitchen - if you could call a few sticks thrown onto a mound of packed earth a kitchen. A kettle was already placed on the fire, steam twisting out into the crisp morning air. Everything was going to change from today. He could feel it.

His stomach rumbled.

'Pass me a cup of tea,' he said to Mazhar, the worker kneeling in front of the kettle.

He had a cigarette between his lips, which he flicked out. 'Got any money?'

Jamil gulped. He was saving every rupee he made. 'No, but I'll pay you back. It's just tea anyway.'

Mazhar chuckled. 'Just tea, huh? Tell that to all the men who paid ten rupees each for the tea leaves and milk. Do you know how expensive everything has become?'

'Believe me, I do,' Jamil mumbled to himself. He put on a bright smile. 'It's okay. I'm not really in the mood anyway.'

Mazhar whistled. 'Looks like Mr Fancy here has a luncheon to get to. Look at him, wearing a pressed shalwar kameez today. Do you have an appointment with your spade?'

'Use your eyes, Mazhar,' Jamil launched back at him. 'Where on earth would I find an iron in this dump?'

'Aww, did I offend, Mr Fancy?'

'Stop calling me that.' Jamil shook his head. He shouldn't be rising to the bait. This was exactly what bullies like Mazhar did.

Everyone broke into a laugh, their mean old faces breaking into a thousand wrinkles as they tried to laugh away their misery. Ganging up on whoever they deemed the weakest was their only means of survival – and entertainment.

'Why have you gone quiet?' Mazhar said, rising from his haunches. 'Cat got your tongue, or are you too fancy to talk to us now? Should I call the overseer and tell him you're getting ideas of dressing up for manual labour? Fancy yourself as an overlord, do you? Now that you have your little friend coming to visit?'

Jamil took a deep breath and stepped back. 'It was just a simple request, Mazhar. If you don't want to give me any tea, that's fine. Besides, I'm leaving today.'

The moment the words had left his mouth, he knew he had made a mistake. The atmosphere immediately became more hostile as all the labourers rounded on him.

'Do you hear that, friends?' Mazhar sneered. 'He wants our tea just so he can make a run for it. I know the right word for vermin like him. Thief!'

Jamil held up his hands. 'I'm only here to look for my daughter. I don't want any trouble. I already have my share of it.'

Mazhar's eyes narrowed. 'Run away, has she? The slut.' He advanced on Jamil, ignoring the protests in the background. 'So, tell us, Jamil. You work here while your daughter spreads her legs for whomever she pleases? Together, you two must be making a killing.'

Jamil's mind had gone blank. All he could hear was the rush of blood in his ears. For a moment it seemed as if the pir was standing in front of him, and a frisson of fear went through him and his hands clenched into fists.

Mazhar was close enough for Jamil to smell the sweat on him.

He looked into the hollow, pitiless eyes, and spotted the fear and helplessness. Right now, all Mazhar feared was Jamil moving up in the world. Jamil had only known him a few months, and yet here they were, squaring up to each other. The fight left Jamil, and he turned away. 'Get lost, Mazhar. There is nothing you can do that will stop me leaving this place.'

Before Mazhar could reply, they heard a jeep approaching. *Finally*, Jamil thought, and sure enough, he spotted Shahid in the driver's seat as he drove towards their tents. Mazhar stared at him for a minute longer before dropping his gaze. 'Let's get to work, men. This place isn't going to build itself. And, besides, we don't have any rich benefactors to take care of us.'

Jamil threw his little pouch of clothes over his shoulder, and hurried to the jeep, glad to see the last of the hovel he had called home for the past few months. He felt sick when he thought of how little money he had made. But, if Shahid was to be believed, where they were going now, money would play little part in the grand scheme of things.

He jumped into the jeep. 'What took you so long?' he said, hating the whine in his voice. Already he was becoming dependent on the boy. He sat up straighter. He couldn't afford to lose focus. He was here to save his daughter, and he had to remind himself not to rely on anyone. He cleared his throat. 'If you could just tell me where they have sent my daughter, I can handle the rest.'

Shahid rolled his eyes. 'Don't be silly, old man. While I admire you for coming all this way to save her, from the time I've spent with you, I can safely tell you that you won't get anywhere without me.'

'Maybe. But how on earth did you convince that horrible woman to give you information about where Abida is?'

Shahid pursed his lips. 'I didn't get it from Apa Ji. I got it from Nargis.'

'Who is that? Another one of the girls that Apa Ji tortures?'

'Hell will freeze over before Nargis was tortured for anything, although God knows I tried my best. She deserved it.' He probably noticed Jamil's face, as he hastily added, 'I did not kill her, and when you hear what they've done with Abida, you'd wish I had killed both her and Apa Ji. I just persuaded her to share Abida's whereabouts with me. She's Apa Ji's right hand, so knows every-thing. She was not very pliable at first, but I've picked up a thing or two from my father. I may hate him for how he treats people, but you cannot deny that man knows how to get his way. Anyway, in short, I know exactly where Abida is being kept, and it's not pretty. I'm sorry, Jamil.'

For a moment, Jamil froze. 'Is my daughter dead?' Nausea suddenly assailed him, but he forced himself not to react to it. Despite the cold, he could feel sweat breaking out under his arms. 'That monster killed her, didn't she?'

'Oh, of course not. She is very much alive. Only she's somewhere much more dangerous than Apa Ji's brothel.' He paused, biting his lip. 'The thing is that Apa Ji has sold Abida to Rana Hameed.'

'Sold?' The words rang in his ears. He realised what type of person Apa Ji was, but he hadn't allowed himself to contemplate that his daughter might be traded like a common mule. A rage he hadn't felt for many years possessed him. 'Where is this Rana Hameed? Take me to him.'

Shahid locked the doors and started the jeep. 'Jamil, in a rage, all you'll achieve is getting caught or, worse, killed. You don't know how powerful Rana Hameed is. Even I didn't know how powerful he was until yesterday when my father finally told me.' He cranked up the heating although the jeep had no roof. 'Now buckle up, will you? I need to make sure I get you to the place in one piece, because everything rests on you. Damn, it was never this cold in November before, was it?'

Jamil took deep breaths to calm himself. Shahid was right. He couldn't allow himself to lose control. Too much was at stake, and Abida had only them to rely on. There was nobody else in the world who could help her. He blinked back tears. 'Thank you for everything you're doing,' he said. 'I don't know how I would have managed without you. I was completely lost.'

Shahid rolled his eyes, but his lips curved in a smile. 'If I had a rupee for every time you've thanked me, I would be a rich man.' His tone grew serious as he glanced at him. 'You've given notice at the place you were working, right?'

It was Jamil's turn to chuckle. 'What do you think I was doing there? I was a common labourer. We don't have any contracts or facilities. It's just backbreaking work for twelve hours a day. Do you think the overseer would care if I were to give notice? He's probably glad that I've left, considering he thought I was in my late fifties.'

'But, you're not, are you? You must be in your early forties.'

Jamil smiled. 'True. The village robs us of everything, starting with our youth and then snatching our children away from us too.' He ran a hand through his hair, feeling the oil on his fingers. It reminded him of Farida and her nightly ritual of massaging his head with a tablespoon of her famous oil cocktail. It was another thing they made a bit of money from: the desperation of balding men. Farida would fill her concoction in used bottles of cooking oil and Jamil would sell it at the butcher's shop. Sales were occasional, but they made Farida happy. He looked out at Lahore, passing outside the window, focusing on the shopkeepers pulling up the shutters as they readied themselves for another day of trade. He knew he would burst into tears if he didn't distract himself. His longing for Farida was almost physical. It constricted his throat, and he wondered how she was managing in the village on her own with the children.

Shahid cleared his throat, bringing Jamil out of his reverie. 'Rana Hameed lives in the outskirts of Lahore, and his estate is heavily guarded, if my father is to be believed. He is never wrong.'

'I'm ready, Shahid. I'm ready to do anything for my daughter.

Just get me a job there, like you said. If I have to sweep the entire estate to free her, I'll do that.'

Shahid clucked as he changed gear. 'It's not as simple as sweeping floors. You will be the eyes and ears of the operation. You will need to look for cracks in the security of the compound. You will need to win the hearts of the people there, anything that might lend us some crucial information.'

'Why would they even hire me? Nobody hires a person who just walks up to the gate to ask for employment. Even I know that and I'm not even from this city.'

'These big houses are always in need of servants, especially ones they can exploit by paying less. We just have to make sure you're dressed in a way that leaves no doubt about your desperation.' He patted Jamil's knee. 'If that doesn't work, we'll try something else, but by God I will get you in that house.'

Jamil picked the dirt from under his fingernails, his head lowered to avoid the gusts of wind whipping his hair. 'Why can't we just take the police with us? If what you say is true, and Rana Hameed makes his money from drugs and selling people, wouldn't the police want to catch him?'

Shahid shook his head. 'I'll tell you what they want.' He rubbed his thumb and forefinger together. 'Money. As long as they're bribed up to their throats, they will keep their mouths shut. Besides, Rana Hameed isn't a fool. He wouldn't keep drugs on his estate. It's all on his farms – at least, that's what my father says.' He drummed his fingers on the steering wheel. 'It's a mark of how powerful Rana Hameed is that even my father doesn't want anything to do with him. I had to lie to him and say I was giving up on Abida too. No, stealth will get us results. We need to be as stealthy as we can.' His tone grew more serious. He glanced at Jamil. 'Will you tell her I'm waiting for her?'

'Quite a thing to ask of a father.'

Shahid shifted his eyes back to the road. 'I'm sorry,' he muttered. 'I don't know what I was thinking.'

'I'll do it,' Jamil grunted. 'God knows I've humiliated myself enough. A little more won't matter.' He couldn't help but smile when Shahid whooped, punching his fist in the air.

Kids, he thought. They were all alike.

Abida

As Rana Hameed's new wife, Abida had been shifted to better quarters. Her bedroom window overlooked the bustling courtyard and beyond that the stunning orange orchards. There was no road that she could see, no way to escape. The estate was surrounded by a brick wall almost three metres high with barbed wire on top. Even if she could somehow reach the wall unnoticed, she could never climb over it, not with that barbed wire. Abida groaned and drew the curtains, almost pulling them off their pegs. She collapsed in the armchair, her head in her hands. She was trapped once again. There was literally no way out, and after what she had done at her *nikkah* ceremony, the little warmth Salma had begun to show her had vanished.

Her body ached all over, as if she had been beaten and poked by bayonets, which in a way she had. Far from being a considerate lover, Rana Hameed wasn't even a considerate man. He had smiled widely as he led her to their marriage chamber on the night of the ceremony, as if he had long forgotten that she had resisted him. His friends had shouted for him to carry her to the bedroom in his arms, which he had, but as he reached the bed, a wheeze making its way in his breathing, he had dropped her onto the bed so that she bounced. The men had laughed.

'Don't break the bed, Rana Sahab,' said one of the men – Harris was his name, she'd later learned – leering at Abida. 'Save it for when you have your fun.'

Rana Hameed had boomed with laughter, before holding up his hand. 'Get out now. I need to spend time with my new wife.'

Abida had implored Salma with her eyes, but the woman pretended not to see, and bringing her hand in a circular motion of goodbye towards her face, she had said, '*Khuda hafiz*, Rana Sahab.'

The moment the door closed, and the sound of footsteps had died away, Rana Hameed had reached for Abida, holding her hand tenderly as he drew her out of the bed. Her heart was beating as if she had run miles, and she was almost panting from fright. He stroked her cheek. 'Panting, already?' He smiled. 'What a slut you are.' The expression on his face changed and the hand that stroked her cheek went to her neck, the other pulling at her hair.

Abida had squealed.

'My house, my rules,' Rana Hameed had whispered to her. 'I like my girls a bit cheeky, but don't let that turn into disrespect, you hear?'

Abida could only splutter in response, his grip on her throat was so tight. She could barely breathe, but Rana Hameed didn't seem to care. It seemed only to encourage him. It was when she felt her vision blurring that he relaxed his grip, giving her time to draw a few shaky breaths before he turned her around and bent her over the bed.

That had been a few days ago, and he had returned to her bed every night since. He never said a word to her, and she knew better than to ask him why. She remained quiet and pliable in his hands, transporting herself to somewhere else, back to her village when she was younger and life was full of possibilities. Each thrust sharpened her memory of the mustard fields, of her mother's yellow lentil curry, of the siblings she had abandoned. It was only after he was finished that she finally returned to the present, and even then she sometimes allowed herself a few seconds more of fantasy, but not too many, for if she didn't seem present enough, she got a slap across the face.

'You've been with so many men that you don't even feel anything now,' he wheezed into her hair. 'God knows what's come over me but I simply can't get enough of you.' When he couldn't perform a second time on the same night, he compensated for it by running his hands all over her, holding her arms so tightly that he left bruises. If she tried to break free, his grip strengthened. So she had learned to act like a living ghost.

Her meals were brought to her by Salma, who didn't meet her eye as she put the tray on the bedside table before hurrying away. Abida didn't bother trying to talk. She was too exhausted, too defeated. She barely ate the rich beef curries and *khameeri* rotis brought to her. She only ate a small portion of yellow lentils as it reminded her of home. She thought of holding the pillow over her face to squeeze the breath out of herself, but her mind rebelled against it. She couldn't consider suicide, not when she had a child out in the world somewhere. She had to remain alive for her, because Kalim, her father, was worse than dead. She didn't even know if he was still alive, and realised she didn't care. There was once a time when she couldn't contemplate life without Kalim, when the mere thought of separating from him meant death to her. Now, he was as good as dead to her. If it wasn't for him, she would be back in her village, back with her father, her family.

Her eyes stung, but she didn't let the tears flow, for once they began, they didn't stop easily. She gulped down her sorrow and arranged herself on the armchair as the key turned in the lock. It would be Rana Hameed again, drunk and ready to rape her. Yesterday, he had been so drunk that he had wet himself while removing his clothes, not bothering to clean himself as he jumped into bed.

She forced a thin smile as the door swung open, but it was Salma who stood in the doorway, and this time, she wasn't carrying a tray.

'Begum Sahiba has summoned you.'

Abida's heart lurched. 'What? Why?'

'Must you always question everything? Begum Sahiba makes a point of meeting each of Sahab's new wives. You must come.'

Despite herself, Abida felt self-conscious. She had never been in such a situation before. What was she supposed to say to the woman whose husband was raping girls half or, in her own case, a quarter his age? She turned away and faced the window. 'Tell her I don't want to see her.'

Salma rushed into the room, and before Abida could turn around, she felt Salma clap her over the head, pulling off her *dupatta*. 'Stupid girl. Two days in this house as Sahab's mistress and you've already forgotten your place. When Begum Sahiba summons you, you come. There is no question about it.'

'I have to do what they say, but why must I put up with you? You don't have a kind bone in your body. You're just like your master. Evil.' She was trying not to break into tears. She didn't want Salma to know how much she craved kindness.

Instead of her usual terse reply, Salma was silent. 'I am nothing like him. He is a dangerous man,' she said finally, looking up to meet Abida's eye. 'In this house, you must not forget your place. You don't want to know what will happen if Sahab tires of you easily. You do not want to invite his wrath.'

She sighed. 'Lead the way.'

If Salma was surprised by her reply, she didn't show it. She just nodded and beckoned Abida to follow her. For the first time since her sham wedding, Abida stepped out of her new rooms. The floors were pure white marble with old-fashioned torches mounted on the walls. 'They're not real,' Salma said, as if reading her thoughts. 'It looks like fire, but they run on electricity.' She gestured towards a table placed against the wall. 'Sahab brought this antique vase on one of his trips to Taxila. Probably just stole it,' she added in an undertone.

Abida didn't rise to the bait. She wasn't going to be friends with someone as unpredictable as Salma.

Rana Hameed's first wife lived in one of the older and more lavish parts of the house. If Salma was to be believed, this house had consisted only of a courtyard and a couple of rooms before Rana Hameed had expanded it to accommodate his growing brood. A long corridor divided Rana Hameed's side from the begum's. As they walked down the torch-lit corridor, Abida sneaked a look out of the windows. Same high walls with barbed wire. She shook her head. This place was even worse than a prison. As they passed through the carved wooden door that led into the begum's inner sanctum, Abida felt a change. Everything became more feminine, even the air, which now smelled of tuberoses. Mauve velvet curtains adorned the windows of the sitting room, and a motley collection of female servants scurried about, some holding trays of food, others dusting. They all paused to look at Abida, before lowering their gaze and hurrying away. Salma led Abida through the sitting room towards another ornate oak door, and knocked twice. A woman's face appeared as the door opened. 'About time, Salma. Begum Sahiba was about to get ready for her afternoon siesta.'

Salma tutted. 'I'm here now, aren't I, Fareena? The new girl needed a little persuasion.'

Fareena's eyes widened as she hitched the *dupatta* back on her head. 'A new girl with some spice. I like it.' She laughed. 'Come in.'

Despite the cold weather, the fan was turned on in the room. As they walked inside, the scent of tuberose became almost over-powering. There was also something else – a cloying smell with which Abida wasn't familiar. She coughed, covering her mouth with her hand. 'Excuse me,' she said, something she had learned from Shahid.

'Finally,' said an authoritative voice, from the direction of the bed. 'A girl with some manners. Come in, for God's sake.'

Salma bounded off towards the begum and sank to her knees. 'I've brought her for you, Begum Sahiba. Here she is, in the flesh.'

'No need to be so dramatic, Salma.'

Abida glanced up, and her eyes landed on a round woman propped up against the pillows, a *hookah* on the floor next to her. A bubbling noise rose from it as the begum sucked in air and re-leased it in a puff of smoke. Abida was fascinated. The cloying smell she now identified as the scent of grapes, yet it came from the hookah. Back in the village, the hookahs smelled nothing like it. Women would smoke one with just a hint of opium, for pain relief.

The older lady put the hookah's shaft aside and surveyed Abida. She was probably in her mid-fifties, but her enormous weight made her look older, and despite covering her head with a *dupatta*, the begum wore thick layers of makeup, her lips so red that it seemed as if she had dipped them in blood. 'So,' she said. 'You are the one. The latest to join the ranks.'

Abida looked down.

The begum laughed. 'Don't feel shy on my account, girl. God knows what you're doing behind closed doors with my husband, so why stand on ceremony here?' Her voice changed. 'Look up.'

Abida met her gaze.

'Where are you from?'

'From a village in Punjab,' Abida murmured.

'I meant which brothel.'

'Sahab got her from Apa Ji's,' Salma piped up.

'Speak when you're spoken to, Salma. How many times do I have to tell you?' As Salma apologised, the begum turned her attention back to Abida. 'How long have you been in the business?'

Abida could feel the damp under her armpits as the blush rose all the way from her neck to her face. She knew her cheeks were bright red. 'Just a few months,' she murmured.

'Carrying any disease?'

Abida shook her head, unsure of what to say. How on earth would she know? She wasn't sure which diseases the begum was talking about.

'Is my husband treating you well, girl?'

'If you consider keeping someone locked in a room and having violent sex with them good treatment, then, yes, he is treating me well.'

To her credit, the begum didn't flinch at the mention of sex.

Rather, she was unfazed. 'Good. That means he's enjoying you. Stay on his good side. My husband...' her eyes assumed a faraway look '...is not a kind man, and capable of far worse.' She shook her head. 'I didn't even introduce myself. They call me Nigaar ... Begum Nigaar.' It didn't seem as if she wanted any acknowledgement, so Abida just bowed her head. 'Did you join that *haramzadi* Apa Ji of your own volition? She attracts all the beautiful girls. She's a girl magnet, I tell you. If it weren't for her powerful clients, I would have had that den of sin shut down years ago.' She spat into a small chamber pot she had on the floor next to her.

'At least that would have saved me,' Abida said, surprising herself.

'What was that?'

Abida looked up and took a deep breath. 'If you had had that den of sin closed, at least I wouldn't have had to enter the trade. I don't know who gives you information, but the majority of the girls there do not enter that house willingly.'

'Pah, what a bunch of lies. I know of Nargis. My husband once paid her a visit but, unfortunately for her, she was a bit too old for Rana Sahab. She was a real piece of work, if word is to be believed.'

'Nargis stopped me escaping. I am nothing like her.'

Nigaar's eyebrows shot up. 'Is that so?' she asked, but Abida noticed a lack of conviction in her voice. Nigaar was not a stupid woman. It was obvious that she had invited Abida to her quarters to remind her of who was in charge, but Abida could tell that the woman was surprised. The meeting hadn't gone the way Nigaar had expected.

She turned to Salma. 'You told me the girl was a harlot.'

Despite herself, Abida felt a pang to hear of Salma's betrayal. Salma was shuffling her feet, looking at the floor. 'She seemed like one, Begum Sahiba. She has a real tongue on her.'

'When did having a tongue make anyone a harlot?'

'She spoke up to Sahab,' Salma said. 'The sheer nerve of this girl.'

'You say that like it's a bad thing. I thought she was a whore.'

Nigaar sagged in the bed. All of a sudden she seemed like a sad old woman, too weighed down by all she had seen in her life. 'I don't feel good, Salma. Take her away. I don't want to see her face any more. God knows I'm troubled enough by the faces of all the others, and by what's happened to them.' She turned her face away, and pretended to focus on the scene outside her window. 'I need to take my nap.'

Abida had rattled Nigaar, but she didn't feel pleased. Something didn't feel right to her, the way Nigaar turned away from her as if she couldn't bear to look at her. Abida thought she'd seen pity in the older woman's eyes. As Salma escorted her out of the room, she couldn't help but feel that she was completely out of her depth here.

It was only when she returned to her room and found Rana Hameed sitting there with an evil grin on his face that she felt the weight of Nigaar's words. *Stay on his good side.* Rana was not a kind man, especially not when he smiled like that.

'Been out for an excursion?' he asked her, patting his knee. 'Why don't you come and sit on my lap? You know you want to.'

With a tremendous force of will, Abida forced a smile. 'Your wife called me for a chat.'

Rana Hameed laughed. 'Did she now? And what did poor, blundering old Nigaar say to you? Her usefulness ended the day she delivered our last son. Now she's just a begum in name, stuck day and night in that lair of hers.' He patted his knee again. 'I thought I asked you to sit here.'

Abida sat on his knee, and Rana slapped her thigh. 'You fool. Do you want to shatter my knee with your weight? Sit closer to me.' He pushed her deeper into his lap. When Abida squirmed, he slapped her thigh again. 'As pretty as you are, I feel you're not compliant enough, my dear. I'm starting to lose interest.'

Abida's stomach lurched. *Stay on his good side.* She ran her fingers down his arm, taking his hand in hers. 'What can I do for you today?'

Rana Hameed's breathing was already shallow. 'That's more like it. But, as it happens, I have another idea to make you more pliable.'

Abida's heart was thudding. She tried not to let her panic show in her voice. 'Oh, you don't need to, Rana Sahab. Remember, I'm your little bird.'

'A bird with a tongue on her,' he replied, pulling something out of his pocket. Before Abida could look around to see what it was, she felt Rana Hameed flip her forearm, feeling for something. 'There it is,' he said at last. She watched in horror as he brandished a syringe in front of her. 'The best part of your life starts now.'

Before she could move, the needle was plunged deep in her arm. She cried out in pain, but the pain quickly turned into something else, something far more powerful. The room brightened around her and her senses heightened. Something like intense joy gripped her, only it was so much more than that. It was as if every nerve in her body was on fire, as if every cell had come alive.

She groaned and writhed against Rana Hameed.

'That's more like it,' he wheezed. 'That's more like it, my girl.'

Jamil

He had spent the last two hours walking around the perimeter of the compound, but other than brick walls and barbed wire, he had seen nothing of importance. No way of escape, either. Whatever Rana Hameed was brewing here, he had taken great pains to keep it safe.

'Drugs,' Shahid had told him. 'He's the biggest drug lord in the city. Maybe even the region. There will be no police raids here. This is his personal territory. If the drugs do arrive in this place, they don't stay for long. No, our only chance is to be on the inside somehow.'

Jamil knew how they could get eyes on the inside. He was well suited to the role after his stint as a labourer. His sunburnt face and calloused hands bore testament to him being a commoner, and commoners weren't considered a threat in Pakistan. In accordance with Shahid's instructions, he waited until midday to make his move.

He approached the gates, but before he could come close enough to touch the warm iron, a guard emerged through a small door embedded in it. He whistled at Jamil and asked him what he wanted.

Jamil drew himself up to his full height, displaying his tattered clothes to full effect. 'I heard you were looking for cleaners, and I'm looking for work.'

The guard stroked his moustache. 'I don't remember us posting an advert. Why don't you just get lost?'

Jamil joined his palms together and drew closer. 'Please introduce me to someone in the house, and I'll be very grateful to you. I really need work.'

The guard narrowed his eyes. 'There is plenty of work to be had in the city. The question is why you've come all this way for work.'

Before Jamil could reply, there was a honk on the other side of the gate, and the other guard yelled, 'Sahab's car is leaving.'

The gate creaked, and the guard Jamil had been talking to rushed back. His heart pounding in his throat, Jamil put the most pitiful expression he could manage on his face and stepped towards the opening gate.

A Mercedes Benz stood waiting to drive through, but before it could move, Jamil threw himself against one of the windows, weeping over the glass.

'What the hell, man?' the guard yelled at him. 'Get away from the car or we'll shoot you.'

Jamil pounded at the window, tears streaming from his eyes. He wanted to see the person behind the tinted glass. He didn't know whether he was faking the tears or not. They poured out of his eyes of their own accord. A surge of hatred coursed through him, almost overwhelming him. His whole body shook as if he was being electrocuted.

He felt strong hands grab him and pull him back, but as they did, the window slid down. The fight left him as soon as he saw the person staring at him. It wasn't Rana Hameed at all. *Damn you, Shahid*, he thought. He had promised him it would be him. 'I've done research,' he had said. What was he supposed to do now? Beg this woman for a job?

The woman was enormous, and she fidgeted constantly, perhaps in a vain attempt to get comfortable. 'Who is this, Tariq?' she asked. 'Did you pull him out of a brick kiln or something? Look at the state of him.'

'Sorry, Begum Sahiba,' Tariq replied, panting from the effort of holding Jamil back. 'He came looking for work, and he wouldn't take no for an answer.'

The woman laughed. 'Is that so?' Her gaze met Jamil's. 'And what do you have to offer that our existing staff cannot do?'

'I can clean, and I can butcher animals. Please, Begum Sahiba, I have seven children in the village that depend on me. My wife is sustaining the family by doing embroidery, but you know how little it brings.'

'We don't want strangers in the house.'

Jamil looked for a chink in the woman's armour, but didn't see any. He racked his brain for something, but nothing came to him. The seconds ticked on as the begum observed him. Finally, she shook her head and instructed the driver to move, in Saraiki – the language of South Punjab.

Jamil launched into an appeal, speaking now in Saraiki instead of the Punjabi he'd been using. 'I had hoped that you would have a bigger heart for the people of your region. We speak the same language.'

'From Multan, are you?' she asked him, signalling the driver to stop.

'Near Khanewal, Begum Sahiba. We are starving. I could really use your help.'

'Oh, to hear my sweet language from a mouth that doesn't belong to me.'

'I won't disappoint you, Begum Sahiba. I have always heard that Saraiki-speaking folk help one another.'

The begum sighed. 'We have been having our meat butchered from outside for a long time now. It would be nice to have someone in the house, and I would like to have people of my region around. They'll make me feel closer to home, to my beloved Multan.' Jamil knew she had made up her mind as she turned to the guards. 'Let the man go, for Heaven's sake. He's not going to attack me. He's from Khanewal. And find him something clean to wear. Tell Salma to show him the places where he will be working. He will be both butcher and cleaner. With the new arrival, we could use the additional help around the house, not upstairs mind you.' She rolled her eyes. 'And make sure he isn't carrying any firearms. Do your jobs, you fools.'

Jamil could hardly believe his ears. He looked at the guard, who looked back at him with annoyance.

'You have a sneaky way about you,' Tariq told him, as he escorted him towards the house. 'I don't like it. Not one bit.'

Jamil couldn't have cared less about Tariq's opinion, but he plastered a broad smile on his face and allowed himself to be herded like a sheep. Within the walls there were orchards that went on for ages until the house came into view. He had been expecting something grand that would fit the image of Rana Hameed, but the house was very old, with peeling paint and rotting doors. It was huge, and he had to admit that some parts seemed newer and better maintained than others, but the overall impression wasn't appealing. His heart sank as he scanned the dozens of windows, all shut with thick curtains blocking everything out. How would he know where Abida was? And then the realisation hit him. After many months, he was in the same place as his daughter. He might not be able to see her yet, but he had found her.

Abbu is here, Abida.

Tariq shook him. 'What is the matter with you? Why are you crying?'

Jamil rubbed at his eyes with his palms. 'Dust got into my eyes.'

'I don't see any dust in the air.'

Jamil was spared from answering as a short, dumpy woman appeared in the doorway. She had her hands on her hips. 'Who is this specimen?' she sighed. 'As if that girl wasn't enough.'

Tariq shrugged. 'He's your responsibility now, Salma. Begum Sahiba hired him off the road just because he speaks Saraiki. I tell you, that woman has an unhealthy obsession with her native city. Anyway, he's to clean the ground floor and do some butchering.'

Salma smacked a palm against her forehead. 'That woman will never learn. She thinks charity will somehow save her from Hell, but it won't. She's as guilty as her husband. And hiring people from South Punjab. How do we trust them?'

'Well, in the begum's opinion, people from that area can do no harm.'

'They are a kind lot,' Salma admitted. 'I've seen them first hand, but the fool can't think all of them are good? Surely not.'

Tariq laughed. 'Better not let anyone hear what you're saying, Salma. Even walls have ears these days.'

Salma spat on the ground. 'Like I care. I've been in this house for decades, and where has it got me? Still cleaning up after the sins of Sahab, which is better than cleaning the sins of the begum, which mostly involves wiping her arse. She can't be bothered to walk to the bathroom.'

Tariq covered his ears and retreated. 'I do not want to hear this.'

As soon as he'd left, Salma turned to Jamil. 'Before I show you to the servants' quarters, I want you to understand one thing. If you try to tattle in front of the begum or Sahab, you will sooner wish you were dead than face the torture I will inflict on you.'

Jamil nodded. 'Understood.'

Salma sneered at him. 'Understood, he says. You're a bloody cleaner here. Act like one. God, if I ever had a husband who looked and smelled like you, I'd commit suicide.'

Jamil saw his opportunity. 'You never married?'

Salma eyed him sideways. 'What's it to you?'

'Nothing.' He shrugged. 'Just wondered, you know, beautiful woman like you. I would have thought you'd have the pick of the land.'

He could sense the barricades shake. He even thought he detected the hint of a smile. 'Well, you certainly have a way with words. Now, stop loitering here at the entrance, and follow me. I'll show you to your quarters first. Once you've cleaned up, we may make a decent man out of you.'

As she led him outside again, Jamil cast a last glance at the doorway that led into the house. Somewhere inside this giant place Abida was waiting for her father to rescue her.

Abida

He was angry today. She could sense it in the way he walked into the room, but in spite of her fear, she welcomed his presence, for he brought something she desired. She tried not to eye his pockets; she tried not to make any sudden movements in case he decided to turn around and leave.

This was the first time in two days that he had visited her, and she was almost out of her mind with need. She had been sweating all day, and twice she had been into the bathroom to throw up what little food she had managed to eat.

'Hit me up.' She realised too late that she had said it aloud.

It was exactly what Rana Hameed had been waiting to hear. He advanced towards her and slapped her face. She fell out of the chair and onto her knees, coughing.

'You stupid bitch. Do you even know what just happened? I had to spend all day at the police station cosying up with the officers so that they would leave me alone. Do you honestly think I'm crazy enough to carry heroin on me when I'm at the station?' He watched her with unconcealed disgust, but she caught the desire in his eyes too. She knew which would win.

She watched as he collapsed onto the bed. 'I'm up to my neck in trouble,' he moaned. 'Someone has been making enquiries about me and complaining to the senior officers. I've had to bribe my hide off to keep them at bay. But I'm sure those bastards at Narcotics won't leave me alone. I can sense it.'

Abida picked herself up from the floor and walked up to Rana. With trembling fingers, she undid his belt, the same one he had used to beat her a few days ago before injecting her with a shot of heroin. She could almost feel the relief it would bring. She was prepared to do anything for it.

She threw herself on top of him, knowing he liked her that way. And then she waited for it to be over.

'Ugh, you stink,' Rana grumbled, but she could feel his desire. 'When was the last time you took a shower?'

'Just today,' she lied, taking care to keep her voice level. She couldn't let him think she was out of control. If he thought for a single moment that she was so out of it she couldn't have sex with him properly, he wouldn't give her the drug. She had to appear composed. 'Do you want me to step into the shower now?'

'Leave it,' he told her, stroking her face with a thumb. 'Pretty little thing, aren't you? But I can sense the need in you. You're dying for a hit. You new ones are the worst. You have no restraint.' His fingers closed around her neck. 'Imagine if I wasn't in the mood to give you any. What then?'

The pressure on her neck increased, but she didn't give in. 'You don't want to damage the sensitive skin around my neck. The bruises wouldn't look pretty for when you're in the mood. They'll keep distracting you.'

Just as she knew he would, he reduced the pressure on her neck and rolled her across the bed so that he was on top. She didn't even feel disgust now, so fixed was she on getting her hit.

Somewhere in her mind, she realised that this was why Nigaar had summoned her, to see whether Rana had turned her into his slave yet. As Rana started going about his business, she retreated into her mind. The funny thing was that she wasn't unhappy any more. It was a torture she had to endure for Rana to give her drugs. And he had told her that if she was good, he would give her a stash. The thought brought tears of joy to her eyes, but even that was nothing compared to how she felt when he reached into his trousers, brandished the syringe, followed by a spoon and a small pouch of white magic.

She smiled, knowing and not caring that she had become his slave. 'You had it on you all along.'

She watched with mounting excitement as the substance sizzled in the spoon until the syringe sucked it all in, and when the needle finally pierced the skin between her toes, she sighed as her head sank into the pillows. This was better than anything in the world ... *better than her baby*. Her eyelids fluttered, but she could neither agree nor disagree with that. At that moment, maybe the heroin was more important than her baby. She felt alive and dead. As if she were somewhere in between. At this rate, Rana could leave the doors unlocked, and she wouldn't escape. Who in their right mind would want to escape this delightful prison? All thoughts of her family and baby fled from her mind, and only a feeling of pure unfiltered joy remained.

Jamil

Jamil was the new servant in the house, which meant he was at everyone's beck and call. Rana Hameed's friends treated him like an animal, bellowing orders at him and kicking him when he made a mistake. Jamil endured everything with his head down, but he was already busy making plans.

He couldn't believe how easy it had been to win over Salma. What surprised him even more was that she had never been with a man before. At first, he couldn't bring himself to flirt with her, but all it took was the thought of his daughter imprisoned upstairs and his mind was made up. Farida would forgive him for this, he thought. When she understood why he had done it, she wouldn't question it. He knew it in his heart. It pained him to lie to her like this, but what was he supposed to do? She was already under tremendous pressure, raising all the kids alone in a village that was no longer a friendly place for them.

'When are you coming back with Abida?' she'd asked him just a day ago.

Jamil had made the first excuse that came to him.

Farida had sighed. 'Sometimes, I feel as if you're lying to me. I sense that in your tone, but then I think that Abida is your daughter too. Your favourite child, no matter how much you deny it. So, naturally you must be doing everything in your power to keep her safe. She is safe, right?'

'Yes,' Jamil had replied in his most soothing voice, but he felt the familiar guilt creeping up on him. 'She is perfectly fine, and I will soon return with her to the village. You'll see, Farida. One of these days, you'll wake up to find us in the courtyard.

'May God make this happen.' Her voice had cracked then, and she'd hastily ended the call.

One day, soon, I will return to the village with Abida, Jamil thought now. There was nothing and no one that could stand in his way.

᳁

For all her bravado, Salma melted immediately. He gave her the small gifts Shahid had packed into his bag in case he needed them for such a purpose – a key-ring, bangles and henna. Jamil had objected initially, and they had argued about morals and self-respect, but he realised now that even a twenty-three-year-old boy had more practical sense than him. Whenever he left her something, Salma would be wearing it later that day. He almost felt bad when he saw her in the bangles, her hair dyed a fierce shade of black and her mouth covered with a thick lipstick, but when he heard her refer to his daughter as that 'filthy girl', his heart hardened, and he redoubled his efforts. Salma had no choice but to fall under his spell. What chance did she stand in the face of a father's desperation? To his surprise, she was quiet in bed, a far cry from her usual self, as if she couldn't quite believe what was going on. In bed, she was off guard, and Jamil enjoyed controlling her. She was at least fifty-five – much older than his forty-two years – yet she trembled like a girl as he touched her, her head rolling back as she moaned. He knew what to do. He had been doing it long enough with his wife.

'Sex means intimacy and intimacy means that secrets are spilled.' That had been Shahid's advice to him. And, sure enough, the whispers started. Trivial things at first, like the titbits Salma stole from the begum and how she sometimes let out her anger by sending up old bread for her. Then, one day, she began talking about the girl upstairs.

'I feel dirty because I have to pimp for that filthy girl.'

Jamil's heart raced, but he kept his face blank and his voice level. 'You mean the begum?'

Salma laughed, not bothering to cover her mouth. Her breath smelled of garlic. 'Girl? The begum? That woman is ancient. Can't even walk to the bathroom. The maids have to help her.' Her fingers played with the hair on his forearm. 'These rich people are very dirty inside, for all their creams and perfumes. I remember once in my early days, I had to—'

'You were telling me about that girl upstairs.'

Salma returned to the present. 'Ah, yes. Don't ask. I hate that little *haramzadi*. She's upstairs in one of the rooms past the landing. Sahab's latest pet. Has a tongue that works like scissors. She has ignored all my useful advice. Serves her right if she dies. Who cares? Let's not talk about her any more.'

It made his blood boil to hear her speak like this about his daughter, but he swallowed his anger and pretended to look at her with such intensity that she turned pink.

'*Haye jee*, you are making me blush like a young girl. Don't look at me like that,' she said, turning her face away from him. But he knew she liked it, and after she'd had her way with him, he knew she would be willing to answer any question he asked. He tried to picture Farida when he was with Salma, but it was impossible. Salma was nothing like his wife.

He shook his head as he extracted himself from her sticky embrace and lay on his side. Their sweat had long since dried. He would have liked to wash himself, but there was no time for that, not when there were a hundred chores to be done and plans to be made. As soon as her snores started, he removed the keys for the upper floor from her shalwar and hid them in his pocket. Judging by the volume of the snores, Salma would sleep for some hours yet. His heart fluttered like a trapped bird as he stole across the small space that Salma called her room and stepped outside. He shut the door as quietly as he could. This was the moment he had been waiting for.

The house was always deserted at this time of day. Nigaar rarely ventured out of her rooms. Her servants stayed there as well. Rana Hameed's children had long since left him, and Jamil didn't blame them. Who would stay with a monster who tortured young girls in his home? A shudder ran through him as he arrived at the main entrance and the grand staircase that led to the first floor. He had never been upstairs before. It was forbidden. However, he had it on good authority that Rana Hameed was not at home, which meant that none of his cronies would be stalking the halls. They would all be outside in the *haveli* getting drunk and making passes at the milkmaids. Most of the female staff were compelled to grant sexual favours to Rana's friends.

'They always considered me too ugly for such things.' Salma had spat on the ground. 'Good thing I was born ugly. I wouldn't be caught dead with one of those rascals. And they call themselves Muslims.'

'You're not ugly. Even a blind person could tell that,' Jamil had replied, and for once, he had almost meant it. Almost. If she hadn't been so cruel about his daughter, he might have felt sorry for her, but her ugliness stemmed from something deep inside her. Perhaps the bitterness of being rejected had ruined her, turning her into a monster in her own right.

He began climbing the marble stairs, careful to step only on the red runner. As grand as the staircase was, the first floor told a different story. Out of sight from downstairs there was a steel mesh door with a heavy padlock. For a moment, Jamil could only stare at it. A prison. A fancy one, but still a prison. He pulled out Salma's keys, his heart pounding now. He didn't even know which was the right one. It was entirely possible that Salma didn't have access to the rooms upstairs and had to ask one of Nigaar's maids to let her in. She might just have been boasting to impress him. She liked to do that.

Stop thinking about Salma, he told himself. If someone saw him now and questioned him, he didn't know what he would say.

To his surprise, the lock clicked open when he turned the key, and within seconds he was in the inner sanctum of Rana Hameed's kingdom. He leaned against one of the pillars, panting. Village life had aged him faster than he'd have liked. A little excitement and he was gulping mouthfuls of air like a man on his deathbed. Rousing himself, he pushed forward. The coast was clear, but there had to be twenty different doors lining the corridor. He knew from Salma that Nigaar's quarters were at the end. 'She likes being as far away as she can from her husband's sinister activities,' Salma had told him, smirking the entire time. 'She doesn't approve of what he gets up to. She especially hates the fact he's bought and sold dozens of girls, each of them his wife for a time. It makes her feel insecure.'

Of course, Jamil thought now. If Nigaar preferred to be far away from her husband, it made sense that Abida would be at the other end. He wished Salma had told him Abida's exact location, but there was nothing to be done about that now. He pulled out the smaller keys for the doors. One must fit each lock. Taking a deep breath, he tried the first door to his right. It was locked, of course, but bending down so that his cheek touched the floor, he noticed that it was completely dark inside. It was a guess, but he didn't think anyone was behind that door. He would come back to it later if the others didn't open. His disappointment mounted as he found the next two rooms empty as well. This was taking too long and if his losing streak continued, someone was bound to find him. He was about to return to the first door, when he thought he heard movement from behind the next. He hurried forward. This had to be it.

This time, the first key he selected turned in the lock. Sure enough, as he opened the door, it became obvious from the smell that someone was inside. It smelled as if the person there hadn't washed in weeks. It was dark in the room apart from a chink of light thrusting through a gap in the curtains. He followed the light towards the bed, and then his heart stopped.

There lay a young woman in only her undergarments, the bed damp with sweat and what he thought could be excrement. It was dark, but even if it was pitch-black, he would have recognised his Abida.

'My *beti*, what have these savages done to you?' He crossed the room and fell on his knees beside the bed. As his eyes adjusted to the darkness, he noticed that Abida's eyes were only half open and she seemed to be in some sort of trance.

'Abida,' he cried, all thoughts of secrecy abandoned. He took her by her frail arms and shook her. 'Abida. I have come to save you. I have come to take you away from this horrible place.'

He could barely see her for his tears. He brought her close to his chest, and racking sobs escaped him. He had utterly failed as a father. Here lay his daughter, worse than a slave. He feared he knew what Rana had been doing to her. He had seen the same look on the faces of homeless youth in the village after they had drunk homemade alcohol. Some of them died from the shock of the drink. He had seen this look on Kalim's face. He also suspected that Abida had been given something far worse. She looked catatonic.

'Abida, can you hear me?' he whispered into her hair. It smelled of her despair, as if she was on the verge of death. He took her face in his hands, dipped his fingers into the glass of water on the bedside table and ran them across her forehead. She didn't respond. He shook her now. 'Abida, wake up.'

She had to wake up. How else was he supposed to tell her about his plan? Before he could whisper again, Abida's dilated pupils fell on him. A frown broke across her forehead, but before she could begin to understand what was happening, Jamil heard a door opening downstairs.

Rana Hameed had arrived. He was sure of it – nobody else used the main door. Even his friends came from the side entrance.

He would have liked nothing better than to confront and kill the man, but Jamil had always been realistic. Perhaps that was what had annoyed the pir. He looked into his daughter's eyes again.

'Remember me. I will come back for you.'

He didn't think he would have the strength to leave her, but what else could he do? He was a realist, and no matter how much he loved his daughter, he couldn't take on the entire household.

Yet.

As he withdrew, Abida reached out and took his hand. He watched as her eyes focused on him, her forehead breaking into a sweat as she tried to concentrate. There were noises coming from downstairs. Jamil couldn't stay, no matter how much he wanted to.

'Abida,' he whispered, but he didn't have to struggle as Abida's grip slackened and her eyes rolled back in her head. She turned away from him with a sigh. She was in her own world again.

Jamil rushed out of the room, shutting the door with as gentle as click as he could. As much as it pained him, he had to lock it. He wiped the tears and snot from his face, and assumed a blank expression. However, before he could move, he found an older man turning into the corridor.

It was as if someone had punched all the air out of him. It had to be Rana Hameed – the posture and expression told him as much. He watched as he stroked his moustache, an expression of mild interest on his face.

'I would like to ask you what you're doing here, but I think the more pertinent question is who are you?'

Jamil said the first thing that came to his mind. 'Salma sent me.'

Rana Hameed raised an eyebrow. 'So, you work here? Wonders will never cease. To think that I'd have men prowling upstairs one day.' His tone hardened. 'I'll ask you again. Who are you and what were you doing in this corridor?'

Jamil couldn't think. He could hardly breathe. He wanted to kill the man standing in front of him, but it was as if all the strength had seeped out of him. He was what he had always been – a coward. It took everything in him not to lose his head while standing there. He cleared his throat. 'I ... I was just...'

'Cat got your tongue?' Rana Hameed pulled something from his pocket, brandishing it in front of him. The light glinted off it, and Jamil realised it was a gun. A proper revolver that might well contain bullets. 'Would this help jog your memory?'

Looking at the revolver and then at Rana's face, Jamil saw that this was how he operated: on fear. So be it. If these were to be his final moments in the world, he would spend them trying to save his daughter. Let the man know that she hadn't been forsaken. He met his gaze head on and drew himself up to his full height.

A shuffling noise came from behind him. He turned to see Nigaar walking over to them, leaning heavily on a stick. 'Damn those maids. They've gone and tripped the entire electricity circuit in my area. The whole place is dark.'

Rana pocketed his revolver. 'Ah, another surprise. My wife walking on her own. You must have been scared. Didn't you even have the presence of mind to open the curtains?'

'Pah, you know how the sun burns my skin.' She was wheezing by the time she reached them. 'And I can walk when I want to. Contrary to popular belief, I walk to the bathroom too. Don't believe everything people tell you.' She put her hands on her waist and surveyed the scene. 'Fancy seeing you here, though. Twice in as many months. I must be a lucky wife.'

Rana grinned, but Jamil could see that he was uncomfortable, and guessed the cause was the presence of his wife. A plan began to hatch in his mind.

'Did you hire this piece of shit?' Rana jerked his head in his direction.

Nigaar looked at Jamil as if she was noticing him for the first time. She put a hand over her chest in mock-horror. 'Why, God save me. A man in Rana Sahab's secret lair? I wouldn't miss this drama for the world.'

'Just answer the question, woman, or I'll shoot him in the head and be done with it.'

Nigaar rolled her eyes. 'Ah, the theatrics. I wish I hadn't fallen for those when I was a young girl. It would have saved me a lot of trouble, and my father a lot of money.' She held up her hand before Rana could speak again. 'Yes, I hired him, and he's an excellent worker if Salma is to be believed. She has been singing his praises, and we all know that the silly old hag doesn't like anyone. Besides, he's from Multan and I like hearing him speak Saraiki.'

'You and your love for Saraiki.'

'It is my language. You can't take it from me.'

'Oh dear God, someone save me from this woman.'

Jamil knew he wasn't in the clear yet, but he could see some of the suspicion dissipate from Rana Hameed's gaze.

'It still doesn't answer my question about what he's doing in my private quarters.'

'Salma must have sent him to clean the area, dear husband. If you haven't noticed, she has the beginnings of arthritis. Perhaps the bitterness she's carried all her life is catching up with her. I don't understand why she's still here. I would have shown the impertinent *kutiya* the door ages ago.'

Rana Hameed grinned. 'She has her uses – for both of us. I trust her.' He turned to Jamil. 'Get out of my sight, and tell Salma that if I ever spot you in my private quarters again, I will burn you both alive.'

I will get you, old man, Jamil thought, as he saw Rana Hameed lead his wife back to her quarters. He noticed a blush of pleasure on Nigaar's cheeks and wanted to vomit.

Abida

Drugs had made her life easier in one way: she didn't have to pretend to like Rana's touch during sex. Now that he thought she was permanently drugged out of her mind, he didn't ask her to be more responsive. In a way, he probably enjoyed the special power he held over her, the power of granting or denying her the one thing she yearned for every hour of every day.

Or so he believed.

He didn't know yet that, for several weeks, she had stopped injecting herself with the poison. She had even avoided snorting the coke he left for her, usually flushing it down the drain. It had taken every ounce of her self-control not to give in to her body, which craved these substances. She was shocked to discover how much she yearned for it, more than she had yearned for anything in her life, even her own child. The first few days had been so bad that all she could think of was that damned needle and the relief that came with it. It didn't help that she shivered uncontrollably and threw up anything she managed to get down her throat. She wasn't a saint. She had gone back to injecting herself several times, but for the past few weeks, she had been clean. She could hardly believe her luck with Rana, though: although he was in the drug business, he didn't seem to recognise the symptoms of withdrawal. The man wasn't a complete idiot though. He knew something was afoot. For many days now, he had been smirking at her, asking her if she was pregnant whenever she vomited.

They say that if you think of something often enough, it happens. She had already missed a period, which she had pinned on her drug use, but when she missed another, having abandoned the drugs, she knew for certain. She was with child. Maybe that was why her symptoms were so bad, and deep down she knew that was part of the reason she had given up the drugs.

She wasn't going to tell Rana. She would rather die before she admitted to the one thing that gave her any kind of power over him. Secrets were strange. They could break you, but under the right circumstances, they could also make you. And, right now, this secret was going to make her. It gave her the strength not to be tempted by the drugs Rana pushed at her every time and it gave her strength now – to endure his thrusts as he groaned her name in her ear. She might be from a village, but she knew what drugs did to unborn babies. She had seen enough drug addicts in the village, doped up on toxic mixtures they got cheap from pedlars and sometimes found dead in ditches or bundled up in shawls. Nobody even bothered checking on them for days, thinking they were just unconscious. It was the smell of their rotting bodies that finally gave them away. She remembered the story of what had happened to one drug addict's baby in the village. It had been so malnourished and simple-minded that the pir had put a steel bowl on the child's head and let him grow into a *Shah Doli's Rat*, to send off to the city for begging. It was a gruesome practice where the heavy, unyielding steel prevented the child's brain from growing, leaving them simple and entirely dependent on others. Such children, when they grew to become adults, fetched good money from begging in big cities with most people stopping their cars just to stare, most finding it in their hearts to give money. These people remained babies in the bodies of adults.

'We've already sent several kids as *Shah Doli's Rats*, and they bring us a steady stream of income,' the pir would say. 'This is exactly why I tolerate the addicts. They provide us with these beautiful rats.'

Years later, when they had removed the steel bowl from a child's head, Abida couldn't help but stare at the tiny skull. The ten-year-old child drooled and babbled like a tiny baby, and was hardly able to walk without support.

'All hail, *Shah Doli's Rats*,' the pir had chanted. 'I will send this gem to Multan.'

Abida shuddered at the injustice of it. That was not what would happen to her baby. Rana Hameed mistook her shudder for pleasure, and his thrusts gained momentum. Abida attempted to remove herself from the present. She couldn't bear to hear his grunts. Her fists clenched as she considered the other secret she was keeping from him, a secret that could potentially destroy her.

Her father.

Her mind had been addled by drugs, but she would have recognised his voice and touch anywhere. He had been in this room with her. She had tormented herself, thinking she must have imagined it, but deep down she knew he had been there. But why hadn't he returned to see her? It had been several weeks and, although she was ashamed to admit it, the thought of her father had encouraged her to avoid the drugs rather than any effect they might be having on her unborn baby. But, then, she hadn't known at the time that she was with child.

Could he really be in this house, biding his time until he could rescue her? Abida screwed her eyes shut. She had to believe that or she would never survive. She had to believe. If she really tried, she could still remember the outline of her father's face as he had bent over her, his hand stroking her forehead. She couldn't be sure, though, not really, not when her whole mind was swimming – but she couldn't deny that she had heard her father's voice. Loud and clear.

He had been here.

She opened her eyes and turned away from Rana's ugly red face. Her eye caught the fruit platter on the side table, a knife stuck into an apple. If she could just reach out with her right hand, she could clasp her fingers around the knife's handle and sink it deep into Rana's neck, putting an end to everything.

'I dare you to try,' Rana panted in her ear. 'I dare you.'

He knew. He always knew.

The thought seemed to give him more pleasure. Abida closed her eyes and dug her nails into his back, hoping he would mistake it for passion. He probably did, as right at that moment, he let out a groan. Abida allowed her body to relax. At least now she would have an excuse for all the sweat that had broken out across her body. Withdrawal could invade her whenever it wanted.

Afterwards, as Abida returned from the bathroom, she found Rana still in the bed, a sheet covering his belly. Despite his advanced age, she couldn't deny that he was in good shape. The hair on his chest had gone white, but there was no sagging. Her eyes travelled up to his face, and she saw that he was grinning.

'Like what you see? Want to have another go?'

Abida almost laughed. As if he was capable of that at his age. She noticed that he held a small packet in one hand and a syringe in the other.

'So, what's it going to be? Coke or heroin?'

'Coke,' Abida said, without thinking.

She could see he was disappointed. 'No fun in coke. I thought you were more of a heroin girl. Here,' he threw the packet towards her, 'have fun with it.' Something seemed to give him pause. 'Come to think of it, you haven't done heroin for a while now. Any special reason?'

His tone was playful, but Abida was not fooled. 'Oh, I'm trying to take it a bit easy. Coke agrees with me better than heroin. With heroin, I am unable to give proper attention to your needs.'

His eyes narrowed. 'You're not pregnant, are you? I don't want a halfwit for a son.'

They all wanted sons, Abida thought, but she kept her face blank. She lifted up her kameez and turned sideways. 'See? No sign of a belly.'

She knew he was testing her. Perhaps he already knew, although she had used the syringe to sprinkle blood on her sanitary pads to fool Salma. She didn't know what he would do if he found out that she was with child, and she didn't want to know. Not yet. Her father was coming to her rescue, and all she had to do was bide her time until then.

She gave him the broadest smile she could muster. 'Now, how about that second time?'

Jamil

His heart was thudding. He was at the point of no return. Once he had done the deed, all he could do was hope and pray that Shahid would stay true to his promise. Shahid could barely conceal his glee when he had called him earlier. Jamil had to retreat far into the shadowy corner of the place where he butchered meat to take his call. His blood-stained fingers had been trembling. Shahid never made the calls. Jamil did. That was the rule.

'They're coming,' he had gushed, as soon as Jamil had put the phone to his ear.

For a moment, his mind drew a blank. 'What do you mean?'

'The anti-narcotics force, who else? They have agreed to raid Rana Hameed's compound.'

The expectations came cascading down. Jamil couldn't believe Shahid was that stupid. 'Have you not listened to anything I told you since I got here? Rana Hameed does not keep any drugs on the estate. He would be mad to do that. He keeps them well away – his people make sure of it.'

Shahid sighed. 'You don't understand. We only need to cause a diversion to rescue Abida. I don't care if the police can't find his stash. All I care about is that they find enough to drag him to the station, leaving the field clear for us.'

'And, how do you hope to achieve that?' he whispered.

Shahid's tone was flat. 'I'm not going to be achieving anything. You are.'

And the plan had brought him close to the gates of the compound. He didn't dare go upstairs again for fear of getting caught, not to mention that Salma had taken him to task. Although she had bought his story that the padlocked door was open and he had simply gone there out of curiosity, there was suspicion in her eyes that hadn't been there before. She was watching his every move.

However, she hadn't said anything to the guards, who let him out for a quick visit to see his 'cousin from the village' after giving him a good pat down.

'You're a nice guy,' one of the guards, Nasir, told him. 'You wouldn't imagine the kind of things we find nestled deep in servants' pockets.' He smirked. 'Some of the men have their underwear stuffed with change and knickknacks. They don't appreciate us fondling them, but what can we do?' He laughed, and gave him a final pat on the back. 'You're always clean. Just make sure you stay that way.'

His 'cousin', of course, was Shahid.

'Got them from the inspector,' Shahid told him, handing him small plastic pouches containing a white substance. 'They cost a fortune, and he needs them back when they raid the compound. Don't let anyone else have them.'

Jamil bristled. 'I'm not stupid.'

'I know.'

Up close, he could see that the strain was showing on Shahid's face. He didn't look like a boy any more. His features had hardened, the jawline sharper than before, and there was hollowness in his eyes, as if he had experienced things beyond his years.

Despite his momentary anger, he couldn't help but feel affection for the young man. He didn't dare wish for anything, but if he could, it would be to see Shahid and Abida settled. Why else would Shahid be helping her? When he asked him, Shahid just shook his head, a thin smile on his face.

'She saved me.'

'Who from?'

'Myself.' His gaze had levelled with Jamil's. 'She came into my life during a time when I wasn't sure of anything, least of all myself. She probably didn't know it, but every moment I spent with her changed me. For the better.' He blushed. 'There were other things too, but those are between us.'

Jamil didn't push him, but he was surprised to discover that he didn't mind. He didn't mind if Shahid and Abida had had a physical relationship. What kind of father did that make him? What kind of a man? He knew what the pir would say: *Coward. Lunatic. Pimp.*

Despite his apparent religious fervour, the pir possessed a very broad vocabulary of abuse when the mood took him.

Jamil patted Shahid on the shoulder. 'You're a good boy.'

Shahid's brows knitted together. 'Just make sure you're not caught.'

Jamil smiled as he made his way back to the compound. It was just as well that Nasir was still on duty when he returned as he waved him through. Jamil had timed his entry at the exact moment he knew the guards would be having lunch. Everyone needed a few minutes off – even the guards. Little did they know that this time his underwear was full of pouches containing a white substance.

He grabbed a broom and a mop, and walked towards the main house. How times had changed. He couldn't care less what the pir thought. After rescuing Abida, he would send for the rest of his family and settle somewhere else. Somewhere close to wherever Abida and Shahid would settle.

One thing at a time, he told himself, shifting the broom and mop into one hand, and rummaging inside his shalwar for a pouch. Naturally, he couldn't plant the drugs anywhere Salma might go – she watched him like a hawk. His only chance was to hide them in plain sight, in places where Salma didn't venture often.

There was only one place he could think of – Rana Hameed's

sitting room downstairs. In a way, it made perfect sense. If the drugs were to be discovered outside, in the stables or the place where meat was butchered, Rana could blame his staff and get away with it, but if they were found in his inner sanctum, even Rana Hameed would not be able to explain them away.

The problem was that his friends were always there. So be it, Jamil thought. Crowding a plastic tray with tall glasses full of orange juice and alcohol (vodka, Salma had told him), he carried it into the sitting room. Since it was early afternoon, only two people were there. Their conversation ceased when he entered. Iftikhar, who was bordering on obesity, spent most of his days on the pink sofa, stuffing his face with sweet delicacies. Sure enough, there was a tray of silky vanilla pastries in front of him, and he was munching imported dates. Apparently he was good with numbers, which was why Rana tolerated him. Jamil's heart sank as his eyes fell on the other occupant of the room.

Shershah, Rana Hameed's second in command. The pouches could wait, Jamil thought, as he retreated. Naturally, Shershah looked up at the worst possible moment, his wizened face tightening as his gaze locked with Jamil's.

He held up a finger. 'Ah, if it isn't the king of the castle.'

Jamil kept his gaze down. Salma abused everyone behind their backs, but even she couldn't bring herself to abuse Shershah. 'He's very evil,' she had told him the last time they'd been together. 'He does everything for Rana Hameed, from abductions to killings. You name it.'

When Jamil had encouraged her to elaborate, she hadn't hesitated.

'He's ancient and has been with Rana Hameed for many years. He used to work for his father as well. In a way Shershah raised Rana to be the animal that he is. Even the begum fears him.'

Salma had begun to trust him. It wasn't just the sex that loosened her tongue. It was something else too. In her way, she had come to like him. Jamil wasn't foolish enough to call it love, but they had a camaraderie, and since he hadn't broken Salma's trust, she had become more honest than ever. He realised now that Salma wasn't as bad as he'd thought. She was a creature of her circumstances, and her circumstances had always been dire. In a household like this, nobody was allowed to get too comfortable.

'Look at me, boy,' Shershah said, pulling him out of his thoughts. 'Put that tray away and sit in front of me.'

Jamil had no choice but to do his bidding. When he tried to sit on a nearby stool, Shershah barked at him again. 'Who told you to sit on the stool? Sit on the floor, like the dog you are. I swear Rana Sahab has really spoiled his servants. His father, Bade Sahab, would never have stood for such behaviour. He was known to slit throats for less. If you worked in my home, I would have skinned you alive for such impertinence.'

Jamil gazed at the wrinkled face. Shershah could have been anywhere between seventy and ninety, but he still sat ramrod straight on the armchair. How could a person be so poisonous?

'Did nobody teach you manners? Do you think that just because you're a houseboy, you can barge in anywhere? We were discussing important business here.'

'Umm, come on, Shershah *bhai*. We were only discussing girls,' Iftikhar put in, but one glance from Shershah silenced him.

'You come in here unannounced, you prance around the house as if you own it, and you have the nerve to enter Rana Sahab's inner sanctum?' He nodded. 'Yes, Rana Sahab told me all about your little excursion. I've been meaning to make some enquiries.'

Jamil gulped. 'I'm sorry, Sahab. I didn't realise there would be people in the sitting room at this time of the day.'

Shershah removed one of his sandals and threw it at Jamil. It hit his shoulder, right on the collarbone, which sent pain shooting through him. He winced.

'Shershah *bhai*, please! Restrain yourself, at least in front of me.'

Shershah hurled such a variety of abuses at Iftikhar that his face turned as pink as the sofa he was lounging on.

Shershah turned his attention back to Jamil. 'My sandal will teach you not to speak out of turn again, filth. If someone had beaten manners into you during your childhood, this wouldn't have happened. Your mothers are all sluts anyway. No wonder you people turn out like this.'

Jamil closed his eyes briefly. His poor departed mother. He said a silent prayer for her soul. His hands clenched into fists. If Shershah abused his mother again, he wouldn't care about the elaborate plan, he would go straight for his throat. There were some lines nobody should cross. He was aware that he was breathing hard.

Shershah continued: 'If you weren't so stupid, I would have thought you had been planted here by one of our enemies.' His eyes narrowed. 'Where are you from, anyway?'

Jamil lied, quoting a village near Vehari he had once heard about.

'Didn't I tell you, Iftikhar, that all of these bumpkins from the villages are the same? No manners and no sense of etiquette. No wonder they're drugged out of their minds most of the time. They're stupid and, on top of that, there are no opportunities in the village. In the end, it is good people like us who have to tolerate them. I tell you, I am so glad that they still have that *jirga* system going on there. It keeps the women in line. Sluts, all of them, but at least they get punished for their sins.'

Iftikhar squeaked. 'What kind of punishments? What jirga system?'

Shershah laughed. 'You are such a nancy, Iftikhar. Do you even live in Pakistan? The *jirga* system is a bunch of village elders who make the rules for everyone. Even the police and lawmakers are scared to question them. Oh, they love to act like they're honourable. They love doing things to their women.' He began counting them on his fingers. 'They burn them, drown them, whip them to ribbons ... and what else? Oh, yes, they drown their illegitimate babies in milk. And if they feel too many girls are being born, they drown a few to balance everything.' He flicked a finger at Jamil. 'You. Get out. The sight of you makes me sick. Remember, if I ever find you again in the wrong place at the wrong time, you will be answering with much more than your tongue.'

Jamil couldn't suppress a smirk as he left the room. If it hadn't been for Shershah, he would never have seen the crevice in the corner, hidden by the plush carpet. While Shershah had been busy talking about village life and Jamil's upbringing, he had reached back and stuffed the pouch into the space. It fitted the crevice as if it had been made for it.

Take that, he thought.

Abida

She fidgeted constantly in Nigaar's presence. It didn't feel right to sit with her and eat dinner. In a manner of speaking, they were both Rana's wives so Abida couldn't understand why she had to stand on ceremony. Every few days, an invitation for dinner would come through Salma. It was always a request, never a command, but how could Abida say no? For all her hatred of Abida, Nigaar couldn't seem to get enough of her.

The dinners always started in the same way, with Nigaar commenting on the weather, then ordering a maid to crank up the heating. She never waited for Abida to reply, but gestured for her to sit at the dining table. A couple of maidservants would bring whatever was cooked for the night, and they would begin. Abida hardly ate anything. In addition to the pregnancy, she was still going through withdrawal, and it took everything out of her not to vomit. Nigaar would talk to her about trivial things, like whether her room was being kept clean and if she had enough to eat. While Abida attempted to answer her questions as best as she could, she still hadn't figured out Nigaar's intent. All she knew was that Nigaar's gaze bored into her the whole time she spent with her. It made her skin crawl.

Today cauliflower curry was on the menu. The smell turned her stomach.

She hesitated. 'May I be excused? I am not feeling well.'

Nigaar looked up from her generously filled plate. She looked surprised. 'My dear, who in their right mind would refuse food like this?' Her mouth stretched into a smile. 'I assumed that, after spending all those months at Apa Ji's brothel, you'd be permanently famished.'

Abida ignored the insult. 'If there was one thing Apa Ji took care of it was food. She had to make sure we looked our best. Shapely thighs are the way to a man's heart, she would say.'

She enjoyed seeing Nigaar's face redden. Two could play at this game, she thought.

'Indeed. And I thought I was the only one with a sense of humour. Perhaps the old saying is true, that wives who share a husband can never be friends.'

Abida pushed her food around with a fork. 'I didn't mean to offend you, Begum Sahiba. I enjoy these dinners, but I don't think you call me here for friendship. What could a woman like you have to gain from a person like me?'

Nigaar brought a loaded fork towards her open mouth and chewed noisily. 'You certainly don't beat around the bush, dear. I wonder if Rana Sahab's attitude is rubbing off on you. All these decades together, and he still hasn't learned to take a joke. You'd think forty years together would afford me some respect in this house but, no, I'm to spend the rest of my days trapped in this gilded cage in the middle of nowhere.'

She was panting as she dug into the cauliflower with a large spoon and dumped it on Abida's plate. Abida breathed through her mouth. She could feel the contents of her stomach rising.

'Something the matter, dear?' Nigaar's eyes were all innocence. She must have been a beauty in her day with those slanted almond eyes and that slender nose. It didn't hurt that she had fair skin. Men in Pakistan were not interested in dark skin.

She considered making up some excuse, but before she could speak, Nigaar shouted at the servants to leave them alone. The maids scurried away, closing the door behind them.

'*Churailain*,' she cursed. 'All of them. They'll be listening at the door, no doubt, ever hungry to feed crumbs of information to Salma.'

Abida was shocked. 'Excuse me? Salma?'

'You heard me. Let's drop the charade, shall we?' She pushed her plate away. 'Disgusting food. I think they do it on purpose. No wonder you didn't eat a bite, but that may, of course, be due to something else.' She allowed herself another smirk, before leaning forward and dropping her voice further. 'Did you honestly think I invited you over here for your company?' She chuckled. 'Far from it, my dear. I invite all of Rana Sahab's mistresses to test their mettle. So far, all of them have disappointed me. Greatly.' Her eyes bored into Abida's. 'You're different, though. I've noticed that Rana has neither won you over nor broken you. I can tell a lot about a person by looking at them. As Rana's wife, I've had to do it for decades.'

Abida tried not to look too shocked. She took care to keep her voice level. 'I'm not sure I understand what you are talking about.'

'He's drugged you, hasn't he? He does it all the time. When he cannot conquer a woman through fear, he conquers her through heroin. But you're fighting it. I can see the withdrawal symptoms. Rana Hameed may be blind to them, but I'm not. Or maybe he just mistakes the sweat for your enthusiasm during sex, my dear.' She laughed. 'For a drug lord, he really is clueless. My poor husband.'

Abida still wasn't sure what Nigaar was angling at, but her silence seemed to spur the other woman on.

'Do you know that we only have sons? Two sons, to be precise. Do you know why?' She didn't wait for Abida's answer. 'Because he killed all my daughters as soon as they were born.'

Abida stared at her, a deep dread rising up her throat. Her nausea was worse than ever. 'How could he?' she whispered. 'I didn't know such things went on in the cities.'

Nigaar's eyes were glassy, and she blinked rapidly. 'He didn't bother with drowning them, oh, no. He'd never consider sparing me pain. He'd be hovering nearby as I delivered my baby. Can you imagine going through labour pains knowing that the child desperate to come into the world may not even live to see the next hour, or the next minute, for that matter? I ignored my pains until I couldn't any more, and the midwife would be called. I'd watch with dread as she rolled up her sleeves and her head vanished between my legs, her fingers poking and prodding me.' Tears were flowing freely down Nigaar's face, the food lying forgotten on the table.

Abida was breathing fast. Her view of Nigaar was changing by the second.

'I could always tell the sex of the child by looking at the midwife's face as she held the baby. If it was pale, I knew I'd had a daughter. Her hands would tremble as she deposited the baby in my husband's arms and whispered something, her voice too weak to reach me. And before I could even think beyond the waves of pain and the afterbirth making its way out of me, the baby's cries would stop. "Dispose of it," he would say. And all I would do was watch my dead daughter's body taken away, the life snuffed out of her.' Her eyes met Abida's. 'I've delivered six daughters. His heart never melted. Not even once. That man is a *Shaitaan*.'

Abida winced as she imagined the scene.

'Afterwards, he would squat next to me and smile. Daughters are a sign of weakness, he would say. They are an insult. Do you really want to spend decades caring for them only to have them betray you or bring shame? They are just a burden. We will try again, and the next time, you will bring me honour. You will give me the son that will look after us, the son that will inherit every-thing.' Nigaar's eyes were closed, a deep frown on her forehead as if she was reliving the experience. 'And just like that, a few weeks later I would be in the marriage bed again, all set to get pregnant.' She opened her eyes. 'I spent the first twelve years of my married life in dread. As chance would have it, my final pregnancy was so difficult and I bled so much during labour that they had to remove my uterus. Good riddance.' She spat on her plate. 'I'll make Salma eat these leftovers.'

'You could have run away,' Abida said, but even as she said it, she realised the foolishness of her statement.

Nigaar laughed and wiped the tears from her cheeks. 'And go where? A housewife like me? At least I had comfort here. And I had my sons. They're gone now. Strange, isn't it, that the very sons Rana Sahab dreamed of day and night abandoned him at the first opportunity? They married women who were sensible enough never to look back at this place.'

Abida spoke without thinking. 'Don't you miss them? How could they abandon you with him?'

Another tear snaked its way down her cheek. 'I couldn't let him poison my sons' minds like my father-in-law poisoned his. I tricked him into thinking boarding school would make them clever young men who could take over not only his drug business but any business in the world. That had him salivating like a dog. I made sure that my sons weren't anywhere near him during their formative years. It broke my heart to send them abroad, but I did it. Rana Sahab was always blind when it came to his sons. He granted them whatever they wanted, but he didn't know that I was the puppet master behind their every move.' A note of pride entered her voice. 'He thinks he's a schemer, but he has no idea he's been thwarted by me every step of the way. I'll never forget the look on his face when they called him to say that they'll not be coming back from Canada. He moped about it for weeks while I celebrated my victory, my vengeance. It pains me not being able to see them, but I've forbidden them from visiting more than once a year. They don't need to take any more of the filth than is absolutely necessary.'

Abida cleared her throat, unsure of how to progress, but now that Nigaar had told her so much, she felt confident enough to open up. 'Someone tried to murder me and my unborn child back in the village.'

'You have a little girl, right?' Nigaar said.

Abida's breath caught in her throat. 'How do you know?'

Nigaar smiled. 'I have my ways.' She reached inside her bra and plucked out a small, square photograph. 'That's partly why I invited you for dinner today. Here, take a look.'

Abida snatched the picture from her. A woman in a nurse's uniform was holding up a baby, about a year old. The little one was smiling at the camera, three small teeth showing in her tiny mouth. She had Abida's eyes and nose. The likeness was unmistakable. The baby was hers.

'Where is she?' Her voice caught. 'Which orphanage? Can you take me to her?'

Nigaar took the photo from Abida, and buried it deep inside her bra again. 'My dear, it depends on how determined you are to see your daughter. You do know that Rana Sahab will not let you see her as long as he has use for you, and don't delude yourself that he has fallen in love with you. Countless women before you thought the same, and look where they ended up. The grave. Even I don't have any such expectations from that monster. That's why I've kept this photo hidden here.' She patted her chest. 'If any one of these maids were to find it lying around, the consequences for me could be catastrophic. I have never before interfered in the private lives of his mistresses. He lets me host these dinner parties because he thinks I'm harmless. After four decades, he still doesn't know a thing about me.' She leaned back in her chair. 'Like I said, everything depends on you.'

Abida was feeling queasy again. She suspected she knew what Nigaar meant her to do, but she didn't think she had the strength. Seeing her daughter had been too much for her. She wanted to be at the mercy of heroin again. They sat like that for a few minutes, Abida rocking back and forth while Nigaar sat rigid in her chair, watching her.

'What would you have me do?' Abida whispered finally.

'The only thing you can do, my dear. The only thing that will make a difference.'

'And what is that?' Abida's tone was icy.

Nigaar reached into her bag and pulled out a pocket knife. She pressed it into Abida's hands. 'His death. Kill Rana Hameed and let us be rid of him once and for all.'

Jamil

Shahid smiled at the police inspector. 'The pouches have been planted everywhere. Jamil here is witness to it. Let's nail the bastard, sir.'

Jamil had even listed all the places where they could find them. He was diligent, Shahid said, but then again, his daughter's life was on the line, not to mention his own. Given what people said about Rana Hameed, there was no telling what would happen if he discovered their scheme.

Jamil looked up to see Inspector Haroon stroking his moustache again. He hated this police station. He had heard a lot about the police force in the cities with their fancy gadgets, luxury vehicles and opulent stations. This station, however, was filthy. Cobwebs hung from the ceiling, the yellow paint peeling in places, the wooden desks straining to hold the tottering piles of yellowing case files, the chipped marble-and-cement floor grimy beyond recognition. The cigarette smoke made it hard for him to concentrate, and it didn't help that all the police officers made fun of him. Some even poked him as he passed.

Despicable creatures. Haroon was more cultured, but for some reason Jamil couldn't trust him. Not completely. There was something elusive about him, the expression on his face resembling that of a cat waiting for a mouse to walk into its trap.

Was he the mouse?

He didn't care. The drug raid had to move forward. Haroon had promised them.

Haroon chuckled at Shahid. 'I hope your little friend hasn't swiped some for himself. These village types love to do that.'

Jamil bristled, but he took a deep breath. This was Haroon's style. Over the past few weeks, Shahid had told him as much. 'I am standing right here,' he said calmly. 'You can address me directly. And, this is my daughter's life we are talking about. It's at risk.'

'Ah, the daughter. The raid is all very well, but I still think that the daughter is making a fool of all of you. Never trust women, if you know what's good for you. I'm sure she's having the time of her life with Rana Hameed. Despite everything that's said about him, he is known to be good in bed.'

Did you sleep with him? Jamil wanted to ask, but he held his tongue. Now was not the time. He took a deep breath, and lowered his gaze, focusing instead on a long line of ants making their way past him.

'When will you conduct the raid?' Shahid asked, nudging Jamil so that he looked up.

Haroon stretched his arms and yawned. 'These things take time, little one, but now that we know the drugs are in place, we will make a move soon. Catch the rat in its nest, and then there is no escape for Rana Hameed, no matter how innocent he might act.' He lit a cigarette and blew the smoke into Shahid's face. 'The raid aside, I'm interested in finding out whether the girl will come with you or not.' He laughed, a short, savage sound. 'I'll bet everything I have that the little slut will reject you without a backward glance. Such is the way of women.'

Jamil watched Shahid as he tried to hold his ground. 'I need to know when and what time. We need to be sure.'

Haroon rolled his eyes. 'What's it to you, boy? The drugs are there, aren't they? They won't run away. We are planning the raid. These things take time.'

'I need to know.'

Haroon sighed and aimed the smouldering stub of the cigarette at a constable's face. The man yelped as it hit him. Haroon laughed. 'Three days. We will be raiding the place in three days. At noon, so that Rana's cronies have already left for work and won't cause problems, but well before Rana himself ventures out of the compound.' He winked at Jamil. 'We know that much about his schedule.'

Three days, Jamil thought. His heart rose, then sank again. Who knew what Rana might do to Abida during the raid? It fell on him to protect her.

⚜

When he got back to the compound, he discovered that all the staff had been ordered to vacate the main house and wait outside while Rana Hameed and his people 'talked'. These talks could last well into the night. Everyone knew what they were about: the men were deciding where to shift the drugs next.

Even before Salma had told him, Jamil knew that Rana wouldn't be so stupid as to keep the drugs in his home. He only brought in the quantity he needed personally. The rest were kept in locations unknown to everyone except those in Rana's inner circle, namely Iftikhar and Shershah.

In the months he had been there, he hadn't seen Rana trust anyone else. Everything was delegated to Shershah, while Iftikhar managed the accounts. The other cronies were only there for support. Even Amjad, who was supposed to be Nigaar Begum's brother, was kept out of the secret talks. Today's meeting could mean only one thing: more drugs were either coming in or being shifted elsewhere, and whenever that happened, Rana's cronies always left the compound for a few days.

Jamil sent up a silent prayer of thanks. A lot of trouble could now be avoided thanks to this stroke of luck. It would be only Rana Hameed that the police would have to deal with ... if they made it past security.

The rest of his day passed doing chores for the house, and by the time Salma nodded at him – her signal that she wanted him in the slaughterhouse, behind the plastic flap where he usually slept – he was exhausted. He sighed. It was going to be another long night with her.

Have faith, he told himself when he was in bed that night. He winced as Salma kicked his shins. The sound of her snoring filled the small room. Although he was used to the smell of a slaughterhouse, Jamil couldn't sleep. Lamb-liver and chicken intestines littered the floor, which didn't bother him generally, but today everything did. Salma, like always, had promptly fallen asleep on the bedding they had unrolled. After they'd had sex, of course. It had become a sort of daily ritual for them, with her waking up earlier than usual and stealing into his private quarters before the day began. Unfortunately for him, she wanted it again in the evening when they had more time on their hands. It seemed worse to him as it lasted longer, and he couldn't bear the thought that he was cheating on poor Farida.

She will understand, he told himself. Besides, what she didn't know couldn't hurt her, could it?

He checked his phone to find five missed calls from her. He stowed the phone back in his pocket. He would call her tomorrow when he'd be feeling more up to it.

Salma's desire shocked him. Back in the village, intimacy was swept under the rug. With Farida, it had started as a duty, a means to procreate. While it had steadily become more enjoyable for Jamil, he still thought Farida looked at it as a duty. The passion he saw in Salma's eyes was something that had always been absent from Farida's. He shook his head. What was the matter with him? The police would be coming to rescue his daughter in a few days and here he was thinking about sex.

It would all end in a couple of days. He didn't feel scared. He couldn't. He was going to rescue his daughter and take her away from this place. If the police didn't, he would kill Rana Hameed with his bare hands. He realised now that no one else would be in the house and, according to Salma, Nigaar hated Rana Hameed so much that she would celebrate his death.

'She's an out-and-out *haram ki*,' Salma had told him once. 'Always simpering around Rana Sahab but, in truth, she hates him. Her personal maid, Fareena, told me so. I used to be her personal maid, but this *haramzadi* is very suspicious and she figured out that my loyalty lay with Rana Sahab,' she had continued. 'She was right. I have always been loyal to him. I even tried to offer myself to him, but he isn't interested in older women. His blood runs hot for teenagers.' She had sniggered then. 'Sluts. They deserve it.'

It had taken all of his self-control not to hit her. Instead he had put a smile on his face. 'How could he not find a sexy little thing like you desirable?' Living with Salma meant picking up her language.

Salma had giggled like a little girl then hidden her face in her hands. 'Uff, you do spoil me.'

Looking at her now, he couldn't believe he had allowed himself to be so thoroughly used. The very sight of her sickened him. Clearing his mind of her, he lay on his side, and nestled his head on his arm. The rhythmic sound of blood pumping through his body calmed him. He closed his eyes. He needed his sleep for what was to come.

Abida

Rana had shot her up with a dose of heroin. Her traitorous body had embraced it like an old friend, and even though a part of her brain wanted to fight it, she knew it was pointless. She allowed the drug to take hold as Rana ripped off her clothes, running his hands over her bare body.

'The food here has certainly fattened you up,' he said, with a smirk. 'Look at those breasts, and what's this?' His hands caressed her small baby bump. 'A little beer belly, is it? Or heroin belly?' He laughed at his joke, his fingers digging deeper into her flesh.

Her lips drew together with the effort of not crying out. He was deliberately hurting her, as if pushing her to reveal the information he wanted. She was not going to give him the satisfaction, no matter how many times he injected her with heroin. In a strange way, the drug was helping her. She just didn't care.

'I hear you're spending a lot of time with Nigaar,' he whispered into her neck.

'Who told you that?' Abida's voice was like a rasp. She could hardly think.

Rana kissed her neck. 'Never mind. Nigaar is not well, physically or mentally. The loss of her baby daughters has addled her. You would do well to stay away from her.'

She couldn't resist. 'What happened to her daughters?'

'Miscarriage.' A lie. She should be furious, but the heroin didn't allow it.

She let him have his way with her, and afterwards she enjoyed the high, knowing but not caring how much it had cost her. She was back at square one.

Maybe not quite, a voice in her head said. In her pillowcase was the knife Nigaar had given her. As Rana settled in for the night, turning his back on her, his deafening snores ringing in the room, Abida clasped her fingers around it.

Not yet, the same voice told her. It wasn't time. She had to plan this. Unripe mangoes were no use to anyone, her mother used to say. She giggled at the comparison, her mind too far gone to care if she woke Rana. He had started spending a lot of time in her room. This was probably the sixth night in a row that he had gone to sleep in her bed, something he was careful not to do before. He was starting to trust her.

Big mistake, Rana. Her fingers loosened around the knife, but she didn't let go.

At least she wasn't powerless any more. She finally had a way to fight back.

Jamil

Today was the day.

With winter finally settling on Lahore, the mornings were chilly enough for everyone to wear proper winter coats. Jamil's teeth chattered as he waited for Shahid. He knew that it wasn't only due to the cold. He had no idea what was going to happen. One wrong move, and the entire house of cards he had built so painstakingly would fall apart.

What if Rana Hameed kills her? his mind screamed at him for the umpteenth time. How would he face Farida back at home?

He glanced at his phone and noticed another missed call from her. He wanted to call her back, but he didn't trust himself. Who knew what he would end up saying.

He rubbed the tears from his eyes and focused on the gate ahead. He couldn't afford to lose concentration. Not today. Not when Abida's life hung in the balance.

It was almost noon when a vehicle finally approached the main gate of the compound. As expected, one of the guards attempted to open the smaller gate to investigate.

Jamil gulped. He knew the guard would be suspicious, but surely he couldn't wave a jeep away, not when it could be carrying someone important. A few more moments passed, and Jamil decided he couldn't take it. He rushed to the gate, ducking under the smaller opening. The sun had peeked through the fog, but it did nothing to warm him up. He could see the anxiety written plain on Shahid's face as his fingers drummed on the wheel.

Anyone with half a brain would be able to tell that the boy was up to no good.

Jamil drew closer, but the guard didn't notice him. He was busy making his way towards the jeep. Jamil sent up a prayer of thanks when he noticed it was Nasir. He was the most gullible of the lot of them, but while he might be duped, Jamil wasn't sure about the others.

He remembered what that hateful Inspector Haroon had said, and he wondered how they were ever going to achieve it.

'Remember Shahid,' Haroon had told him over the phone. 'You must make sure the guards are knocked out. We don't want to give Rana Hameed time to escape. If we're held up by the guards even for a few minutes, we risk him getting away with his wives and blaming everything on someone else. That man has sharks for lawyers.'

Jamil took a deep breath as Nasir finally reached the jeep.

'*Assalam alaikum*,' Shahid mouthed, rolling down the window. 'How are you?'

The guard poked his head into the jeep and sniffed. 'Who are you and what do you want?'

'I'm here to see Rana Sahab,' Shahid replied, without missing a beat. 'I have an appointment.'

The guard's eyes narrowed. 'Rana Sahab's men have all left the compound for work. There is no one here, so I'm not sure what kind of appointment you're talking about.'

Excellent, Jamil thought. Nobody except Rana Hameed was here. He cleared his throat and assumed a tone he had heard the pir use when talking to his subordinates. 'Rana Sahab sent me to receive him. He is at home. Maybe he invited him over because everyone else is out.'

Nasir looked back at him with narrowed eyes. 'What the hell are you doing here? This is guard business.'

Jamil held his ground, even though he felt some of his conviction falter. 'Do you want me to disturb Rana Sahab by calling him down here? Because I will do that. Only, it will be you people who will have to deal with his rage.'

He waited for the guard to call his bluff, but he knew he wouldn't. The fear on his face said as much. Still, the guard hesitated.

With a wink behind Nasir's back, Shahid went in for the kill.

'Tell you what, why don't I share some of the cold drinks I've brought with me, and we can discuss everything in detail before you let me into the main house? I don't think he will be down for an hour yet.'

Nasir checked his watch. 'He comes down at precisely twelve-thirty, which means you'll have to wait for another half an hour.' He eyed the drinks Shahid had on the passenger seat, the straws already placed inside the open bottles. 'I could guide you into the main house, or you can wait with us here if you wish.'

'Perfect.' Shahid gave him a broad smile as he waited for the gates to open. 'Why doesn't this good old man accompany us while we wait,' he said jerking his head in Jamil's direction. 'He looks like he could use a cold drink.'

Nasir shrugged as he called to his fellows to open the gates.

They spent the next twenty minutes talking about everything and nothing with the guards in their little room, until the four men had slumped forward in their seats, the empty bottles rolling on the concrete floor.

Jamil rubbed his palms together. 'Well, that wasn't too hard, was it?'

His heart fell when he noticed how Shahid's face had crumpled.

He checked his phone again. 'Nothing from Haroon.'

Jamil cursed under his breath as Shahid dialled his number. It was now or never.

No reply.

'Goddamn it!' Shahid shouted, throwing an empty bottle at the wall.

You could never trust the police.

Just as the bottle shattered, and the pieces rained on the floor, the door to the guard's room opened.

'About ti—' Jamil began, but he froze when he heard the voice.

'Rana Sahab is sleeping in. I'm here to tell his driver to wait.'

It was a woman's voice, and before Jamil could do anything, he was standing face to face with her.

Salma's face paled as her gaze travelled to the unconscious guards, at that moment one of them sliding down the wall to the floor, his wrist bending at an awkward angle as his body sprawled out.

Time stretched on as her eyes finally came to rest on Jamil. 'You killed them?' she whispered.

Jamil shook his head. 'You must listen to me. I haven't harmed anyone. The police are on their way.'

'Police?' squeaked Salma. He didn't like the way her eyes darted around the room, as if she was looking for something to hit him with.

He took a step towards her, his finger still held to his lips. 'You must keep quiet.'

It was a mistake.

She gave a terrified cry and turned to flee, screaming, 'Police raid! Police raid!'

Jamil stood still as the woman's screams receded into the distance. Finally, he collapsed into a chair, and held his head in his hands. 'What have I done?'

Right at that moment, Shahid's phone beeped. His face went deathly pale. 'Oh my God, Jamil. They're not coming. Inspector Haroon just messaged.'

Abida

You didn't dream under the influence of drugs. That was what Rana Hameed had always told her. Yet she always dreamed. She was back in her village, the air so crisp with cold that even her nose released mist when she breathed. She could almost taste the mutton fat as her mother seared meat in a pan, preparing for lunch later on. She saw her throw the mutton into a steaming pot of curry to soften it, and then with a final drizzle of oil, take it off the heat. The younger kids were being called by name for their morning porridge. Usually only her father and the older children got to try the curry with the specially prepared *khameeri roti*, but today there seemed to be enough for everyone. Abida waited for her mother to call her, but Farida called everyone but her. She was already forgotten. Judging by her mother's smooth forehead and carefree gait, it was as if Abida had never existed.

She was hungry. She tried to call out to her mother.

Why have you forgotten me?

No sound came from her mouth. She looked about for her father, but he was nowhere to be found. A cloud was descending over their house, a black shadow that threatened to destroy everything in its path. A whirlpool of air. She rushed forward to warn her mother, but found she couldn't move. The steaming pot of mutton had congealed into an unrecognisable mess. The shadow assumed the shape of a hand with long fingers and sharp nails, and before Abida could blink, it had reached inside her and stolen her baby.

Her eyes flew open. She was sweating, her body shaking as if she had run miles. Beside her Rana was still sleeping. What time was it? She knew enough from the light through the window that it was past midday.

The fool was still in bed. He was supposed to have gone by now. Abida closed her eyes and tried to calm her breathing. It wouldn't do to appear anything but calm in front of Rana. He would just inject her with another dose if he suspected she was unwell. She couldn't risk sliding into that pit of need again.

She remembered her silent scream in the dream when the shadow had stolen her baby. There was a warm wetness between her legs. Had she wet herself in the night? Was urine usually so sticky? She reached down. The whole bed was soaked. Her fingers came up scarlet with her blood. She knew it was hers because more was leaking out of her.

'The baby,' she croaked. The shadow really had taken her baby. She squeezed her eyes shut, ignoring the pain in her lower abdomen. She didn't dare look down.

A scream was building inside her, but before she could even think of releasing it, another scream sounded from outside.

'Police raid!' It was Salma's voice. 'Raid! Raid! Raid! The guards are down. Somebody wake Rana Sahab.'

Rana Hameed was up in an instant. He launched himself out of bed, still naked, pulling the curtains apart. 'The police.' He swore. 'After all I pay them, they still pull these tricks on me?'

Abida covered herself with the bedspread and searched for her shalwar. Thankfully, it lay draped over the edge of the bed. She snatched it up.

Salma was now pounding on their door. 'Sahab! Sahab! Open the door. Someone has killed the guards and will be coming to kill us all any moment.'

Rana stumbled as he tried to dress. 'Which police is it?' he roared. 'Anti-narcotics or the regulars?'

'Not the police yet, Sahab. They'll be arriving soon. Right now, it is some boy. The devil incarnate. He has killed the guards. He

has called the police. And – and you won't believe who else...'
Salma's voice drowned as she launched into a fit of sobbing.

Good, Abida thought. *Let her cry*.

'Why are you crying, you stupid woman?' Rana Hameed had
finally managed to pull on some clothes and was panting with the
effort. He slapped Abida across the face. 'What are you lying in
bed for? Waiting for that person to come and have his way with
you?' He threw her a shawl. 'Get dressed.'

Abida blinked past the drugs that were still in her system and
stretched. She couldn't let him see the miscarriage. He would beat
her to death for hiding the news from him. She was grateful for
the dry shalwar. She edged out of bed, throwing the comforter
over the mess. 'The day hasn't even begun and I'm already tired.'

Rana Hameed gave her a withering look before removing his
pistol from the bedside drawer. 'Let that bastard come to me. He's
clever, though. He's come when there is nobody in the house.'
With his other hand, he dialled a number and barked at whoever
was unfortunate enough to receive the call. In the flurry of abuse,
Abida only made out that the person at the other end of the line
was a policeman.

Poor guy, she thought. She didn't believe any of the story Salma
had just fed Rana. There would be no raid – Rana would make
sure of that. She was surprised she didn't feel lightheaded. There
had been a lot of blood.

While Rana shouted into the phone, she slipped the knife into
her shalwar. Should she just go ahead and do it? Strike him when
he was distracted? If what Salma had said was true and the guards
were dead, the compound would be easy to flee. Rana's men were
not here, and she could easily push aside people like Salma.

And then what?

She didn't even know where the compound was. They were in
the middle of nowhere. Even if she managed to escape this place,
where would she go? She'd probably be raped by the first man who
saw her, and where would that leave her?

What a thought. What had this place done to her? Of course she should try to get out. Just as Rana opened the door to the sobbing Salma, something occurred to her, and she cursed herself for not thinking of it sooner.

Nigaar.

Jamil

Salma had just run off to the main house, screaming her head off. That meant Jamil's cover was blown. Rana Hameed would know. And with no police around, it meant certain death for both of them, and where would that leave Abida?

How could he have trusted the police, and how could he have let himself be tricked into this false sense of security? He cursed aloud, then ran towards the main house himself, the gravel crunching beneath his shoes. Everything be damned. He was going to see this to the bitter end.

Shahid followed him, breathless, his face a mask of panic. He kept wringing his hands. 'I've ruined everything. Everything.'

Jamil knew he had to think quickly. 'You need to leave now,' he told Shahid.

Shahid's mouth dropped open. 'What?'

Jamil grabbed him by the elbow and steered him to the slaughterhouse. The smell of rotting innards was overpowering, but even so it couldn't stifle the stench of fear.

'Listen to me. Rana is armed and dangerous. There is no way we'll get past him with these knives. He'll kill us on the spot, and where would that leave Abida?' He held up a hand when Shahid opened his mouth. 'Let me finish.'

Shahid pursed his lips.

'You need to go now, or you will end up dying with me' – Jamil closed his eyes – 'and Abida.'

When Shahid didn't move, Jamil shook him. 'What is wrong with you? Do you want to get killed?'

'We won't get killed.'

Jamil threw his hands in the air. 'Oh, really?'

He reached into his jacket, pulling out two handguns. 'Not if we have these.'

⁂

Shahid climbed the stairs with an urgency Jamil had never seen before. He was surprised to see how few staff were in the house. Apart from the maids, who screamed when they saw the revolvers, they didn't encounter a single man.

'Rana Hameed has a mortal fear of employing male staff indoors. He thinks they will run away with his wives. God knows how Nigaar persuaded him to hire me, and how he let himself be persuaded.'

'Perhaps he's going senile,' Shahid suggested.

Jamil shook his head. 'It would be foolish to underestimate the man.'

They took the stairs two at a time as they neared the landing.

'Hurry, Shahid,' Jamil said. 'We can't let him call in his people. If they arrive, everything is lost.'

'The guards will be coming round soon,' Shahid mumbled. 'I didn't mix much Rohypnol into the drinks.'

Jamil increased his pace.

They had almost reached the landing when they heard someone sobbing. Jamil peeked around the corner.

'It's Salma,' he whispered. 'You stay back. Let me handle this. I'll make up a story.'

He turned the corner. Salma was hunched over the closed door, sobbing and crying out for Rana Hameed. The door clicked open and Rana Hameed's face peered out. Without warning, he punched Salma's face. The shock put an end to her sobbing.

'Will you just shut your trap for once?' he spat. 'Now, where is the man you've been bleating about?'

Salma turned. Her eyes locked with Jamil's. He was pleased to see the terror in them. She screamed. 'There he is. And look, there's the other guy.'

Jamil wasn't scared. He felt as if this was what he had been hurtling towards all his life. It was now or never.

'You *khanzeer*. You dare to pull this nonsense with me?' Rana shouted at Jamil.

Jamil didn't even blink. He pushed past Salma and held his palm against the door, one hand gripping the pistol in his pocket. He had no idea how to use it, but he was going to rescue his daughter today, no matter what.

'Let me in,' he said softly.

Rana's eyes widened. 'Have you gone barking mad? Why should I let you in? Is this what I've been paying you for? How dare you.'

'Let me through.' Jamil increased the pressure against the door.

No sooner had he shouted than they heard a loud cry from inside.

'Abbu?'

Jamil

It was his Abida.

He used the moment of confusion on Rana Hameed's face to shoulder his way through the door. Before Rana could even realise what was going on, he'd stumbled backward into the room. He crashed into a table, a lamp falling on his head and smashing into pieces.

The moment Jamil's eyes found Abida's, he forgot about Rana Hameed. Her hands were pressed to her mouth and she looked so much older than she was. It was as if an age had passed since he had last seen her. There were dark circles beneath her eyes, eyes that had seen so much over the past year. Too much.

His poor daughter – what a terrible price she had paid for love.

He opened his mouth, but no sound came out. Instead, he inched closer. What wouldn't he give to take her in his arms like he used to? But he hesitated. He didn't know what was going on in her mind. He didn't know how her circumstances had damaged her. Would she push him away if he drew any closer? He deserved it.

'I've failed you so badly,' he said at last. 'I am so sorry.'

Abida didn't reply. She simply launched herself at him, throwing her arms around his neck. 'You came,' she croaked. She was trying not to sob. 'I knew it was you all those weeks ago. I just knew.'

She smelled of cigarettes, and something he couldn't put his finger on. He closed his eyes and returned the hug. He remembered how many times Farida had reprimanded their daughter:

'Grown-up girls don't hug their fathers. What would people say if they saw you two?'

The thought of Farida did it. Jamil dissolved into sobs. He couldn't help it. He didn't care that men weren't supposed to cry, and he didn't know how long they stood like that, father and daughter, reunited at last.

'How touching.'

His voice was ragged, but firm. Jamil and Abida sprang apart. Rana Hameed sat in the armchair, the revolver pointed in their direction. The smile on his face bordered on crazy. It chilled Jamil to the bone.

He pushed Abida behind him. 'You will not torture my daughter any longer.'

Rana Hameed scratched his beard. 'Is that so? Do you honestly think I've been torturing her all this time? You've worked here long enough. You do know she's my wife, right?'

'Salma told me,' Jamil replied coldly. 'It doesn't matter. I am taking her away from this place.'

'And how will you do that? You may have bypassed the guards, but I have called reinforcements. Any moment now, this place will be teeming with my men. What will you do, then, hmm? And where did that other man go? Did good old Salma entice him too?' He smirked. 'Yes, I've heard the rumours about you and Salma. Who knew she still had it in her.'

'Don't listen to him, Abbu,' Abida whispered. 'Just go before his men arrive. It is enough for me that you care, that you love me enough to come for me.' Her voice broke. 'I can spend the rest of my life with that thought.'

'What a martyr your daughter pretends to be.' Rana held his tongue between his teeth before running it over his lips. 'For an imprisoned woman, she's surprisingly passionate. Since you've been spying on everything, I hope you had the chance to hear her moans at night.'

Abida whimpered, but Jamil wasn't going to be led into hating his own daughter. He reached into his pocket and took out the pistol, aiming it in Rana Hameed's direction. 'I'm going to leave here with my daughter now, and you'll let us go. Otherwise, I'll kill you.'

Rana threw back his head and laughed. 'Look at the way you're holding the pistol. Do you even know how to use that thing? Why don't you return my wife to me, and maybe I'll let you live? Maybe. That is, after I've murdered Salma, who let you into the house in the first place.'

'Your wife let me into the house.'

'Ah, yes, dear old Nigaar. Always the fool.'

'She hates you, you know,' Abida said. 'She hates what you did to her daughters.'

'Our daughters!' Rana's voice boomed around the room. 'It had to be done. Do you think I wanted to? Do you think I would have let her brand me as a father of daughters? The humiliation would have been enough to kill me. And, besides, nobody would have respected me in the business if I had daughters prancing around the house. The female sex is weak. It is not to be trusted, especially not with men in the house.' He spat on the ground. 'Look how trustworthy you've proven to be, my dear. The moment your father came, you abandoned your husband.'

'You are no husband to me.' Abida's voice dripped with hatred.

Rana's face assumed an ugly look. The revolver remained pointed at Jamil's chest. 'Let's cut the charade, shall we? Abida, you come here this instant or I will kill your father. Your useless father who doesn't even know how to hold a gun.'

'He may not know how to shoot a gun, but I do.'

Shahid walked into the room, his gun aimed squarely at Rana's chest.

'Shahid. What ... what are you doing here?' Abida's eyes had gone round. 'How do you know my father?'

'And another saviour arrives.' The smile had returned to Rana's face. 'I do like a man who knows what he is doing, but unfortunately for you, my boy, you've chosen the wrong person to save. This girl will never be yours.'

'Then I shall kill you.' Shahid's voice brooked no argument. Looking at his face, Jamil knew he would do it.

'Shahid—' he began, but Rana Hameed cut him off.

'Do you imagine that Abida will leave with you, no questions asked? Has she not told you her dirty little secret yet?' He smirked. 'You see, she isn't such a martyr as you think she is. Here, I'll show you.' He dropped the gun in his lap, and pulled a packet from his pocket. He poured something from the packet into a spoon and held it over a flame from his lighter.

A sudden fear clutched Jamil's chest. He knew what that was, and he knew how destructive it could be. A bitter smell filled the room.

Rana's smile widened. He winked at Abida. 'Would you like some, my dear wife?'

Jamil turned to his daughter, and his stomach dropped. She was gazing at the bubbling drug as if transfixed. Her forehead had broken into a sweat even though it was cold in the room. For a moment, it seemed like she wanted to reach for it, but then her expression cleared. She cocked her head as she met Rana's gaze.

'You really think you've got me addicted to this, don't you?' Her mouth curved into a slow, brittle smile. 'I've been flushing all the drugs down the toilet for weeks.'

For the first time that day, true shock registered on Rana Hameed's face. 'Is that so? What about the dose I gave you yesterday?'

'What about it? I'm stronger than you realise.'

'Then maybe you'd like to know where your daughter is, hmm?'

The effect was immediate. Abida's face went blank. 'You're bluffing.'

Jamil shook his head. 'I have a granddaughter? Kalim told me she died during the birth.'

Rana Hameed produced a plastic syringe from his jacket and filled it with the amber liquid. 'Come to me, Abida, and I promise

I'll reunite you with your daughter. She is very much alive, I assure you.'

'I know.' Abida's voice was flat, defeated. The fight had left her. She stepped towards Rana. 'Nigaar showed me a photograph.'

'My wife never did learn to mind her own business, but I have to admire her for her resourcefulness. She has never taken such an interest in my previous girls.' Having filled up the syringe, he threw away the spoon. 'Come to me.'

'Abida, no...' Shahid cried. 'You can't let him play you like this. Let's just run. He isn't even holding a gun right now. This is our chance.'

But Jamil knew his daughter well enough to realise that she was not listening to Shahid. She was in another world.

'Yes ... yes, there's a good girl,' Rana cooed. He unbuttoned his trousers. 'Come to me.'

Abida stepped around Jamil and moved towards Rana, her eyes locked with his. She was shaking all over.

There were loud shouts from outside, which could mean only one thing. The guards had awakened.

'Abida,' Jamil called. 'Abida, come back. We need to go. Don't believe his lies. We will find your daughter together.'

Rana laughed. 'And where, may I ask? There are hundreds of orphanages in this country. You wouldn't even know where to begin, *chutiye*.' Abida wasn't listening. She inched closer to Rana. 'There's a good girl.' His eyes met Jamil's and there was triumph in them. 'As long as I have this, she will never leave.'

Shahid pulled at Jamil's sleeve. 'We need to go. Now.'

'No!'

Abida was sitting on Rana Hameed's lap now. He whispered in her ear, licking her earlobe.

Jamil closed his eyes. 'Abida, please.'

Shahid was tugging hard at his sleeve now, practically dragging him out of the room. 'We need to go, Jamil. We will come back another time.'

Jamil's vision was blurred with tears. He knew they would never come back. He couldn't bear to look, and yet he couldn't bear to take his eyes off her. 'Abida,' he cried again. 'Don't do this. Please, don't do this.'

Abida turned to look at him. Her face was devoid of expression, but a tear rolled down her face. 'Just … just go. Now.'

Abida

She knew she had done the right thing. After all her father had been through, she couldn't have him beaten and killed by Rana's men. There would be nobody to save him. It broke her heart, but right now, she had to be fully present with Rana. It was her turn to save her father.

She watched as Rana fiddled with the syringe. 'Resistance was never your strong suit, was it, my dear? First you went against everyone in your village to run away with some fool, who ultimately sold you to Apa Ji because you couldn't resist the desires that plague young ladies. And, look at you now. Desperate for another kind of pleasure.' He slapped her thigh. 'Some girls never learn.'

She took a deep breath. 'Look, I've never asked you for anything, but if I ask for something now, will you grant me that?'

Rana laughed as he put the syringe aside. 'If you want more drugs, I hate to break it to you, my dear, but they will kill you. You can only inject a certain dosage.'

'I'm not talking about the drugs. I don't want them.' *Are you deaf,* she wanted to add. She shifted herself closer to Rana so that her face was inches from him.

'Then, pray tell me, what is it that you want?'

'If your people catch my father and Shahid, I want you to promise me that no harm will come to them. If you do that, I will willingly stay with you for my entire life.'

Rana's fingers were inching up her leg. She swallowed the disgust that rose up her throat. 'With your addiction, my dear

Abida, you will be staying with me anyway. What else do you have to offer?'

'I told you: I'm not addicted to this stuff any more. Don't you listen?' She took a deep breath, putting a smile on her face. 'You're right, of course. What else do I have to offer?'

He slapped her thigh. 'That's more like it, girl. You should be thinking how much dirtier you can get in bed.'

Watching him smirk before revealing those ugly gold teeth, she realised she could do it. Looking closely into that lined face with the shadow of white stubble, she saw him for the first time as a human. A human with flesh, blood and bones. Someone who could be broken. She had been unsure of whether she was up to the task ever since Nigaar had handed her that dagger, but sitting on his lap now, with him grinding against her, his eyes boring into hers, she knew that she had hit rock bottom. And she knew just the thing that would shock him.

'I'm with child,' she murmured. 'It's yours, of course.'

'What?' The grinding stopped. The smirk vanished. Rana's hand withdrew from her thigh. The eyes that, moments ago, had been filled with lust were now filled with surprise ... and was that concern? 'Why on earth did you let me inject you with drugs? How long have you known? You foolish, foolish girl.'

She found she didn't care much for his concern. Besides, the child was gone. Abida was surprised at how little she cared for this one.

As Rana attempted to dislodge her from his lap, she pulled out the dagger from the belt strapped around her shalwar. She had heard that when a person took another's life, there was a moment when their entire life flashed in front of them. It was called the moment of weakness.

Abida encountered no such moment.

With a grunt, she pushed the dagger's blade deep into Rana's ribs.

He screamed as a spurt of blood erupted from him. She lurched back as some of the blood sprayed right in her face, the coppery tang of it on her lips. She gagged. She didn't want to look at him for another moment. A burst of laughter erupted from her. It seemed as if it came from someone else, not her. She shrank from it, but couldn't help continuing to watch him in horrified fascination. And suddenly, her life did flash before her. Her beautiful village came to her as if she was standing there, knee deep in the muddy fields, helping her father pull out weeds. She watched how that girl lost her innocence and then her life as she knew it. Her destruction hit Abida like a punch in the stomach, and she staggered back, turning away from the sight of Rana gasping for breath. There was nothing more to see here.

Jamil

The hallway was empty. Salma had fled, or maybe Shahid had killed her. Jamil didn't care. All he cared about, all he had ever cared about, was in that room right now, being injected with heroin.

He brushed the tears from his cheeks. He couldn't believe he was abandoning his daughter, but what else was there to do? She had made her decision.

The voices outside were louder, and Shahid's terrified voice finally broke through to him. 'I don't think we can escape. They are too close.'

A small part of Jamil grieved that Shahid would go down with him, but as for himself, he was done. He didn't want to live any more.

Before they could run down the stairs, there was a crash, followed by an ear-splitting scream.

The scream was shrill, but it was difficult to place. What the hell was going on in that room? Jamil was rooted to the spot, his hand clutching his heart. 'He's done it,' he whispered. 'He has killed my daughter. I'm going back.'

But before they had taken a step, the door of the room burst open, and out came Abida.

She was ashen-faced, a bloodstained knife clutched in one hand. Some of the blood had splashed across her kameez. She was shaking all over. 'I finally did it. I ... I stabbed him. Deep. Twice.'

'Abida!'

'He would never have stopped looking for me. I don't want to run from him my entire life, so I stabbed him. Abbu, I ... I killed him. I really did.' She burst into tears.

Jamil was aware that his mouth was open. He was staring at his daughter – in wonder or terror, he didn't know. There was no time to find out. The guards outside were almost upon them. They were pounding at the main door. A couple more minutes and they would find the three of them standing there, Abida with a blood-ied knife in her hand and Shahid, the person who had given them the spiked drinks. And if memory served, he was sure he had heard one of the guards say that Rana's cronies would be returning soon too. That meant a war on all fronts. There was no conceivable way that they could win.

There was really only one thing they could do.

'We need to hide. Now.'

His words broke the spell, and Abida's sobbing ceased. 'I know a place, Abida, but I'm afraid Salma knows about it too.'

Jamil shook his head. 'She will immediately give us away.'

Shahid looked around the hall. 'You've been here for months, man. You must know of somewhere else.'

Jamil looked down. 'There's the butcher's area.'

'That's outside, Jamil. Outside, where men are baying for our blood.'

He shrugged. 'We should at least get out of the way. Out of the main hall.'

'We could—' Abida began, but Jamil cut her off.

'I am here now, Abida.' He put his arm around her shoulders. 'You don't need to make decisions now. I am here to protect you.' His voice broke. 'I will never let you out of my sight again.' Her shirt was sticky with Rana's blood, and the metallic smell of it filled Jamil's nostrils. In his peripheral vision, he saw Shahid rolling his eyes.

'There is no time for this.'

Abida removed her father's arm from around her. 'You're not listening. I don't need your protection, Abbu. I just need you. Alive. I think I know a way out of here.'

Jamil's heart was pounding. He held on to the banister. 'You do?'

Abida took a hold of his hand. 'Follow me.'

Jamil pretended not to notice the stickiness of the blood in his hand as Abida led them down the long corridor. All of a sudden, everything became clear. 'Abida, why are you taking us to—'

Abida threw open the door at the end of the corridor. 'Nigaar will help us.'

'Help you with what?' a voice said.

They all watched as an older woman walked towards them, leaning heavily on a walking stick. A female maidservant followed her, clearly horrified when she spotted the knife that Abida was still clutching.

Now Abida brandished it towards Nigaar. 'I did like you said. I stabbed him.' Her voice trembled as if she had just understood what she had done.

Nigaar's maid screamed and clapped a hand over her mouth.

Nigaar hit the maid on the legs with her walking stick. 'Keep your voice down.' She turned to Abida, her face shining with hope. 'Abida, you've done what nobody else could. You've achieved the impossible. Did you drive the blade right in his heart?'

'I don't know. I just stabbed him. There was so much blood.'

Nigaar frowned. 'But did you give him a fatal blow?'

Jamil didn't like where Nigaar's line of questioning was headed.

Abida simply shook her head. 'I stabbed him in the ribs twice, and then left him.'

'You did not check to see if he was dead?' Nigaar gestured towards her heart. 'You left him like that? Oh, you fool.' She uttered the last words with a sigh.

Abida shook her head, her voice breaking. 'I didn't look. I couldn't. Did I do something wrong?'

Nigaar closed her eyes, the disappointment radiating from her. 'Monsters like Rana Hameed don't die so easily. I'd shake you for this blunder, but I don't have the strength. My body can hardly support me. He will kill you for this. All of you.'

Jamil put a protective arm around his daughter. 'Begum Sahiba,' he began, but Nigaar held up a hand.

'Quick, let's go into my room,' she said, and turned. 'You're lucky it's just Fareena here and not the other girls. Nobody will think to look in my quarters. At least, not for a little while.'

'What are you doing, Begum Sahiba?' Fareena cried. 'What if he is not dead? How will he react when he finds out that you helped her escape?'

Nigaar snatched her arm away from her and almost tipped forward. She leaned heavily on her stick. 'Fareena, I may not have been able to save my girls, but I can help save this one. She was brave to stab him, the only one who could, so if I can do something to make her life better, I will.'

Jamil felt a sudden wave of gratitude for the lady. 'How could we ever thank you, Begum Sahiba.'

'Don't thank me yet. I just hope Rana is dead.' Although she had her back to them, Jamil could hear the smile in her voice. 'Oh, I will have a nice time dismantling his empire. I'll have his cronies sent to jail – Shershah, and my traitorous brother.' She looked back to see them still standing huddled together. She nodded in Jamil's direction. 'Salma told me that you're Abida's father. You've gone to great lengths to save your daughter. I just don't understand why Rana couldn't have done that for his baby girls? How was it 'honourable' for a father to kill his daughters?' She shook her head. 'Didn't you hear me? You all need to come into my room.'

'Why are you helping us?' Jamil asked.

Nigaar rolled her eyes. 'Silly man. If we were to have this discussion right now, we would all be dead, for I assure you those guards outside, now threatening to break down the door, do not suffer fools gladly. Let's go.'

They followed her without argument. Fareena had taken her

arm again. Nigaar was wheezing from the effort of trying to walk fast and speak at the same time.

'As soon as I had heard the commotion, I ordered the maids to their quarters. Drug raids have become less frequent recently, but if bullets were to be exchanged, I wanted them out of harm's way. Fareena was the only one who wouldn't leave my side. But as the minutes had ticked on, I realised that it wasn't a drug raid. No policemen had come in, looking for evidence. There were no more shouts from outside. It was only after Salma burst into the room screaming that hope finally took root inside me. Despite Fareena's protests, I pushed myself out of my armchair and made my way outside. If Rana was going to be killed, I wanted to witness it. I wanted to spit in his face.' The hand on her cane shook.

'Why don't you catch your breath for a moment?' Inside, Jamil was desperate to get going, but there was no point in killing the woman. They wouldn't get anywhere without her.

Nigaar collapsed into one of the armchairs in her room, her head leaning against a tapestry.

'You probably think I am an evil person,' she panted. 'But this man deserves to die.'

Jamil looked back at the way they had come. His eyes met Shahid's. There was no time to lose. 'Begum Sahiba, about the escape...'

Nigaar didn't seem to have heard him. '"You must be less assertive, more subservient to me", she said, mimicking her husband. '"It is because of your wilful nature that your body keeps making girls. If you obeyed me more, your body would finally learn to obey."' Her eyes filled with tears, but she rubbed at her eyes in anger. 'You don't know how many years I spent beating myself up for giving birth to girls. Why couldn't I be more subservient? I endured Rana's beatings silently. I let him have his way with me, even when it involved mindless pain. I allowed him to do things that no sane woman would. My legs are lined with cigarette burns. Parts of my upper arms and breasts have small chunks of flesh missing. I don't even want to think of what he did to me down there. It is too painful to recall.'

Abida was crying too now. Jamil stared at the woman panting in front of him. All the money and luxuries in the world hadn't saved her from enduring these unspeakable horrors. If Rana had done this to his first wife, the mother of his children, he couldn't begin to imagine what he could have already done to his daughter. They had to get out of here.

'Abida,' he said, but she wasn't listening. Her eyes were locked with Nigaar's. At that moment, both women were experiencing something profound and that seemed to have connected them.

Nigaar was the first to break eye contact. 'Fareena, I want you to open the window to the terrace. Walk out like you don't have a care in the world and check how many guards he has stationed around this section of the house.'

As Fareena opened the window and slid outside, Abida asked, 'What happened next?'

A dam seemed to have broken inside Nigaar. She didn't seem to mind sharing the most intimate details of her life. 'I kept giving birth to girls,' she continued. 'I kept piling on the pounds. And then, out of the blue, the first boy arrived. And another.' She laughed. 'I had finally done my duty. After that, Rana left me alone. Every night my heart would be in my mouth as I dreaded his arrival, but he never visited my bed again. When a year had passed, I began to relax, and for the first time in my life, I began to live. I found solace in my quarters, my little kingdom, where I could order people around and pretend to be queen. I loved my boys, and was delighted when they left, never to come back. I rejoiced when it broke their father's heart, but deep down I hated myself for caring how it affected him. In my own way, I loved that monster and perhaps that's what made him into what he is today. I did nothing to stop him.'

Jamil glanced at the window, but Fareena hadn't returned yet. Time was running out. Any moment now the guards would break through the front door and swarm the place. Despite Nigaar's assurances, he knew they would barge into her quarters too. The doors sounded like they were about to give way. And here, the way Nigaar told her story, it seemed that nothing out of the ordinary seemed to be going on.

As if on cue, Fareena materialised in the window, ducking her head to get inside.

'Well?' Nigaar asked.

Fareena's face was triumphant. 'Not a single guard to be seen near this part of the house, Begum Sahiba. I looked for ages.'

A shadow of a smile spread across Nigaar's lips. 'I knew it. He has always underestimated me. A few years ago, when there was a drug raid, Rana had an escape route constructed down from my terrace. He thought I'd be too lazy to even bother looking, but I like to keep tabs. There's a steel tube at the end that hides a ladder. I've heard rumours that it is hot as hell inside, but it's an escape.' Her eyes gleamed. 'Rana has always kept the door that leads outside of the property guarded, but today's chaos must have rattled the guards. They've left it unattended.' She clapped her hands together. 'Opportunities like this don't come often. Go ahead and run. The only reason I was talking was that this may be the last time I get a chance to tell my story to Abida. You see, I'm a coward. I don't have it in me to kill someone, Abida. Let's just say that when I saw Abida I knew that my saviour had arrived.'

Abida was quiet, but at these words, she reached out to take Nigaar's free hand. 'I had no idea you had suffered so much.'

Nigaar brushed her off. 'Ancient history. Now run along before those bastards burst in.'

At that moment they heard an almighty crash. Jamil's stomach dropped. He took Abida's hand and urged her to move. 'Run, Abida!'

Abida tried to follow, but something seemed to be slowing her down. She had her hand pressed against her lower abdomen. She noticed his gaze and gave him a weak smile. 'You go on ahead. I'll be right there.'

'If you think I am letting you out of my sight ever again, you're sorely mistaken.'

'Ah, the melodrama,' Nigaar muttered, but her lips were drawn into a tight line. As the distant noise of the guards filled the place, another sound joined the chorus – another door being thrust open and someone letting out an earsplitting shout. They didn't need to guess who it was. It was obvious.

'You hear that?' Nigaar said. 'Why didn't you stab him in the chest, Abida? That monster would have died then and there.'

Abida whimpered. 'He's not dead?'

Despite the fear, Jamil felt a weight lift from his chest. 'Just as well,' he told his daughter. 'I wouldn't want murder to be on your conscience. Whatever happens now, we will face it together.'

They heard bullets ricocheting off the walls. 'You *gushti*!' It was Rana Hameed yelling, but it was unclear to Jamil who he was referring to – Nigaar or Abida.

'Go now,' Nigaar said. 'Take Fareena with you. Make sure she gets to her village safely.' She pressed Fareena's arm. 'Use the money I have given you, my girl, and make a life for yourself.'

Fareena was weeping. 'Begum Sahiba...'

'Won't you come with us?' Abida asked.

Nigaar laughed. 'If you have to ask that question you're an even bigger fool than I imagined. Look at the state I'm in.' She flapped her hand at them. 'Go. Leave me. I have unfinished business with my dear husband.'

They didn't need telling twice. Jamil dragged Abida away, but not before Abida had managed to wrap her arms around Nigaar for a second. 'I will never forget this kindness,' she whispered. 'Thank you.'

'For once in my life, Abida, I am not afraid. I am done watching him ruin the lives of girls.' A sob broke out from her. 'He should have let our daughters live. He should have given them a chance.'

'Come with us,' Jamil said, but he knew it was futile. Nigaar's mind was made up.

She wiped the tears from her eyes and gave Abida a shove. 'Go and never come back.'

As they ducked under the window and out onto the terrace, Jamil turned back to see Nigaar watching them, a faraway smile on her face. If they reached safety, she would have saved not one but several lives.

She turned just in time to face Rana as he came limping towards her. Jamil only had time to steal one glance at him, but it was enough. The man would not survive. He was soaked in his own blood. His face was deathly pale as he staggered towards his wife, his hands pressed against his wound, but the expression on it was murderous.

He only had time to hear Nigaar say, 'My heart sings to see you like this—' before they were out of earshot.

Abida

After climbing down the ladder that led away from Nigaar's terrace they ran faster than they had ever run in their lives. The pain in her lower abdomen bothered her, but she pushed on. They didn't look back as they made for the nearby village, Shahid leading, as he knew the area better than she or her father did. When they paused to catch their breath, Jamil cupped her face in his hands and wept. Until now he hadn't let go of her arm. It was as if he feared she would dissolve into thin air.

'I can't believe I found you. Will you ever forgive me for being so late? For being in the house where you were abused and unable to do anything?'

She grabbed his shoulders. 'Forgive you? You didn't give up on me and you loved me enough to come for me. For as long as I can remember, you've been saving me, first from those beatings from Ammi and then from the pir. And now—' Her voice broke, but she pressed on. She had to get the words out. 'You've done what no other father would do. You've gone against your very nature for me. That alone is all I need to get through the rest of my life. And you talk of forgiveness?'

She would have dissolved into tears if Shahid hadn't urged them to hurry on to the village. On the outskirts of Lahore, it was at the crossroads of the old and new.

'This is a very dangerous place,' Shahid said. 'Unlike traditional villages, this one has more access to technology, but it has none of the anonymity of the city. So if someone is looking for us, it would be easy for them to find us here.'

'We might still have some time,' Jamil said. 'It will take Rana's men a while yet to figure out we've disappeared – that is if he has survived. If he hasn't they'll be too busy dealing with his body.'

They didn't dare venture into the village proper as it would be impossible to make a run from there, so Shahid led them to an old petrol pump at the far end of the village, where a few trucks idled.

Abida noticed a passing woman giving her a strange look. She glanced down to see a spattering of Rana's blood on the hem of her kameez. She hastily spread her shawl to cover it.

Shahid left them in the shade of a towering peepal tree and then approached one of the truck drivers. Abida watched with her heart pounding in her throat as the truck driver gesticulated wildly, shaking his head several times.

'It doesn't look like it's going well,' her father murmured. 'Be prepared to make a run for it.'

Fareena whimpered.

Just as it seemed that Shahid would have to retreat, the truck driver began to nod and drew him away to the back of the truck. Abida was sure money then changed hands, because when Shahid reappeared he had a smile on his face and beckoned them to join him. Abida saw the truck driver pocketing something before opening the back of his truck to them.

'Make yourselves comfortable, but remember not to touch or damage my carpets.'

There were dozens of rugs, rolled up and stacked neatly inside the truck, but there was still enough room to fit a few people.

'If anyone asks anything, stay silent. Let me do the talking.'

'I'll be in the front to keep an eye out,' Shahid told them. 'Our first stop is the bus station near Ferozepur Road, where we will see off Fareena. Then, we proceed from there.'

It was dark inside the truck, but air came in through the gaps in the sides, and no one could see them as they entered Lahore at Thokar Niaz Baig. Thankfully, nobody stopped them either.

The truck deposited them at the bustling bus station on Ferozepur Road, where they were finally able to see Fareena onto the bus bound for her village. It was a quiet farewell. Fareena didn't really know them, and the few sniffles she had were probably for Nigaar. Abida was sure Fareena was happy to see the last of them.

Once the bus had pulled away, Shahid turned to Abida and announced that he would be taking them to the orphanage.

Abida blinked, taken completely by surprise and struggling to read his expression in the grey Lahori afternoon. The mist descended in waves, obscuring everything within a few metres. Her heart rose and then fell. 'Who told you where she is? My daughter. How do you know?'

'My father says a lot of things when he's drunk. Apparently, Apa Ji used his help to make your daughter disappear. But she didn't really disappear. He is a horrible person, but I've come to realise that he needs me.' Shahid looked down as if the very thought disgusted him. 'If his only son were to cut ties with him, he fears that he wouldn't have anyone to care for him in his old age. I told him that if he wanted to see my face again, he would do this for us – he would help get your daughter back. I called him while we were in the truck.'

Abida couldn't form the words to thank Shahid. Thanking him for this would be like thanking Majeed, and she wasn't sure she was ready to do that. Majeed was doing this to regain his son's favour. She owed him nothing. She looked out at the city she had come to hate. Lahore. It had taken too much from her. These foggy, polluted skies had robbed her of her innocence.

❦

Now that they were in the city proper, it was easy to hitch a ride to the orphanage. They piled into a stuffy old wagon that took them to the other side of the city – crowded Shahdara. Entering the black steel gates of the orphanage, they spotted a gleaming police van waiting for them. A well-turned out policeman greeted them, shaking hands with Shahid.

'Your father is already here,' the policeman informed him, his gaze travelling over the rest of the party. Abida wondered what he thought of the state of them. They were all wearing shawls over their clothes, but they'd had no time to wash their faces and they must look exhausted.

'Look at the act they are putting on,' Shahid muttered to Jamil. 'All this respect, bowing and scraping. My father loves this, but I couldn't care less. It doesn't hide the fact that they're plain incompetent. I only wish my father had influence over that bastard Haroon. He's the one who ruined the plan.'

Abida tuned them out. Her heart had started to pound. Would she really find her baby here?

Inside, the place was teeming with people, most of them desperate. Some had the desperation to have a child written over their faces while others wore the desperation of having rid themselves of one. Although it was a cool day, the cluster of people packed together in the hallway made the place stifling. However, Abida dared not take off her shawl. She couldn't risk people seeing the blood.

As the minutes ticked by, she grew more frantic. What if Rana's men came to the orphanage to look for her? Would they drag her off in the presence of all these people? Majeed appeared and nodded at Shahid, but ignored Abida, then walked down one of the corridors, promising to be back shortly. Abida was growing suspicious now.

'I hope your father doesn't intend to arrest us,' Abida murmured to Shahid. 'I don't trust him.'

Shahid took her hand and patted it. 'He's evil, I grant you, but in this instance, he will not betray us. He knows I will leave him forever if he does that.'

It seemed like hours later, but could only have been minutes, when Abida caught sight of Majeed's familiar face among the sea of unfamiliar ones. He was walking towards them, a baby in his arms. She held on to Shahid for support.

It was her baby – her daughter.

Her knees threatened to buckle, but somehow she summoned the strength to remain upright, holding out her arms for the child.

'Give her to me.'

Feeling her small weight in her arms, she tried not to press her too close to her chest. The child already looked worried. A disapproving frown had settled on her face, and Abida burst into tears. *Don't you recognise your own mother?* Of course, she couldn't. Abida laughed, a wet throaty sound, as she blinked hard to rid herself of the tears that prevented her from seeing her baby properly. She only had to look at that face, so much like hers but with Kalim's features, and she knew she was hers. Majeed had brought her her baby.

She looked up to see that her father was in tears too, his arms open for his grandchild. He planted a large kiss on her forehead as he took her.

'My granddaughter. Oh, Abida, she looks exactly like you, doesn't she?'

'She's beautiful,' she whispered.

Majeed cleared his throat. 'If I may?' He ushered the group into a private corner, away from the crowds.

No matter what her feelings for Majeed might be, it would have taken weeks or months to get her daughter back had it not been for his intervention. Abida nodded, gesturing him to continue.

'Rana Hameed is dead,' Majeed told them. 'It has been confirmed. I've tried feeding information to my police colleagues saying that his wife killed him, but Rana's associates ... they will know the truth. They're not stupid. It is not safe for you to be in this city. His closest men will not let this slide. Shershah, in particular, will be eager to hunt you down. He has eyes and ears everywhere in Lahore. They all do. They're like a bunch of rabid dogs. They will come for you all. It's not just Rana Hameed that's died. With him gone, their business will die a slow and painful death. You've just robbed them of their income. Killing a person like Rana Hameed is no easy feat. The entire city is buzzing with the news. Make no mistake, they will come for you.'

'Of course they will,' Jamil said. 'Salma will tell them everything. Fortunately, I never told her exactly where I was from.'

Majeed couldn't meet Abida's eyes, so he spoke to her father. 'Did anyone apart from Rana Hameed know where you are from?'

Abida answered: 'Kalim, of course, and perhaps Apa Ji. I don't know how many people Rana told.'

Majeed scratched his head. 'My guess would be that nobody apart from Rana Hameed knew of your village. He liked to keep his secrets. As for Apa Ji, she won't be blabbing to anyone in the near future because she has been arrested for trafficking girls. I can protect you, but there are leaks in the police all the time. Someone could easily give away your location. No, this has to be done right. You need to either go back to the anonymity of the village for a time or you need to be together as a family in one of the cities. Lahore would not be safe for you, and I don't have any influence beyond it.' He put his arms behind his back. 'I'm sorry. As much as I would love to help, I can't. Not unless Rana Hameed's men are all either arrested or killed – which could take time.'

Shahid took a step forward. 'Can't or won't?'

'Shahid, I've already risked my neck doing this. I'm not invincible. And, you be careful with that tone. I'm doing this for you.'

Despite everything he had done to help her, Abida couldn't forgive him. He was Shahid's father, but she would never forget that he had left her to suffer in Apa Ji's house. He had abused and raped her. She couldn't forgive that.

But he had brought her to her baby. When her father passed the child back into her arms, she felt complete. She looked into the child's grey irises, so much like Kalim's. Abida vowed that her daughter wasn't going to be anything like that coward.

'Shakila,' she said. 'I will call you Shakila.'

Her father's eyes glistened as he spoke, 'You're naming her after my mother.' It wasn't just love in his voice. There was also pride. He was very protective of his mother's memory – he hadn't named a single daughter of his after her because nobody could match his mother; but looking at him now, she knew he approved and that she had made the right decision.

'From the little you've told us about her, she was one of a kind.'

'Oh Abida, she was … she was.'

The little one looked at her as if she was a stranger, which, of course, she was. Her miniature eyebrows furrowed into a frown and her mouth turned down as if she was about to cry. Abida had hoped that some connection, no matter how tenuous, from when she had carried Shakila inside her would bring a glint of recognition to her eyes. It didn't. She kissed her forehead and whispered, 'You are my baby.'

Her father had his arms folded across his chest, a frown of deep concentration on his face. He turned to Majeed again. 'So, am I to understand that you cannot protect my daughter while she is in Lahore.'

Majeed shrugged. 'Look, it's not like that. I could send her to a safe house, and chances are that she will be safe, but Rana Hameed's associates are not like ordinary people. They have a vast network of spies and they have connections in the police force. One tip and they'll swoop in on her within minutes.'

Shahid stepped forward. 'I will stay with Abida. You go and get your family from the village, Jamil.'

Majeed snorted. 'Don't be a fool, Shahid. You've never lived on your own. You'll get yourself killed.'

Jamil shook his head. 'I am not letting my daughter out of my sight. Never again.'

'You'll take her to the village, then, where the pir is baying for her blood?'

Abida had a sudden idea. 'You come with us, Shahid. We'll say we are about to get married.' The realisation dawned on her then, and she lowered her eyes. 'You don't have to marry me. I'm sorry, I didn't think. I just—'

Not caring that they were standing in the reception of an overcrowded orphanage, Shahid embraced her. 'After all this time, do you still question my love?'

'Shahid, please, my Abbu is here.'

Jamil laughed as they broke apart. 'After the horrors I've witnessed in Lahore, I don't think an innocent hug will affect me much.'

Majeed looked like he had bitten into something sour. 'So, you intend to marry her?' He almost spat the words.

Shahid's face grew hard. 'I do, and nobody can stop me. That is, if Abida would accept me with all my faults.'

'You don't have any,' she whispered, before she allowed him to embrace her again. 'You have only goodness in your heart.'

'Go to your village, then,' Majeed said to them. 'I can assure you Rana's men wouldn't be able to follow you there. Once they're arrested, I'll give you the signal to return, but right now, you must hurry.'

'How will we get there?' her father asked. 'I don't want to take the bus. We can't subject the baby to that torture for fifteen hours.'

'Shahid's jeep is parked outside,' Majeed mumbled. 'I rescued it from the compound.'

As they stepped out in the open air, Abida let out a deep breath she didn't even know she'd been holding. Freedom, at last.

Before they left, Shahid embraced his father. 'This doesn't absolve you of your sins, but it's a start. Do better, Abbu. Be a better man.'

Abida looked away as the older man wiped a tear from his eye. She was not going to feel sorry for that monster.

When Shahid asked her again to marry him on the way back to the village, she said yes. Her father raised an eyebrow, but he was smiling. 'Now it is confirmed that Rana Hameed is dead, you may indeed be married. Your *nikkah* with him is broken.'

Shahid punched his fist in the air. 'I can't wait for you to be my wife, Abida.'

Abida attempted to smile for him, but another fear had blossomed in her heart. The thought of facing the pir again made her blood run cold. She had almost let him kill her the last time she'd been in the village. What if he tried something like that again? Was it really wise to be returning to the village after all? Wouldn't they be safer elsewhere? But then, she had trusted Kalim once, and where had that got her. No, she had seen how the city leeched the goodness out of people. She wondered if she would ever be able to trust someone as blindly as she had trusted Kalim, but she immediately quelled that thought. One look at Shahid told her he was worthy of her trust, but she also knew she couldn't part from her father. Not yet, at least.

Jamil put an arm around her shoulders. 'I've always been able to tell what you're thinking from the expression on your face. Don't worry, *beti*. Everything will be fine. Right now, you must focus on healing, and your marriage to Shahid. It is very important that you two understand this. You must not give anything away about your time with Rana Hameed and Apa Ji.'

She understood what her father was saying, but as she sat right now with the people she loved, her long lost daughter nestled against her chest, the wintry breeze blowing at her face from the open window, she wondered if her life was finally improving.

Jamil

The drive through the countryside should have been liberating, but all he could feel was dread. The moment they passed through Khushab, where people swapped the Punjabi language for Saraiki, his mood darkened. Soon they would cross Khanewal and be on their way to Khan Wala Village. He wondered if he was making a mistake, taking his daughter back into such danger. Should he have allowed her to make a life with Shahid in some strange city where they knew nothing about how things worked? He glanced at Shahid's profile, the serious expression on his face, and thought of the sacrifices he had made for Abida, the things he was still doing for her, and the pit of worry in his stomach grew heavier. Hadn't Kalim professed his undying love for Abida as well and promised her the world, only to ruin her life? He had put her through the kind of humiliation nobody should have to suffer; his actions had pushed her to the very brink of death.

Jamil shook his head. No, he was not going to leave his daughter alone with another man. Not until he was absolutely sure that she would be safe. What if Rana Hameed's men caught up to them? Shahid was loyal, but he was young, and he was just one person. How would he be able to defend her against a bunch of those hooligans Rana Hameed had commanded?

He wished he could have called the rest of his family to Lahore, but he knew Farida would never be able to manage it. The poor woman had never been outside the village. She hadn't even been on a train before. She'd had no reason to. And he didn't want her to. He'd seen what happened in the big cities. His family would be robbed, or worse, raped. He knew Shahid would have arranged something, but he wasn't putting the lives of his family in another person's hands ever again. He'd called Farida in advance, warning her to stay at home and wait for them, but he knew she would be dashing through the fields right at this moment.

'I'm desperate to see her,' she had gushed. 'After all these months, I will finally lay eyes on my husband and daughter.'

'Your granddaughter is coming too,' Jamil had told her, which had produced a squeal of excitement from her.

'I had almost forgotten about her. Please tell me good days are finally coming, husband. We will be alright, won't we? I don't think I can go on like this.'

'I was penniless when you married me, remember? Your father had so many children he couldn't wait to get rid of them. If we survived those days, we can survive anything.'

Just as he'd known she would, she had laughed at that. 'All these years later, and you still don't hesitate to make fun of my poor father.'

Her father was long dead now in a faraway village, but Jamil had to admit that he couldn't have had a better wife. If Farida could see him now, with his eyes glistening with tears for her, she would never let him hear the end of it.

He smiled as he looked back at Abida, sleeping with her head thrown back, mouth open, Shakila splayed across her chest.

Shakila, he thought, swelling with pride. She deserved that name. If his mother had been alive, she would have been proud to lend her name to her son's grandchild. Like her, he had put love before honour.

Abida

A great congregation assembled as Shahid's jeep made its way through the village and into the square. Abida had covered her head and took pains to keep her eyes down, but whenever she raised them, she could see the hate-filled looks the villagers were directing at her. Nobody had forgiven her for her transgressions, but she knew that they also remembered the intervention of the police, and nobody liked to get mixed up with them. They kept their distance. It was almost like a political procession, the way people had lined up on either side of the dirt road. A large vehicle entering the village was always a big deal, but this time it carried a person they knew and probably hated. A few elderly women spat on the ground but, to her surprise, some of the younger women smiled secretly at her when their eyes met, and not every man looked at her as if she was the carrier of a plague. The children were utterly taken with Shahid's jeep. They dared each other to touch the bonnet, and sprang back when they felt the hum of the engine. Yet, there was something in their midst, a kind of evil with which she was familiar. The air pulsed with it.

The pir stood at some distance from the crowd, blocking their way.

'I'm sorry,' Jamil whispered to them. 'We have to pay our respects to him if we are to survive in this village. I wish there was somewhere else I could take you, but this is the only place far away from Rana. For now.'

Shahid nodded. 'You're right, of course. We had to leave Lahore. It wasn't safe for me either. Rana's men will be combing the city for us. My father would have helped us hide, but even he has his limitations. He says that with these drug cartels, one person holds the reins and if he dies or is killed, it takes a long time for the business to recover, if at all. Rana's men will be vying to take over the business, but the loss of their leader will hurt their pockets and they will want the people responsible killed. No place in Lahore would have been safe. Not until they arrest all of them. But they're vulnerable now, after the loss of their leader. There is a good chance they might get arrested or killed. Then, we can return to Lahore.'

'Let's get this over with,' Abida said, holding Shakila, who was fast asleep. 'What's the worst the pir can do? It's not like he's caught us doing something. He has nothing on us. I'm done being scared of men.'

The pir surveyed them as their vehicle approached, his face breaking into a winning smile. His kameez was speckled with red. Was it blood? Had he been killing people again? Despite her earlier bravado, a frisson of fear sliced through her.

She was back in hell.

Their jeep stopped and they stepped out.

'Our daughter returns with her child and a new man,' the pir said. 'I may be getting old, but if memory serves, you were initially married to Kalim, were you not?'

'They're divorced, Pir Sahab,' her father replied for her. 'This is Shahid. He is from Lahore and will be marrying Abida soon. I wanted to show him our beautiful village.'

'Indeed. And have you told him all there is to know about your dear daughter?' He turned to Shahid. 'For a marriage to succeed, honesty is imperative. As much as I love my people, I feel it is important always to reveal the truth.' He pointed at Shakila. 'The baby she carries in her arms was conceived out of wedlock. They married later, but the damage was done. If it hadn't been for the local police, Abida would have died to restore honour to her family.' He sighed. 'Alas, that wasn't something her father wanted. They remain to this day a family living in dishonour.'

'Kill her. Let's stone her to death,' someone shouted from the crowd, but not many other voices chimed in. Many villagers stood silent, their heads lowered.

The pir held up a hand. 'Now, now, let's not get ahead of ourselves.' He smiled again, revealing those brilliant white teeth. 'What can I say? The bloodlust in some of them knows no bounds.'

'We can't let them pass,' a woman shouted. 'She bears a bastard in her arms. Burn her. Stone her to death.'

Abida's heart began to thud. Had they just stoned another girl to death?

A few others joined in the shouts, but then silence quickly descended. Was that shame she saw in some people's eyes? The pir noticed the silence too and she could tell that it disturbed him. His eyes darted across the silent crowd and a shadow crossed his face before he smiled again. 'The village remembers.'

Her father bristled. 'Pir Sahab, it would be wise to allow us to pass in peace. I want to take my daughter, my future son-in-law and the child home. There will be no honour killings in my family.'

The pir spread his arms. 'Of course. We respect the decision made by the police. I forbid anyone in this village to disturb this peace. There will be no honour killing of anyone in your family here.' His eyes gleamed, and Abida thought his suggestion was that killings might happen elsewhere, and behind closed doors. 'Not in public, at least. You've already reminded us that love comes first for you and that you have no problem letting your daughter's desire triumph over your family's honour. So, no, we will not get in your way.'

Abida's heart sank, but her father stepped forward, smiling broadly. 'I'm happy to hear that, Pir Sahab, especially given that our Shahid's father is a senior policeman in Lahore, one who wields significant influence throughout Punjab. It would be a shame to see his daughter-in-law harmed. In fact, he said that he would be joining us here as our esteemed guest.'

The smile vanished from the pir's face. 'You dare threaten me, Jamil?'

'Only stating the facts, Pir Sahab.' Her father sniffed the air. 'Do I smell blood? What have you been up to now? With the police almost at our doorstep, I'd say you have bigger things to worry about, Pir Sahab, than whether or not we pass.'

The pir's face paled. 'And do you intend to keep your future son-in-law with you in the same house with your divorced daughter?'

Her father remained unfazed. 'I think I am alive and well to look after my daughter's honour. And besides, Shahid will be sleeping in the courtyard with me, not with Abida.'

The pir scoffed. 'We all know how attentive you are, my dear man. You let her roam free in the fields, with the result that she returned with a swollen belly.'

Her father turned to Shahid. 'I want you to start recording this on your phone and I want you to send this to your father so that he can inform the nearest police station of the warm welcome we are receiving in this village.'

The pir clenched and unclenched his jaw. 'I'm not scared of the police, but if the father of a girl is unwilling to consider her honour, then what can I say? However, if we were to catch them doing something improper, or if I were to get an incriminating report from one of my people about your dear children, I will not be as accommodating.' With a curt nod, he moved aside to let them through.

Abida sighed as she climbed back into the jeep, realising only now that she had been holding her breath.

'Was it a mistake to come here?' Shahid asked, as they drove through the gap the pir had cleared for them. 'Should we turn back?'

Her father shook his head. 'It may have been a mistake, but we're here now, and the pir won't try anything if we lay low. He may sound as if he's all-powerful, but deep down, he is mortally afraid of the police. Like all bullies, he is a coward at heart. He will not try anything now that he knows of your father's position. He will only be concerned with clearing up his mess. We will soon be out of here.'

They had to use Majeed's name to instil fear in the pir, which Abida didn't like, but she hadn't objected to. She couldn't help feeling she had only narrowly escaped death again. She should not have expected things in the village to have improved while she'd been away.

⁂

She watched Shahid as he peacefully slept. She wanted to wrap her arms around him, but she didn't. He needed his rest for their journey back to Lahore, and besides, her father was sleeping right next to him.

After lying low in the village for several weeks as Jamil and Farida scrambled to pack as much as they could without arousing suspicion, they would be returning to Lahore. Abida didn't like the thought of facing Shahid's father, but he had rented a house for them in one of the wealthier neighbourhoods of the city and that was where they would live. Away from all the madness. With Rana Hameed gone, the umbrella of protection over his cronies was gone too and it hadn't taken the police long to arrest them. Her father had heaved a sigh of relief when he'd heard of Shershah being arrested.

'Now I feel like I can breathe.'

They still had no idea what they were going to do in Lahore. Majeed had promised to support his son, and with his years of accepting bribes he could, but naturally, Shahid would need to find a job. He didn't seem too worried about it. The real worry was what her parents would do in Lahore. Even if they sold their house in the village, they couldn't hope to buy property in Lahore.

She thought of her mother. Farida was realistic at heart. As soon as she had heard that they were to move to Lahore, she had said, 'If this is what we're supposed to do, then this is exactly what we'll do. I just hope and pray that you are happy in your new home, my dear girl. If anyone deserves it, it's you.'

To her surprise, even her father was optimistic. 'I think I've had enough of life in the village. I'll find something to do in Lahore. Maybe I'll open a butcher's shop. People in Lahore can probably afford more meat in any case.' His eyes had shone with excitement. 'It's like a whole new world for me.'

The sky was lightening. Dawn was approaching. She rose from her bed, scooped up a sleeping Shakila in her arms and, careful not to make any noise, went outside into the courtyard. It was the end of winter, but her breath still came out as mist in the cold morning air. Abida drew her shawl around the already bundled Shakila, holding her against her chest for warmth, but the baby didn't stir. She was fast asleep.

Abida walked down the road leading into the village proper. There was one last thing she needed to do.

She knew it was dangerous to walk alone in the village that had bayed for her blood not long ago, but this was something she had to do alone. Gravel crunched against her *khussas* as she made her way to the more prosperous part of the village. The house she was going to wasn't very far from the pir's house, and there was no telling what he might do if he found her now. She covered her entire face until only her eyes were visible and knocked on the gate.

She kept knocking until finally Kalim's mother appeared. She was no longer the arrogant figure Abida remembered, back straight as a ramrod, eyes narrowed in what seemed like permanent disgust for her. Before her now stood a woman who looked much older than her years, with a bent back and dark circles beneath her eyes.

She burst into tears as soon as she saw Abida. 'Why have you come here? To rub salt in my wounds?'

Abida didn't know what to say. Why had she come? She considered comforting Kalim's mother, but thought better of it. A woman of her stature, no matter how far she had fallen, would never receive comfort from someone like Abida.

'I was your daughter-in-law once,' Abida began. 'I ... I just thought I would ask how ... he is doing ... How is Kalim doing?' There. She had said his name.

It wasn't until she had said the words that Abida discovered how much she wanted to know about Kalim. Had he found happiness after selling her? Had he ever tried to track down his daughter? Maybe he had married again, although she couldn't imagine how anyone in their right mind would have him and his addiction.

Kalim's mother, Ayesha, simply stared at Abida. 'You don't know?'

'I was told that he had verbally divorced me when he ... he left me. I haven't seen or heard from him since.' The woman might have hated her, but it wasn't her fault that her son had sold Abida to Apa Ji. It would be cruel to tell her that.

Ayesha's face crumpled. 'We don't know where he is. We put him into a hospital when word reached us about his addiction. His father found him in some ditch in Anarkali. Rail thin and shouting nonsense. But now they tell us he has escaped, and they don't know how to find him.' She wrung her hands. 'My only son. Whatever will I do?'

'Thank you for being honest with me.' Abida had thought that discussing Kalim would evoke anger or sadness in her, but she felt nothing. It was as if she had heard news about some stranger. That was wrong: she would have felt something even for a stranger, but for Kalim she felt nothing. He really was dead to her.

Ayesha wiped the tears from her face and put on a brave smile. 'I apologise for my earlier behaviour. None of it was your fault. We've been able to piece together some of the story from Kalim's friends, and we want you to know that we don't blame you for what happened. Not in the least.'

Abida said nothing.

'Won't you come inside? As you said, you were once our daughter-in-law.'

'Not any more,' Abida said, and almost turned away. But then, she remembered why she had come here in the first place. She uncovered Shakila's face. 'You have a granddaughter.' She held her out to Ayesha. 'Would you like to hold her?'

It warmed her heart when a big smile lit up Ayesha's face.

When she returned home, she found she wasn't the only one who had woken early. Her father was up too. He had his back to her, but he must have heard her approach for he turned and smiled at her. 'Where were you? I was so worried.'

'How did you know it was me?' She put Shakila back in bed before stepping out to stand beside him, watching the sky turn orange. 'I felt like taking a walk,' she said. Before he could speak she added, 'I know it is dangerous for me to be out and about, but nobody was awake. The streets were empty.'

Her father let it go. She knew he had learned to let go of a lot of things over these past months.

'You're more like me than you know,' he said. 'I also wake up in the early hours and have to persuade myself to go back to sleep. But I can't do it now. Too much has happened.'

'I agree.' She put her hand over her father's. 'I will miss you. We're leaving.'

'What? Already?' He looked away, but a tear trickled down his cheek. 'I don't want you to go. I brought you all the way to this village just so you would never be out of my sight. And now, you suddenly want to leave again. What's happened? Why don't you wait a few more weeks for us to be ready to leave the village with you? That was the plan.'

Abida patted her father's hand. 'Abbu, I know what you are thinking. You are worried that Shahid will turn out like Kalim, and you won't be there to save me yet again. But Shahid is nothing like Kalim. You've known him for months. I will be fine. His father has given us the all clear. Those monsters have all been arrested. Shershah has been arrested. So now it is probably more dangerous staying here than it is returning to Lahore.'

He cleared his throat, flicking a tear from his cheek. 'I don't trust Majeed. How do you know he's telling the truth?'

'Then trust me. For the first time in my life, I am sure of something. Shahid isn't someone who can be pushed around any more. His father wouldn't dare lie to him. Besides, he was implicated in the death of Rana Hameed as well, so it is only natural that Majeed wouldn't want to risk his life. Let me go with Shahid to Lahore. Making him stay here isn't fair, and besides we don't know when the pir might blow his fuse.'

Her father's eyes drank her in as if he was never going to see her again. 'I am just a phone call away. It must never be like before. I will be checking up on you every day.'

Abida laughed. 'I will take care to answer your calls. I don't want you running all the way to Lahore for nothing. Besides, Yousaf is accompanying me. My brother will look after me, and he will give you daily reports too.'

Her father gazed at her. 'You are the most important thing to me in the world. You know that? I will always love you, no matter what happens.'

'You have other children too. You shouldn't have favourites.'

'But you're my only firstborn.' His smile crinkled the skin around his eyes. Although time had passed since the events of that fateful day, he was still tired, Abida thought, and his forehead was still creased with worry.

She knew he wouldn't rest until they were all safely back in Lahore. But, then, was anywhere truly safe? She had thought Lahore was the answer to all her dreams, yet the time she had spent there had been worse than she could have imagined. She wondered if she was putting too much trust in Shahid. Like her father said, maybe he would betray her as Kalim had. She immediately stifled the thought. She was being ungrateful. Shahid had come into her life when she was at her lowest, and he had helped her father at great personal risk. Shahid could never be like Kalim. He loved her in a way Kalim never did and never could.

She'd considered the possibility of staying in her village as well, especially since, over the past few weeks, something strange had happened. Despite her family's apparent dishonour, people had started buying meat from her father again, and the women who had secretly bought embroidery from her mother were now open about it. Rice would be harvested in the fields soon and for all intents and purposes, life seemed to have gone back to normal.

But, she also knew that true change didn't happen in a matter of weeks. They would never trust the pir. They could never trust these villagers who had allowed so many crimes to go unpunished. Change might be taking place, but it had cost too much. She did not want to stay in this place for a day longer than was necessary.

She'd never had a very loving relationship with her mother. Perhaps it was the sheer scale of her father's love that had dwarfed hers, but Abida had never felt close to her. However, these past few weeks had taught her how complex love could be. Her own love for Shakila ebbed and flowed, but it never really died. It would often get replaced by frustration when she wouldn't eat or anxiety when she was sick, but all these feelings stemmed from love. She realised now that the same was the case with Farida. When Abida had asked her if she would miss her embroidery business, her mother had scoffed at her.

'My eyesight was failing in any case, although whether it was from the embroidery or worry for you, I will never know. I am just relieved that at least one of my children will be settled soon. That is one less burden I need to carry.' Everyone had their own way of expressing love. That was her mother's. She never told Abida in words that she loved her, but let it show by her actions, giving Abida the best bits from the chicken curry, or sending the village girls packing when they came to gawk at Abida and ask questions. 'My daughter will be married to a rich city boy now. She doesn't need the likes of you. You never once stood up for her, but now that she is someone, you all come crawling here for gossip. Go away.'

Abida and Jamil still laughed about that episode.

'Will you be alright?' her father asked her, his thumb caressing her hand. 'Isn't it strange that while I know you're not entirely safe here I'm selfish enough to want you to stay?' He held her chin between his thumb and forefinger and turned her face towards his. 'Tell me, honestly, will you be safe?'

'You're asking this for the thousandth time, Abbu.'

He shrugged, dropping his hand. 'I can't help it. I'm your father.'

She threw her arms around him and hugged him hard. She didn't care that she was once again breaking the rules. She had been reminded time and again by her mother that daughters didn't hug their fathers, but Abida didn't care and neither did her father. 'I will be fine,' she whispered.

And she meant it.

Three Years Later

The girl flinched as the door closed.

'You've got nothing to worry about. You're safe now.'

She flinched again. She was sitting on the grey cemented floor with her legs drawn up against her chest, her head bowed. The *dupatta* on her head had large holes in it, and when Abida drew nearer she could see that the poor girl hadn't had a chance to wash for days. Weeks maybe.

Not that long ago, she had been like that as she had cowered by the river, the pir urging her father to drown her. She remembered her ragged kameez, the way they'd torn it all the way up to her breasts, letting everyone see her belly. It wasn't her belly that had shamed her. She was proud of it, proud of the fact that she was carrying something made of love inside, a new life she would soon care for. No, what had shamed her were the looks she got from certain men who seemed like they couldn't wait to run their hands all over her. To this day, the thought made her sick.

Despite her large belly, she lowered herself to the floor to sit next to the girl. The baby kicked her in protest.

'Ow.' She massaged her belly with one hand while with the other, she touched the girl on the shoulder. 'I know what you're going through.'

'You know nothing about what I am going through,' she spat, her eyes red-rimmed, a wild expression on her face. 'You sit in your comfortable house in Lahore. What do you know of the injustice I have suffered?' She burst into tears. 'I barely escaped with my life. They … they killed my baby.' Her eyes widened, her breath coming out in gasps. 'You know nothing.'

Abida closed her eyes for a moment before opening them. How long would women in Pakistan continue to suffer like this? It was at times like this that she questioned the point of what she was doing. It was like a drop of kindness in an ocean seething with violence. What hope did she have of making things right? She shook her head. She was being silly. If she could make a difference in even a single person's life, she should count herself lucky. She squeezed the girl's shoulder.

'What's your name?'

The girl sniffed. 'Bahaar. What's it to you? A fancy girl like you doesn't care. The person who helped me escape to Lahore said you helped people, not interrogated them.'

Abida breathed in. 'Some time ago, I was nearly drowned in the river myself for being with child before marriage.'

Bahaar looked up, the tears running down her cheeks all the way to her neck. She glanced around the room, her eyes tracking the *charpai* in the corner with its clean bedspread, a side table with a jug of water and an extra comforter for the cold weather. 'Unbelievable. I've heard so much about you, but I never thought you'd have actually been through it yourself. What makes you so strong?'

Abida felt her chest swell. 'My father.'

Bahaar was dumbstruck. 'Since when did fathers help their daughters? Mine wanted to burn me alive for dishonouring the family name. Honour is above everything, he told me. The only reason I survived is because I was being raped by the village elder. He couldn't bring himself to kill me, so instead, he killed his own baby and sent me away.' She shuddered. 'The monster. He asked me to return to him when the dust settled. *Haramzada*, I wish him the most painful death.'

Abida wondered what the pir back in the village must be doing right now. Thanks to Shahid, they'd managed to get some police presence in the area with plans to make a permanent station there. That was one of his conditions before agreeing to join Majeed in his new side business, which he was intending to run after his retirement from the force. Abida wasn't very happy about it, but Majeed was Shahid's father after all. What could she say? And the money didn't hurt. It was with that very money that she had managed to set up a small sanctuary in their rented house. Instead of settling in one of the crowded areas of Lahore, Majeed had found them a nice place just outside of Defence. It was thinly populated, but not deserted.

It was perfect.

It had a large garden and a small annexe, where they currently sat. Abida pushed herself up, holding her belly. To her surprise, Bahaar helped her stand, already warming to her.

Abida smiled. Bahaar had a small, heart-shaped face and large eyes that seemed to peer right into your soul. 'Let's go to the basement of the main house.'

'Why? What's there?'

The poor girl had suffered so much that she still couldn't bring herself to trust Abida. And why should she? Abida remembered trusting Nargis and realised that Bahaar was more sensible than her. She had been through a lot, but she hadn't given up like Abida had back when Apa Ji bought her like a toy. She could see the fire in Bahaar, and knew she would go far. Saying nothing, she walked towards the basement on her own, but before she had reached the bottom of the staircase, she heard Bahaar coming down after her, her face wary but curious. Meeting her eye, she shrugged. 'Couldn't be worse than what I left behind.'

She gasped when Abida threw the doors open. Abida tried to see everything from Bahaar's perspective. She wondered how she would feel if she saw fifteen girls of her age, all of them involved in some sort of activity. The basement was one large space divided by a glass pane so you could see what was going on in each room. On one side of the hall was her mother, teaching embroidery to a bunch of girls. Abida noticed how her mother's eyes lit up when a girl did a stitch correctly.

'My own kids are so bad at embroidery I was worried I would die without the chance to pass on my skill to others. Now I feel like my life has a purpose. I like to think I am finally making a difference.'

And she was. Lahore was a booming market for clothing, and hand embroidery was a valuable skill to have. Shahid had a friend in the textile trade who paid them for the hand embroidery, and the girls used the money to support themselves. They all had traumatic pasts, and Abida knew that sometimes waking up in the morning seemed like a struggle, but they were trying to put their pasts behind them.

'What do you think?' she asked Bahaar. 'Would you like to work and live here while we find you a more permanent place? You'll earn money.'

Bahaar's mouth was open. 'I love it. I ... I don't know what to say.' She looked back at Abida with tears in her eyes again.

Abida flicked the tear from her face. 'Say nothing. Why don't you go and see what my mother is teaching the girls?'

As Bahaar bounded away, Abida wondered how old the girl really was. She seemed like a child. Now twenty-one herself, she felt like a much more grown-up person. Maybe her circumstances had shaped her that way. Whatever the case, she felt much older than her years. She massaged her belly. The fact that she would soon be taking care of two young lives was also a factor, she mused.

On the other side of the basement, she saw her father and brother, Yousaf, hard at work. Today Yousaf was teaching another group of girls how to string words of the English language together. He glanced at her mid-sentence and paused, with a mock frown on his face. Abida remembered she was supposed to be present for the lecture. Like many of the other girls, she was learning English too. Her father placed a hand on Yousaf's shoulder and shaking his head at Abida, the boy continued.

Jamil's face broke into the huge smile, the kind of smile he reserved just for her. She knew he was waiting for Yousaf to finish the lesson so he could take the girls outside and teach them the art of butchering. Thanks to her father, there were several girls in Lahore that now apprenticed in meat shops, with dreams of opening their own someday. Abida knew they would achieve their goals. If they could endure the trauma inflicted on them, they could endure anything. Abida was working on bringing other professionals in to teach other types of skills to the girls, but for now she was happy with how everything was going.

Her father came up to her and threw his arm around her shoulders. Abida expected her mother to disapprove, but Farida had rediscovered herself over these past three years. She only gave them an indulgent smile before busying herself with her girls.

'This group is really doing well,' her father said. There was a note of pride in his voice. 'I expect them to find permanent work soon. How is the little one inside?'

Abida made a face. 'She's not in a very good mood these days. Lots of kicking.'

'So, it's a she?'

'I'd like to think so.' Abida hadn't had it checked, but she hoped the baby would be a girl, a sister for Shakila. 'That reminds me, I need to check on Shakila upstairs. God knows what my sisters are doing with her.'

Her father squeezed her shoulder. 'You worry too much. The girls are perfectly capable of looking after Shakila, but if you're worried, I'll go up. You shouldn't climb so many stairs in your condition.'

'You sound like Shahid.'

'That boy is very good to you – to us. Without him, we'd have nowhere to live.'

'Oh, Abbu, you do go on. You and Ammi work so hard at helping us run this organisation. You hardly pay attention to your butcher's shop.'

Jamil sighed. 'If I could, I'd spend all my time here. It feels so good to be able to help these girls. It makes me feel like I'm helping my own daughters.'

Abida rested her head on her father's shoulder. 'Did you ever think we'd come this far? When I look at these girls and their talent, I am hopeful for our future.'

'I always had every confidence in you, *beti*, even if I didn't say it aloud.'

A hand brushed against her belly and she sprang apart from her father. 'Who's there?'

Before she could turn around, someone put their hands on her eyes. 'Guess who?'

Abida gasped. 'Shahid, you're so silly. You scared me. Can't you behave like a normal person for once?'

'Where's the fun in that?'

Her father was laughing. These past few years, his face had become fuller and he looked a decade younger. 'I'll go and check up on Shakila.'

Abida allowed Shahid to put his arms around her belly. 'You're such a joker.'

'That's me,' he whispered in her ear. 'What say we go upstairs for some fun?'

'Shahid, I am six months pregnant.'

'That didn't come in the way last night.'

Abida laughed, batting at his hand. 'You're too funny.'

'If I told you that a major charity organisation wants to partner with us to support the work we are doing, would you like to have some fun then?'

Abida's eyes widened. She turned around to face him. 'Are you serious?'

'They want to meet you first. They've heard about all you're doing for underprivileged, traumatised girls and they want to help.'

'How did they even find out about me? I'm nobody.'

Shahid brushed a piece of lint from his sweater. 'Please give your husband some credit. He's learned a thing or two about marketing while working with you on this project.'

'Oh, Shahid, I could kiss you right now.'

He raised an eyebrow. 'What's stopping you?'

They laughed as Shahid guided her back upstairs. 'You're making a difference, Abida. Your fight against honour killings is bearing fruit. We're getting calls for help from all over the country. Your parents are proud of you. I am proud of you. Soon, the world will be proud of you.'

'Oh, Shahid, you do go on. I'll tell you what, I'll meet you halfway. Let's have some fun eating lunch, alright? The other fun can wait.'

Shahid kissed her on the forehead. 'Sounds good. We need to get some food inside you so we can properly nourish our Suzy.'

'Her name is not Suzy. It's Sharmeela.'

As they emerged outside in the cool, wintry afternoon, the sun warming their skin, Abida knew she hadn't felt happier than she did right now. She looked up at the forget-me-not-blue sky and wondered if it was the same in her village. The more girls she helped, the more she thought of the ones left to suffer their fates in silence. There had been a lot of noise in the government about cracking down on those who killed for honour, but that's what she had never understood. Honour. A word that had brought death to countless girls. How was it that a bunch of men sitting under a peepal tree got to decide whether a woman was honourable or not? How was it that they had the right to pass judgement on whatever she had or hadn't done, that they had the audacity to rip a woman's shirt and stone her to death. Or to drown her in a river. Why didn't these jirgas have female representation?

She knew the practice wouldn't end in her lifetime – it was too deeply engrained. But she also knew that she had to keep trying. Perhaps, someday, she'd even be able to talk about this to someone in the government. Stranger things had happened.

For now, though, as Shahid squeezed her hand and smiled at her, she was sure of one thing: she was finally home.

Acknowledgements

As ever, I would like to thank:

My parents and entire family for their staunch support.

My publisher, Karen Sullivan, for seeing the potential in this book and bringing her vast amounts of energy and expertise to the table. I cannot thank her enough for her trust in my talent and for her passion and diligence in bringing this book out in the world.

My agent, Annette Crossland, for being my biggest champion and for always believing in my work and pushing me to finish writing this book.

Hazel Orme, who has always been my first reader and constant guiding light.

West Camel, editor extraordinaire at Orenda.

Faiqa Mansab, Alex Chaudhuri, Paula Robinson and Alan Gorevan, for being true friends, honest critics, and for always standing by me as I weathered the highs and lows of publishing. I'd be nowhere without you.

Juliet Mushens, for her friendship, expert advice and sound feedback.

Sabine Edwards and Kirstie Long, my A team!

Kirsten Arcadio, Anita Chaudhuri, Shirin Azari, Sirah Haq, Heleen Kist and Damien Hine for their enduring support

Liam Chennells, for inspiring me to think out of the box and reach for the stars.

Helen Edwards, for loving my work enough to take it on.

Zaeem Siddiqui and Shireen Quraishi, for opening up their home in London for me while I worked on *No Honour*.

For all their support over the years: Ayo Onatade, Sean Coleman, Carla Webb, Alex Morrall, Jacky Collins, Danielle Louis and Avkirat Dyal.

My students at The Writing Institute who inspire and impress me every single day.